Alice M. Frere

'Ilâm-en-nâs

Historical Tales and Anecdotes of the Time of the Early Khalîfahs

Alice M. Frere

'Ilâm-en-nâs
Historical Tales and Anecdotes of the Time of the Early Khalîfahs

ISBN/EAN: 9783337336516

Printed in Europe, USA, Canada, Australia, Japan

Cover: Foto ©Andreas Hilbeck / pixelio.de

More available books at **www.hansebooks.com**

'ILÂM-EN-NÂS.

HISTORICAL TALES AND ANECDOTES

OF THE TIME OF

THE EARLY KHALÎFAHS.

TRANSLATED FROM THE ARABIC AND ANNOTATED

BY

MRS. GODFREY CLERK,

AUTHOR OF "THE ANTIPODES AND ROUND THE WORLD."

LONDON: HENRY S. KING & CO.,

CORNHILL, AND 12, PATERNOSTER ROW.

1873.

I DEDICATE THIS WORK

TO

FREDERICK AYRTON, ESQ.,

OF CAIRO,

THE KIND FRIEND

WHO SUGGESTED MY UNDERTAKING, AND WHOSE HELP

AND ENCOURAGEMENT ENABLED ME TO PURSUE,

THE TRANSLATION OF THESE TALES.

TRANSLATOR'S PREFACE.

" I ENTREAT gentlemen who may hereafter attend my lectures, to bear in mind this last saying. If they wish to understand History, they must first try to understand men and women. For History is the history of men and women, and of nothing else; and he who knows men and women thoroughly will best understand the past work of the world, and be best able to carry on its work now. . . . If, therefore, any of you should ask me how to study history, I should answer—Take, by all means, biographies; wheresoever possible, autobiographies; and study them. Fill your mind with live human figures; men of like passions with yourselves; see how each lived and worked in the time and place in which God put him. Believe me, that when you have thus made a friend of the dead, and brought him to life again, and let him teach you to see with his eyes and feel with his heart, you will begin to understand more of his generation and his circumstances than all the mere history-books of the period would teach you."

Thus spoke Dr. Kingsley, when, as Professor of Modern History, he delivered his inaugural lecture before the University of Cambridge. His advice is sound, but good advice is seldom the worse for wear. And in the present day, when, for the most part, every one, whether educated or uneducated, is content to adopt the thoughts of anonymous writers, how can it be possible to "see with the eyes " and " feel with the hearts " of those old-world giants of thought and research ? In European history, moreover, the vast change which has taken place even during the last few centuries, not only in the physical and religious distribution of power amongst nations, but in customs and habits of thought, and even language itself, raises a barrier against the assimilation of the modern with the ancient mind. In Oriental history, however, particularly the history of the Arabs, this barrier need not stand in the way of an earnest student. Language, habits, mode of life, amongst the Arabs of the desert are little changed from what history represents them to have been more than twelve centuries ago. This fact may possibly create an interest in a record of those times.

When, at the instance of my kind friend Mr. Frederick Ayrton, of Cairo, I undertook the translation of the following tales and anecdotes, it was with no idea of appending historical notes. But when, in connection with the translation, I studied the history of the times to which these tales refer, I felt that in submitting them to the public, it would be advisable to add such explanatory notes as might possibly induce some of my readers themselves to engage in researches into the history of that interesting period.

I have rarely given my authority for the notes, because they are for the most part condensed from various authors. But I subjoin a list of the principal works whence they have been drawn :—

Abu 'l-Fedâ, *Annales Muslemici* - - - Hafniæ, 1789-94.
Badger, *Imâms and Seyyids of 'Omân* (Hakluyt Society) - - - - - London, 1871.
Burton, *Pilgrimage to El Medinah and Meccah* - - - - - - London, 1857.
Caussin de Perceval, *Histoire des Arabes* - Paris, 1847.
D'Herbelot, *Bibliothèque Orientale* - - Paris, 1697.
Gibbon, *Decline and Fall of the Roman Empire* - - - - - - London, 1797.
Ibn-Khallikan, *Biographical Dictionary* (translated by Baron Mac Guckin de Slane) Paris, 1871.

Lane, *Modern Egyptians* - - - - London, 1846.
Modern Universal History - - - - London, 1780-84.
Playfair, *A History of Arabia Felix or Yemen*
   (printed for Government) - - - Bombay, 1859.
Sale, *The Koran* - - - - - - London, 1812.
Weil, *Geschichte der Khalifen* - - - Mannheim, 1846.

The Reverend George Percy Badger, to whom I am indebted for much valuable help, informed me that some of the tales in the following volume had been already translated and offered to the English public in the notes to an edition of Mr. Lane's "Thousand and One Nights" (commonly called The Arabian Nights). I was unaware of this at the time of translating the tales, and since referring to Mr. Lane's volumes, have found that the rule which applies to most of the Eastern tales with which I am acquainted holds good in this instance, viz., that though the foundation of the story may be the same, yet that the details have been varied. This may be partly caused by the fact of so many Oriental tales and anecdotes having been handed down orally for several centuries. And it may be due in part to the flexibility (if I may use such a term) of the Arabic language, which admits of considerable latitude in translation, while the sense in every case is, according to the view taken of the subject as a whole by the translator, substantially correct. This remark applies also to the original works, and to the interpretation put upon words by natives of the country reading them in their mother-tongue. I have therefore retained the stories and anecdotes as originally translated by myself.

In spelling proper names and places, I have followed the plan adopted by Mr. Badger in his "Imâms and Seyyids of 'Omân," and I cannot do better than quote his words upon this subject :—

"As a recognized transliteration of the Arabic into Roman characters is still a desideratum, I have eschewed any attempt at etymological exactness in that respect, and have simply endeavoured to convey the correct sound of the original as nearly as possible, without resorting to expedients unfamiliar to the general reader. I give to the *consonants* the same power as in English; to the *vowels* the same sound generally as in Italian; *a* as in *far;* *e* as in *beg;* *i* as in *pit;* *o* as in *store;* *u* as in *lunar*. The diphthongs *ai* and *ei*, like the *ie* in *pie* and the *ei* in *vein* respectively. The vocal sound of *ow* in *how* I express by *au;* when doubled in the same word, by *aww*, as in *Tawwâm*.

"The Arabic suffix, when used to denote an ordinary or gentilic adjective, I have represented by *y*, which somewhat in the same way constitutes the formative of many of our English adjectives, *e. g.*, *windy* from *wind*, *stormy* from *storm*, etc. This terminal *y* should be pronounced with a ringing Italian *i* sound.

"The acute accent (´) over a vowel denotes the syllable to be accentuated : attention to this expedient will prevent such mispronunciations as Maskát instead of Máskat. The circumflex (ˆ) over a vowel prolongs it : *î* is equivalent to *ee*, *û* to *oo*. The apostrophe before a vowel is intended to express the guttural *'ain ;* before a consonant, the ellipsis of a preceding vowel."

I trust that with the foregoing explanation readers will have no difficulty in giving to every word its correct pronunciation, and that the object attained by following the above rules will compensate those not acquainted with the original language for the unfamiliar appearance of the words.

I must say a few words respecting the verses which appear in the following pages. I do not possess, alas! "the gift of linking measured words" into rhyme, and am, moreover, by no means sure that English rhyme would convey so good an idea of the rhythm and flow of Arabic verse as does the measured prose in which I have rendered it. With the concurrence therefore of better judges than myself, I have left the verses in their rhymeless form, striving only in the poetry, as in the prose, to give not merely the general sense of the original, but the very words and idioms used therein.

It is not for me to point out what I may deem the merits of the various stories. But it may not be considered out of place if, recalling the truth of the old saying, "History repeats itself," I draw attention to the tales of "The Young Man who was deemed Mad," p. 158 *et seq.*, and "The Three Educated Young Men," p. 168 *et seq.* The former might well form the groundwork of as thrilling a romance as any modern writer has produced; while in the latter, the remarks made upon the subject of education by the tyrant el-Hajjâj might have been uttered to-day by our foremost advocates of universal instruction.

I wish to offer my grateful thanks, not only to my friends Mr. Ayrton and Mr. Badger, but also to Dr. Rost, librarian to the India Office, and to Mr.

Eggeling, librarian to the Royal Asiatic Society, through whose courtesy I have been enabled to refer to books the want of which I much regretted while abroad.

In conclusion, I would express my sincere hope that those who read the following pages may enjoy in their perusal some portion of the pleasure I have experienced in their translation. And I beg that if any charm be found in these tales, it may be ascribed to the fascination of the Arabic language ; and that all defects may be attributed, not to want of will, but to want of power in the Translator.

ALICE M. CLERK.

SOUTHSEA, HANTS :
   March, 1873.

CONTENTS.

TABLE OF CONTEMPORARY SOVEREIGNS.

MUSLIM EMPIRE.	A H.	A.D.	EASTERN EMPIRE.	WESTERN EMPIRE.	ENGLAND. SAXON HEPTARCHY.	
Muhammad	el-Hijrah	622	Heraclius I. and II.	Clothaire II., King of Burgundy and Austrasia. Dagobert I., Neustria.	Edwin of Northumbria, King of all England except Kent. Eadbald in Kent.	In drawing up this "Table of Contemporary Sovereigns," it has not been my aim to make a complete list of the kings and princes who held sway during the century and a half over which these tales extend. Such a task would be not only foreign to the subject, but within narrow limits impossible, considering the many divisions into which both England and Europe were then broken. I have only sought by means of a more or less familiar name amongst the rulers of those times to bring before the minds of readers more clearly than mere dates would bring it, the remote period at which the events treated of in the following pages occurred.
Abu-Bekr	11	632				
'Omar-ibn-el-Khattâb	13	634		Sigebert II., King of Austrasia.		
'Othmân	23	644	Constans II.			
'Aly in Arabia }						
Muâwiyah in Egypt and Syria }	35	655	Constantine III.			
Hâsan for six months, then Muâwiyah alone	40	660		656. Clothaire III., King of Neustria.	Oswy of Northumbria.	
Yezid I.	60	680				
Muâwiyah II., and in the Hijáz, 'Abd-Allâh-ibn-Zubair	64	684	Justinianus II.	Childeric II., King of Austrasia. Pepin le Gros (d'Héristal) becomes master of Austrasia. Sole ruler of France, 687.		
Marwân I. In the Hijáz, 'Abd-Allâh	64	684				
'Abd-el-Málik	65	684				
el-Walid I.	86	705		[trasia.		
Sulaimân	96	714	Anastatius II.	715. Charles Martel in Austria. Chilperic II. in Neustria.		
'Omar-ibn-'Abd-el-Aziz	99	718		720. Thierri IV. in Neustria, Burgundy, and Austrasia.		
Yezid II.	101	720				
Hishâm	105	724			731. Ethelbald of Mercia, King of England south of the Humber, 737. also of Northumberland.	
el-Walid II.	125	743	Constantine IV.			
Yezid III.	126	744		741. Carloman and Pepin.		
Ibrahim	126	744		742. Childeric III.		
Marwân II.	127	744				
Abu'l-'Abbâs, es Saffâh	132	749		752. Pepin le Bref.		
Abu-Jaáfar el-Mansûr	136	754				
('Abd-er-Rahmân in Spain, A.H. 139.)				768. Charlemagne and Carloman.		
el-Máhdy	158	775	Leo IV.	771. Charlemagne alone.		

ERRATA.

Page 65, line 4. *instead of* note *, *read* note †.

  ,,   81, last line, *instead of* note *, p. 13, *read* note *, p. 143.

  ..   155, last line, *instead of* note p. 31, *read* note p. 37.

     275, third line of note, *instead of* Muhammad, *read* Marwan.

HISTORICAL TALES AND ANECDOTES

TIMES OF THE EARLY KHALÎFAHS.

AUTHOR'S PREFACE.

PRAISE is to God* who caused to descend upon the most noble of prophets and apostles the

* The true sense of " el-Hámdu l'Illâh " is, that "all praise is (due) to God" as of necessity and right, since He created all things, including the power of appreciating what is praiseworthy —that is, the faculty by which praise is recognized to be due. So that nothing can be conceived of which the praise is not due of right to God.

The correct idea is conveyed as nearly as our language will admit of by the translators of our Bible, who render עֹז לֵאלֹהִים Power unto God, by " Power *belongeth* unto God ;" and so of salvation, righteousness, etc., the *belongeth* being introduced by way of explanation in italics.

el-Farrâ, a celebrated grammarian who lived during the reign of el-Mamûn, the seventh Khalîfah of the Benu-'Abbâs, dynasty, and died at the age of sixty-three, A.H. 207 (A.D. 822-3), when dictating a complete commentary on a treatise on the Kurân which he had written, employed no less than a hundred leaves upon the words " el-Hámd " alone.

Book of Manifestation (of His commands); and related to him histories of the past and of things to come (in this and the next world as well); and taught him what was and what will be until the Day of Judgment. We praise Him for having appointed us His people. And we thank Him for His gifts and His grace. And we bear witness that there is no god but God. He is one. He hath no companion. Behold! of His goodness He hath vouchsafed to us knowledge of the state of those who have preceded us among nations. And He will not raise His mantle (of protection) from over us, even though our footsteps fail us. And He made us a people just, and above others, and testified unto us thereof in the great and honoured Book. And thus spake the Most High: "Ye are the blessedest of people that hath appeared among mankind. Ye shall exhort with kindness and forbid from iniquity." And virtue appeareth through that which He hath made excellent by it, and glorified.

And we bear witness that our lord and our prophet Muhammad is His servant and His messenger, who (Muhammad) said: "My Lord instructed me, and therefore gave me the best instruction." And he is lord over all the prophets, and before them all. May God bless and grant salvation to him* and his family and his associates!†

To proceed : There are the words of the poor and feeble slave, endowed all his life with weaknesses and deficiencies, and much error and many sins—

---

* This formula, *Sálla Alláhu 'alaihi wa-sállama*, is always used by Muslims after naming the Prophet. The expression is not easy to translate idiomatically. It means literally, " May God look with favour upon him, and grant him salvation." Either the first or last verb, but more especially the last, is like " God save (the Queen)." In a somewhat similar formula, " *Salawátu 'láhi 'alaihi wa-salámáhu*," the first word is equivalent to Mercy, and the last to Salvation, or Eternal Peace ; and the whole means, " May the mercy of God be upon him, and His salvation." Perhaps the first-mentioned phrase may be rightly translated, " May God grant him grace and salvation." Redhouse has it : " May God grant him eternal peace," *i. e.*, salvation. But there is a double meaning in the formula to the sense of a Muslim. The verbs being in the past tense, the phrase would abstractedly mean, " God *has* blest and granted to him salvation." But a Muhammadan whilst uttering the formula must also inwardly pray that God will continue to bless and grant him His grace.

† The word *suhábah*, " friends," also means "companions" or "associates," and when applied to followers of the Prophet, signifies those who were personally acquainted with him, and those only. Their names to the number of 7,500 are given in the *'Usd-el-Ghábah fi Ma'arafat es-Suhábah* by *Ibn-el-Athír*, 5 vols. large 8vo, Cairo, A.H. 1280 (A.D. 1863). *Ibn-el-Athír* died A.H. 630 (A.D. 1233).

Muhammad, who is known as Diyâb-el-Itlîdy, from the region of el-Minych-el-Khasibiyyeh.*

Some of the pious brethren whom it would be impossible for me to refuse, have asked me to collect for them accounts of events which occurred during the times of the early Khalîfahs of the Benu-'Omeyyah and the Benu-'Abbâs. And I consented to do this, though knowing myself to be unequal to it ; for verily it is said : Obedience is better than Politeness.

And I called my work, Warnings for Men, or *'Ilâm-en-Nâs*, on account of what befell the *el-Barâmakah* at the hands of the Benu-'Abbâs.†

And I have begun my subject with the Commander

---

* A town so called after *el-Khasîb-ibn-'Abd-el-Hamîd*, who was the collector of the revenues of Egypt for *Harûn-er-Rashîd.* It is in Upper Egypt in lat. 28° 5′ N., on the west bank of the Nile.

† I have not in this volume reached the point here alluded to. The el-Barâmakah were one of the most illustrious families of the East, being originally descended, according to some authors, from the ancient kings of Persia. The uncertainty of human happiness is the moral which the author in alluding to them evidently intends to point. For during the reign of Harûn-er-Rashîd, A.H. 171 to 193 (A.D. 787 to 808), the whole family fell under the Khalîfah's displeasure ; and from the topmost pinnacle of wealth, consideration, and power, descended to the lowest depths of poverty and misery. Different reasons are assigned for the change in er-Rashîd's feelings towards these great men, into which it is useless now to enter. But I may remark that after

of the Faithful, 'Omar-ibn-el-Khattâb [may God be satisfied of him],* in whom, and in the mention of whom, I, the author, am blest.

this illustrious family had been abandoned by fortune, the people had a more lively sense than ever of the important services the members of it had rendered them. Their exalted merit and excellent qualities then appeared in a stronger light than even when they were in the zenith of their power, and in after ages they found as many historians to celebrate their virtues as did the greatest conquerors and most powerful princes of the East.

  * This formula is used after mentioning the names of the first Khalîfahs, and of the Associates of the Prophet, and of the disciples of Christ. It is more honourable than the formula "May God have pity upon him," which is used for doctors of the law and other persons of note. "May God bless and grant salvation to him," is used only for the Prophet. I may remark here, once for all, that these formulæ are always used, but they cause such awkwardness in breaking the sentence, that I have in almost every case omitted them. Even Muslims abbreviate them to the utmost.

ANECDOTE OF 'OMAR'S JUSTICE.

TRANSLATOR'S PREFATORY NOTE.

'Omar-ibn-el-Khattâb was the second Khalîfah of the Rashîd *
dynasty, and traced connection with the Prophet through
Ka'ab the son of Lúwa, from whom the Prophet was
descended in the eighth generation. 'Omar was born
thirteen years after the Prophet, and was the fortieth person
who professed el-Islám, which profession greatly increased
the spread of the true faith. Muslims affirm that his conversion was a miracle wrought in answer to the Prophet's
prayer. 'Omar-ibn-el-Khattâb and Amr-abi-Jahl were two
of the Prophet's bitterest enemies, and were of high estate
and greatly esteemed amongst the Arabs. The Prophet,
therefore, knowing that the conversion of either of them
would much aid the progress of el-Islám, prayed that God
would cause one of them to profess. And in answer to
this prayer 'Omar-ibn-el-Khattâb became a true believer,
but Amr-abi-Jahl died an infidel. Hafsah, 'Omar's
daughter, was one of the Prophet's wives. 'Omar succeeded Abu-Bekr in the Khalífate A.H. 13. He was murdered by a Persian of the Magian religion named Abi-

---

* *Rashîd* means taking a right course, holding a right belief,
orthodox. It is an appellative specially applied to the four first
Khalífahs, Abu-Bekr, 'Omar, 'Othmân, and 'Aly ; but also ap-
plicable to other Imâms who followed the same course as those
four.

Lŭlŭah el-Fayruz, who was a slave belonging to el-Mughîrah-ibn-Shuàbah, in A.H. 23, aged 63 years. He was buried at el-Medînah, in the same building as the Prophet and his first successor Abu-Bekr.

IT is related of 'Omar that on his return from Damascus to el-Medînah, he withdrew himself from the public in order to study more minutely the circumstances of his subjects. Happening to pass by the hovel of an old woman, and turning towards her, she addressed him, saying, " And what is 'Omar doing ?"

" He has returned from Damascus in safety," was his reply. Whereupon she exclaimed, " Has the fellow, indeed ? May he obtain no recompense from God on my account !"

" And wherefore ?" asked 'Omar.

" Because," she replied, " since he has held rule over the Muslims he has never given me one dinâr ; no, nor even a dirhem." *

* " The dinâr of the Arabs was a perpetuation of the golden solidus of Constantine, which appears to have borne the name of denarius in the eastern provinces, and it preserved for many hundred years the weight and intrinsic value of the Roman coin, though in the fourteenth century the dinâr of Egypt and Syria had certainly fallen below this. The dirhem more vaguely represented the drachma, or rather the Roman (silver) denarius, to

"But," said he, "how is it possible for 'Omar to know anything of your condition ; and you living in such a place as this ?"

"The Lord be praised !" she cried. "By Allâh ! I could not have supposed that a ruler over men existed, who was in ignorance of anything that occurred between the east and the west of his dominions."

Then 'Omar wept, and said inwardly, "O 'Omar ! every one is better acquainted with the Divine law than thou, even old women. Alas, O 'Omar !" Then he said to her, "O handmaid of Allâh ! for how much will you sell me the injustice you have received from 'Omar ? For I would redeem him from hell-fire."

"Do not mock me," she cried, "as God may have mercy upon you."

which the former name was applied in the Greek provinces." (See *Castiglione, Monete Cufiche*, lxi. *seqq*.)

In these pages I have not attempted to render the sums mentioned, in even approximate sums of English money ; and for this reason : according to the period and the place, the worth of the dinâr varied between 9s. 6d. and 14s. 1od. And in like manner the dirhems were at different times and places valued at from ten to twenty-five to the dinâr. Those who are curious will, however, find an interesting note upon this subject in the second volume of Col. Yule's *Cathay, and the Way thither*, from which work I took the extract given above.

The oldest gold dinârs are of A.H. 91 and 92. The following is

" I am not mocking you," said 'Omar. And he did not leave her until he had bought her injustice for five-and-twenty dinârs.

Now whilst he was thus occupied, behold! 'Aly the son of Abu-Tâlib,* and 'Abd-Allâh the son of

a description of the oldest dinâr I have seen. It was struck in A.H. 96 (A.D. 714-15), during the Khalífate of el-Walíd-ibn-'Abd-el-Málik, the sixth of the Benu-'Omeyyah Khalífahs :—

INSCRIPTIONS.

Obverse.	(Area)	There is no God but God. He is one. He hath no partner. (Negation of the Trinity.)
	(Circle)	Muhammad is the Apostle of God, Who hath sent him with the true Guidance and Religion, that he should manifest it above all other religions.
Reverse.	(Area)	God is one. God is eternal. He neither begets (negation of Christ being the Son of God) nor is begotten. (Negation of Christ being God.)
	(Circle)	In the name of God. This dinâr was struck (in the) year 96.

* 'Aly, the son of Abu-Tâlib, became in after-years the fourth Khalífah of the Rashíd dynasty. His father, Abu-Tâlib, was the Prophet's paternal uncle ; and he ('Aly) married Fâtimah-ez-Záhrah, the Prophet's daughter. He was born thirty years after the Prophet, and professed el-Islâm two days after the Prophet received his mission, being the first who did so after Khadíjah daughter of Khuilíd, the Prophet's wife. 'Aly was the father of Hásan and Husein, and succeeded 'Othmân-ibn-'Affân in A.H. 35 (A.D. 656). He was murdered by 'Abd-er-Rahmân, ibn-Mulgâm, el-Murâdy, in A.H. 40, aged 63 years, after a reign of four years and nine months. He was buried at el-Kúfah, and his grave is famous. To this day it is visited by the pious.

Mas'ûd,* arrived at the place, and cried, "Peace be upon thee, O Commander of the Faithful!" Upon hearing which the old woman smote her head with her hand, and exclaimed, "Alas! what a misfortune! I have insulted the Commander of the Faithful to his face." But 'Omar said to her, "You have done no wrong. May God have mercy upon you!" And then he asked for a piece of parchment, that he might write upon it; but as none could be found, he cut off a piece of his shirt, and wrote upon it, "In the name of God, the Compassionate, the Merciful:

* 'Abd-Allâh-ibn-Mas'ûd was one of the first to profess el-Islâm, and was amongst those who fled into Egypt from the persecution of the Kuraish. He was a learned man, and celebrated amongst the Associates, to whom he was known as *Sahib es Sawâd wa 's Siwâk* (lord of blackness and toothsticks), the former probably because he was lord or proprietor of the rural districts (called *Sawâd*) of el-Kûfah, to which place he belonged; and the latter because he may have possessed a district or plantation of a certain tree called *Arâk*, from the branches and roots of which the *Siwâk* or *Miswâk* (toothstick) is made. Sawâdi means *belonging to the Sawâd* (or *cultivated plains*) of 'Irâk. This region was so called because the Arabs of the desert, when they first saw the verdure of the trees, exclaimed, "What is that *sawâd* (dark thing)?" and this ever afterwards continued to be its name. 'Abd-Allâh died A.H. 23 (A.D. 653), at el-Medinah, aged between 60 and 70 years, and was buried there in the cemetery called el-Bâkiyâ, in the reign of 'Othmân-ibn-'Affân, the third of the er-Rashíd Khalífahs.

this is what 'Omar has purchased from Such-an-one—The injustice which she has suffered from the time he began to reign over the Khalîfate, to such and such a day, for five-and-twenty dinârs out of what she may claim from him on his appearance at the Resurrection before God Almighty—and 'Omar is exempted from it.* Witnesses to this—'Aly, and the son of Mas'ûd."

Then 'Omar gave the writing to his son, and said, " When I am dead, lay this in my winding-sheet, that I may appear with it when I rise in the presence of my Lord.†

* Attention to the affairs of the poor, and almsgiving, are amongst the first principles of Muhammadism. But the old woman condoned the injustice she had experienced by receiving compensation for it at the time.

† The circumstance related in the above anecdote would seem to have occurred on the return of 'Omar to el-Medînah after the reduction of Jerusalem in the 16th year of the Hijrah. After several conferences between the patriarch of that place and the Muslim general, it was finally agreed that the city should be surrendered to the Arabs on condition that the inhabitants should receive from the Khalîfah's own hands the articles of their security and protection. On receiving tidings of which, 'Omar therefore set out from el-Medînah, attended by a numerous retinue. He rode upon a red camel, and carried with him two sacks—one of which contained his provision, consisting of barley, rice, or wheat, sodden and unhusked, and the other fruits. Before him he carried a leathern bottle to contain

water, and behind him a wooden platter, out of which every one of his fellow-travellers, without distinction, ate with him. His clothes, according to Theophanes, were made of camel's hair, and were in a very ragged and tattered condition. The same author relates that when 'Omar entered the Church of the Resurrection at Jerusalem, he appeared in such sordid and filthy attire as gave great offence to the patriarch Sophronius, who with much difficulty prevailed upon him to put on some clean clothes till his own foul rags were washed. After the reduction of Jerusalem, and whilst the Muslim general was besieging Antioch, one 'Omar-ibn-Rafa'a, who had been taken captive by the Greeks, embraced Christianity, and was after his baptism received with great kindness both by the bishops and the Emperor Heraclius himself. The latter questioned him concerning the Khalífah, and desired to know what could induce him to appear in such mean attire, so different from that of other princes, when he had taken so much wealth from the Christians. "The consideration of the other world, and the fear of God," replied 'Omar. When further asked what sort of a palace the Khalífah had, "One of mud," he answered. "Who are his attendants?" asked the Emperor. "Beggars and poor people." "What tapestry does he sit upon?" "Justice and equity." "What is his throne?" "Abstinence and certain knowledge." "What is his treasure?" "Trust in God." "Who are his guards?" "The stoutest of the Unitarians. And knowest thou not, O king!" continued 'Omar, "that some have said to him, O 'Omar! thou possessest the treasures of the Cæsars; kings and great men are also subdued unto thee; why, therefore puttest thou not on rich garments? To whom he made answer, Ye seek the outward world, but I the favour of Him who is Lord both of that and the other."

THE YOUNG BÉDAWY WHO FULFILLED HIS PROMISE.

SHÁRAF-ED-DÎN-HUSEIN, the son of Riyân, relates : " Marvellous are the anecdotes which I collected, and wonderful are my reminiscences of the excellent things which I noted down from one who was present at the Council and heard the words of 'Omar-ibn-el-Khattâb, the Khalîfah of el-Islám."

He stated that one day whilst the Imâm was sitting in council with some of the chief of the Associates, and others to whom he referred for judgment and advice, and whilst he was giving his decisions in causes, and issuing his commands among his subjects, a young man of comely appearance and in clean attire, appeared, in the grasp of two other young men, also well-favoured and well-dressed, who dragged and pulled him until they brought him in, and placed him

before the Amîr-el-Múmanin.   And when they thus
stood in his presence the Amir looked at the two
young men and at the other, and then commanded
them to take their hands off him.   Upon this they
drew near and said : " O Commander of the Faithful !
we are brethren, sons of the same mother and father,
and are accustomed to speak strictly the truth.   Our
father was a sheikh advanced in years, excellent in
administration, respected among his tribes, free from
vice, known by his virtues.   When we were children
he educated us ; when we grew older he treated us
with consideration, and amassed for us a large inherit-
ance.   As it is said :

> Had there lived amongst men one other father like our
>   father,
> The world would have grown rich in virtues.

This morning he went out into his garden to enjoy
himself amongst the trees, and while he there gathered
the ripe fruits this youth killed him and turned from
the way of righteousness.   And we ask from you the
retaliatory retribution for his crime,* and the decree

* Wilful murder, though one of the most enormous crimes
that can be committed, is yet allowed to be compounded for, on

for the same according to that which God has revealed to you." (*i.e.*, in the Kurân.)

The historian then relates that 'Omar looked upon the young man and said to him : "Verily you have heard. What is your answer?"

And at this the youth's heart was calm and void of apprehension. Truly he flung off the garment of fear, and cast aside the mantle of trepidation. Then he smiled like a pearl,* and speaking with a most eloquent tongue, saluted the Prince in beautiful language. Then he went on, saying : "O Commander of the

payment of a fine to the family of the deceased, and freeing a Muslim from captivity. The next of kin, however—or, in the language of the Bible, "the revenger of blood"—has the option of accepting or refusing such satisfaction, and may insist on having the murderer delivered into his hands to be put to death. Manslaughter must be redeemed by fine, and the freeing of a captive ; which atonement if a man be unable to make, he must fast two months together by way of penance. The fine for a man's blood is set down in the *Súnnah*, or Traditions of the Prophet, at a hundred camels, to be distributed amongst the relations of the deceased. If the person slain be a Muslim of a nation or party at enmity or not in confederacy with those of the slayer, the redemption of a captive is declared a sufficient penalty.

* That is, he opened his mouth slightly to laugh, and exposed white teeth like pearls. I may mention here that the people of the East have always been intense admirers of the

Faithful! by Allâh! they have well recollected in making their plaint; and have spoken truly in what they have said; and have made known that which took place; and have described that which occurred. And I will now recount my story before you, and judgment thereupon rests with you.

"Know, O Commander of the Faithful! that I am an Arab of the Arabs.* I was reared in the dwellings of the desert, and years of misfortune darkened my life. So I came to the outskirts of this city with my household, and my goods, and my children. I followed one of its roads which led me between gardens, having with me she-camels, beloved by me, dear to me; and amongst them a he-camel of noble race, the sire of a large progeny, of beautiful form, an excellent breeder, who walked in their midst like a

beauty of youth—and which is in truth the kind of beauty that most appeals to a pure heart. Even in the streets of Cairo one may see a mother or other relative take up a little child, and exclaim, "O thy youth! O thy youth!" (*Yâ shabâbak! yâ shabâbak.*)

* That is, an Arab of Arab descent, and not *must'arâb*—that is, made an Arab by lapse of time, and birth in Arabia, though the original progenitor was not of Arabia. (See Note *, p. 79.)

crowned monarch. One of the she-camels approached a garden over the wall of which trees were visible that she could reach with her lips. So I drove her away from that garden, when lo! an old man appeared, panting with rage. And mounting on the wall he presented himself, carrying in his right hand a stone, and raving like a furious lion. Then he struck the he-camel with the stone, and killed him—it fell on a fatal spot. But when I saw the camel fall on his side and roll over, live coals of rage were kindled within me. I seized the very same stone and struck the sheikh with it, and that was the cause of his end. He met evil in his turn, and the man was slain by that with which he slew. After that he had cried a great cry, and had screamed a terrible scream for help, I hastened from the spot. But haste was of no avail against these two young men. They laid hold of me and brought me here as you see me."

Then said 'Omar: " Behold! you have confessed the crime you have committed, and your acquittal is impossible, and retaliation is imperative, and there is now no refuge."

Then said the young man: "I obey that which

has been decreed by the Imám, and am satisfied with what the law of el-Islám ordains. But I have a little brother whose aged father before his decease left exclusively to him a great deal of wealth and much gold. And on his death-bed the old man brought him into my presence, and committed his affairs to me, and said, 'This is in your keeping for your brother; take it and guard it zealously.' And upon that I made choice of a spot for burying it, and placed it there. And no one knows of it except myself, and if you order my immediate execution the gold will be lost, and you will have been the cause, and the child will demand his reckoning from you on the day when God shall judge between His creatures. But if you will grant me a delay of three days, I shall have nominated some one to take charge of the boy's affairs, and will return obedient to the rein. And I know one who will guarantee these my words."

Then 'Omar lowered his eyes and was silent. Presently he looked at those who were near, and asked, " Who will stand surety for him, and for his return to this place ? " Then the young man studied the countenances of the spectators of the Council, and

pointed towards Abu-Zarr,* amongst those who were
present, and said, " This one will answer for me, and
will become my surety."

Said 'Omar: "O Abu-Zarr! wilt thou become
surety for these words ?"

He replied: "Yes, I will be answerable for him
for three days."

And the two young men, the accusers, were satisfied
with the suretyship of Abu-Zarr, and granted the
delay determined upon.

But when the time had expired, and the hour was
at hand, if not already past, they again presented
themselves at the Council of 'Omar, who was seated,
with the Associates around him, like stars around the
moon.   Abu-Zarr was also present, and the accused
alone was absent.

Then said the two young men: "Where is the
culprit, O Abu-Zarr?   How shall he who has fled
return?   Thou shalt not quit this place without
redeeming thy pledge."

Then said Abu-Zarr: " By the truth of the Omni-
scient King! when the whole of the three days shall

* Abu-Zarr, el-Ghifâry, one of the chief of the Associates of
the Prophet.

have elapsed, if the young man does not appear, I will redeem my pledge and resign myself, so help me God!"

Then said 'Omar: "By Allâh! if the young man delays, I will surely execute upon Abu-Zarr what the law of el-Islám ordains."

At these words tears fell from the eyes of the spectators, and sighs for Abu-Zarr broke from all who were present; and great was the sorrow, and deep the regret.

Then some of the chief of the Associates suggested to the two young men to take the price of blood, and so obtain the praise bestowed upon those who are merciful. But they would none of it, and refused everything excepting vengeance for him who had been slain.

And while the people were swaying to and fro with grief at what was passing, and commiserating Abu-Zarr, lo! the young man approached, and stood before the Imâm, whom he saluted with a perfect salutation. And his countenance was radiant as the rising sun, and shone with sweat. And he cried, "Behold! I made over the boy to the care of his mother's brethren, and acquainted them with the secret of his condition, and discovered to them the place of his property. Then I hastened here, in the heat of the sun, to fulfil the obligation of a true-born man."

And the people marvelled at his honesty and fidelity, and at his intrepidity in meeting death. But he said, "He who acted perfidiously was not pardoned by the man who had him in his power. But upon the one who was faithful the avenger had pity, and pardoned him. And I was also certain that when death presented itself, there was no guarding against it by flight. And let it not be said, Fidelity has gone from among men."

Then said Abu-Zarr, "By Allâh! O Amir-el-Mûmanîn! of a truth I stood surety for this young man, though I neither knew to what people he belonged, nor had seen him before that day. But he looked towards me only amongst those who were present, and turned towards me, and said, 'This one will be surety for me.' And it did not seem right to refuse him; and humanity forbad that his hopes should be frustrated when there was no harm in consenting to his wish, lest it should be said, Goodness has gone from among men."

Thereupon said the two young men : " O, Amîr-el-Mûmanîn ! verily we give our father's blood to this young man, that his trouble be changed into gladness—lest it should be said, Benevolence has gone from among men."

Then the Imâm rejoiced that the young man had received pardon, and at his truth and fidelity.   And he declared the humanity of Abu-Zarr to be greater than that of any of the Associates seated with him. And he approved the benevolent intention of the two young men, and praised them in the warmest terms.   And he quoted this couplet :

> He who doth good shall not want for his rewards ;
> That which he hath done will be forgotten by neither God
>   nor men.

Then he proposed to them that he should pay the price of their father's blood out of the Treasury.*

* *Bait-el-Mâl el Muslimîn:* a treasury into which was paid—a fifth part of the spoils of war—the remainder of the wealth of one dying without heirs and leaving no will, after payment had been made of his debts—tribute levied on conquered countries—duties imposed upon foreign merchants—and taxes claimed from foreign settlers in Muhammadan cities.   From it were paid—soldiers— men of learning—those who committed the Kurân to memory— the descendants of holy men—the expenses of fortifications, bridge-building, and the materials of war—poor and needy persons, and destitute orphans—and the funeral expenses of paupers. Such was the Bait-el-Mâl in the palmy days of el-Islâm.

But they said, " Surely we have pardoned desiring to
.please God the Merciful ; and he who proposes this
to himself must carry out his benevolence neither
dishonourably nor injuriously."

The historian adds : " So I inscribed this in the
collection of Marvellous Tales, and inserted it in the
' Accounts of Wonders.' "

THE PROFESSION OF EL-ISLÁM BY THE PERSIAN PRINCE HURMUZÂN.

TRANSLATOR'S PREFATORY NOTE.

According to most Oriental authors, the 15th year of the Hijrah was rendered famous by the battle of el-Kâdisiyyah, (so called from a city of that name bordering upon the deserts of 'Irâk), wherein the Persians were signally defeated by the Arabs, and in consequence of which their capital city, and the greatest part of their dominions, fell into the hands of the latter. Hurmuzân, a noble Persian who had possessed himself of Khuzestân, after this complete defeat surrendered that province to the Khalîfah, and at his request embraced Muhammadism in the manner related below. Hurmuzân's dominions lay, says D'Herbelot, fifty leagues from el-Wâsit, on the Tigris, and eighty leagues from Isfahán.

HURMUZÂN was brought bound as a prisoner into the presence of the Commander of the Faithful, 'Omar ibn-el-Khattâb, who called upon him to profess el-Islám. Upon his refusal so to do, 'Omar gave the order for his execution. But he cried, "O Commander of the Faithful! before you kill me give me a draught of water, and do not slay me parched with thirst." So 'Omar ordered some water for him, and so soon as Hurmuzân had the goblet in his hand he asked, "Am I safe until I shall have drank it?" To which 'Omar replied, "Yes; safety is yours for that time." Then Hurmuzân flung the vessel away from him, and spilt the water, and cried, "Your promise, O Commander of the Faithful!" So 'Omar said to the executioner, "Leave him, whilst I find out what is to be done with him."

And when the sword was removed from over him, Hurmuzân exclaimed, "I testify that there is no God but God, and that Muhammad is the prophet of God!"

Then said 'Omar, "Verily thou hast professed the best form of Muhammadan faith. What caused thy delay in doing it?"

"I feared," he replied, "that it might be reported I had professed el-Islám through dread of the sword."

"Of a truth, thou art wise in judgment," said 'Omar, "and art worthy of the dominion thou hadst." And after that time 'Omar consulted him about the going forth of his armies into Persia, and acted according to his advice.

THE APOSTACY OF JÁBALAH SON OF EL-AIHAM.

AND now comes a somewhat similar story in so far as it regards obtaining safety by a trick. It was told by 'Abd-el-Málik, son of Badrûn, the commentator upon the Kasîdah of 'Abd-el-Majîd, son of 'Abdûn, and relates to what befell Jábalah,* son of el-Aiham, when he struck the Fazâry in the face for treading upon his Ridá.† 'Omar having said to him, "Let the

---

* Jábalah was the last chief of the Christian tribe of the Benu-Ghassân, which must have had its dwellings to the east and north of the Lake Tiberias. Their ancestor was Jáfnah bin-'Amr, bin-Thalabah, bin-'Amr, bin-Muzaikiyah (of the tribe of Azd) bin-Ghauth, bin-Nabt, bin-Málik, bin-Udad, bin-Zeid, bin-Kahlân, bin-Sába (also called 'Abd-esh-Shems), bin-Yashjub, bin-Yaárab, bin-Kahtân (supposed to be the same as the Joktan of our Scripture). The Ghassân section of the tribe of Azd left el-Yémen on occasion of the *Sail-el-Arim*, or flood of Arim, at Máreb, and migrated to the Syrian desert, wherein they settled near a stream called Ghassân, whence their subsequent name. Abu'l-Fedâ's *Mukhtásar fi Akhbár-el-Báshar.* —Abridgment of the History of Mankind.

† The Ridá was a piece of stuff, usually cotton, resembling it

man retaliate upon you," or words to that effect, Jábalah asked, "And are we upon an equality in this matter?" To which 'Omar replied, "Certainly; the law of el-Islám is the same for both of you." Then Jábalah said, "Let me wait until to-morrow." And when day dawned he went off to Cæsar, Emperor of Rome, and apostatized. Afterwards he repented, and composed these lines :—

A Prince has apostatized by reason of a blow !
But had I pardoned it, what were the harm ?
Obstinacy and pride have hindered me,
And on its account I bartered true vision for one-eyedness.
Would that my mother had never borne me ! and would that I
Had hearkened to the words which 'Omar spake !

is said the *herám*, worn at the present day by pilgrims on passing within certain limits of the holy towns of Mekkah and el-Medînah. This piece of stuff, in the form of a long white cotton (or sometimes woollen) shawl, is wound about the upper part of the body. Another white piece of stuff, called the *Izár*, is worn round the waist. The shoulder-piece might in Jábalah's days have been broader than is now worn. I find this anecdote shortly related in *Modern Universal History* (London, A.D. 1766). It is there stated that Jábalah and the men of his tribe having embraced el-Islám, performed the pilgrimage to Mekkah. And whilst walking in procession round the Káabah, a man of the tribe of Fazâreh accidentally trod upon Jábalah's vest, whereby it fell from his shoulders ; upon which, though the man swore he did not mean to affront him, Jábalah struck him, broke his nose, and beat out four of his front teeth.

> Would that I were herding camels in Káfrah,*
> Or were a slave to the Rabîa or Múdhar !†
> Would that I had in Syria the scantiest portion,
> Dwelling among my people, tho' deaf and sightless.‡

And when Jábalah-ibn-el-Aiham had returned to Christianity, he became a follower of Heraclius, lord of Constantinople, who allotted to him lands and money; and so he remained according to the will of God. And some time after this, 'Omar sent a messenger to Cæsar (Heraclius) to give him his choice of professing el-Islám, or of paying the capitation tax.§

---

* Káfrah means in the abstract a barren valley, but it is probable that Jábalah here alludes to some known place connected with Ghassân on the confines of Syria.

† Arab tribes of the 'Adnanîyeh. Múdhar was the earliest well-ascertained ancestor of the Prophet.

‡ All this sentiment refers to his position in Syria before the Christians conquered it. And for the sake of his former home he wishes that he had, after becoming a Muslim, remained one instead of returning to Christianity. At the battle of Yermûk, which decided the fate of Syria (A.H. 15, A.D. 636), Jábalah at the head of his Christian Arabs fought for Heraclius, and it was after the signal defeat of the Greeks in this battle that Jábalah became a Muslim. Yermûk is the name of a river (in Latin Hieromax, and in Greek νερωουκα), five or six miles east of the south end of Lake Tiberias. .

§ In the infancy of Muhammadism, all the enemies of that religion taken in battle were doomed to death without mercy. But when that religion was firmly established, this sentence was

And when the messenger was about to return, Heraclius asked him : " Have you seen your paternal cousin who is with us ? I mean, Jábalah who came here wishing to rejoin our religion ? "

" No," replied the messenger.

" Then go and see him," said Heraclius, " and afterwards come to me, and I will give you an answer to your letter."

The messenger relates : So I went to the house of Jábalah, and behold! about it were household officers, and janitors, and splendour, and a great concourse like that around the door of Heraclius. And I did not cease begging with all courteousness for permission to enter until leave was granted me. Then I went in to him, and I found him with a light-

deemed too severe. So afterwards the Muhammadans, on declaring war against a people of a different faith, gave them choice of three courses : to embrace Muhammadism ; to submit and consider themselves as subjects of the Khalîfah, and pay an annual tribute and the usual capitation tax of four dinârs a head, in which case they were allowed to profess their own religion, provided it was not gross idolatry ; or, thirdly, to decide the quarrel by the sword. If it was decided to fight, and the Muslims prevailed, the conquered women and children became absolute slaves, and the men were either slain or otherwise disposed of according to the will of the Khalîfah, unless they professed el-Islám.

coloured beard and with long moustaches, though my recollection of him was with a black beard and head. So I did not at once recognize him ; but lo! he verily called for gold-dust, and sprinkled it upon his beard until it became red. And he was seated upon a chair of state of polished silver, on the legs of which were four lions of gold. And when he recognized me, he placed me with himself upon the seat. And he began asking me about the Muslims. So I gave him good news of them, and said : " Of a truth they have increased much beyond what you remember them." Then he said : "And how did you leave 'Omar-ibn-el-Khattâb ? " I replied, "In excellent case." And I saw anguish in his face when I spoke of 'Omar's health.

Then I descended from the chair ; whereupon he asked, "Why do you refuse the honour with which we would honour you ?" I replied, " Because the Messenger of God (may God bless and grant salvation to him !) has prohibited us from this." And he said, " Yes. He has prohibited it. May God bless and grant salvation to him. But nevertheless your heart is pure, and do not think of what you have been sitting on." And when I heard him saying, " May God bless and grant salvation to him," I yearned

over him, and said to him, " O unhappy Jábalah !
will you not return to the Faith ? for you certainly
had knowledge of the law el-Islám and the excellence thereof."

Then he cried, "How can I return after what I have
done ? "

I replied, " You certainly can return, for verily a
man of Fazârch did more than you have done.   He
apostatized from the true faith, and fought against
the Muslims with the sword.   Afterwards he returned
to el-Islám and was received ; and I left him at el-
Medînah a Muslim."

And I only told him that he who did this deed was
of Fazârch, and that he fought against the Muslims
with the sword, and apostatized, and returned to el-
Islám, because the man upon whose account Jábalah
apostatized when he had struck him, and 'Omar
wished the latter to retaliate, was also a Fazâry.
And I added, " It is even easier for you to return
to el-Islám, for you have not fought against the
Muslims with the sword as did he."

Then he said : " I should like to hear more about
this.   If you would assure me that 'Omar would give
me his daughter in marriage, and would appoint me

to succeed him in the government, I would return to el-Islám."

So I promised him the marriage, but I could not promise him the succession to the government.

And after we had been thus talking for a while, he motioned to a servant standing near him, who went out quickly, and lo! a train of servants came in bearing boxes containing refreshments. These were set down, and tables of gold and platters of silver were laid out. And Jábalah said to me, "Eat." But I drew back my hand, and said, "The messenger of God has prohibited from eating off vessels of gold and silver." He said, "Yes. He has prohibited. May God bless and grant salvation to him. Therefore let your heart be pure, and eat off whatever you like." So he ate off gold, while I ate off Khalanj.*
And after we had done eating, he called for lavers of gold and ewers of silver. And he washed his hands in the gold, but I washed mine in yellow brass.

Presently he made a sign to a servant in front of him, who went out quickly. And soon I heard a slight noise, and lo! a train of servants appeared

* The name of a certain kind of wood of which bowls are made, or other vessels of wood, having variegated streaks.

carrying chairs encrusted with precious stones. And these they placed, ten on his right hand, and ten on his left. Then came slave-girls wearing coronets of gold. And they seated themselves upon the chairs on his right hand, and on his left. And they were followed by another slave-girl, like unto the sun for beauty. Upon her head was a coronet, and on the coronet a bird, than which I have never seen one more beautiful. And in one hand she had a vase of powdered musk, and in the other a vase of rose-water. And she made a sign, and whistled to the bird which was upon her coronet, and he flew down into the vase of musk and bestirred himself in it. Then she whistled to him a second time, and he flew into the vase of rose-water, and splashed about in it. And then she made a sign to him, and he flew up, and alighted upon the cross which surmounted Jábalah's crown, and did not cease fluttering his wings until he had scattered what was on his feathers over Jábalah, who laughed in the excess of his delight until his eye-teeth were visible.

Then he turned to the slave-girls who were upon his right hand, and said to them, "Make us laugh." So they broke forth into singing, and

began sounding their lutes, and sang the song which
begins—

> May God reward the companions with whom
> I consorted in early days in Gillik——*

until it says :

> Sons of Gáfnah around the grave of their father,
> The grave of the generous, the excellent son of Mariyah ;
> They gave to drink to their cup companions
> Ice-cold drinks mixed with the sweetest wine.

And when Jábalah heard this, he laughed until his
eye-teeth appeared, and asked me, " Do you know
who composed that ?" I replied, " No." He said,
" Hásan-ibn-Thábit,† the Prophet's poet."

Then he made a sign to the slave-girls upon his
left hand, and said, " Make us weep." So they burst
into song, striking their lutes, and recited this poetry :

> By whom were desolated the homes in Ma'aân,
> Between the heights of Yermûk and Khimân ?

until the song runs :

> 'Twas a dwelling for the tribe of Gáfnah for a time,
> But now a place for tales in future ages.
> Verily they regarded me there as of authority awhile,
> With the master of a crown was my resting and dwelling-
> 　　place.

* Damascus and surrounding villages. All this evidently
alludes to some story (perhaps also poetry) well known to the
hearers at the time.

† See Prefatory Note, p. 64.

And Jábalah wept until the tears streamed down his beard. Then he asked me, "Do you know who was the composer of that?" And upon my answering that I did not, he said, "Hásan." And he then repeated to me the lines beginning—

A prince has apostatized by reason of a blow!

to the end. And presently he asked me about Hásan: "Is he alive?" And when I said "Yes," he ordered for him a robe of honour, and another like it for me. And he also ordered treasures for Hásan, and she-camels laden with wheat; and said to me, "If you find him still alive, make over the gift to him, and transmit to him my salutations. But if you find him dead, give the presents to his people, and slay the camels on his grave."

And when I returned to 'Omar, and gave him an account of Jábalah, and told him of the conditions which the latter had imposed upon me, and of the answer which I had given, 'Omar said, "And why did you not also promise him the succession to the government? For if the Most High chose to give the power into his hands, and to decree against me, it would be in His wisdom. Nothing would happen except what He had willed."

And after this, 'Omar sent me a second time to Heraclius, and commanded me to agree to Jábalah's conditions. But even as I entered Constantinople, I met the people returning from his burial. And then I knew that his name had been written among the condemned, in the Almighty's Book of Reckoning.*

* *Umm-el-Kitáb*, The Mother of Books. On one page are inscribed the names of all good Muslims ; on the other, the names of infidels, and of those Muslims who do not live up to their religion. My sheikh gravely and persistently asserted that, be as perfect as I might (according to my lights *bien entendu*). I could as a Christian never hope that my name would be written upon the former !

HOW EL-MUGHÎRAH THE SON OF SHU-'ABAH BECAME GOVERNOR OF EL-KÛFAH.

TRANSLATOR'S PREFATORY NOTE.

The province of 'Irâk, answering to the Babylonia of Ptolemy, had for its capital el-Hîrah, a city founded by Mâlik, one of the descendants of Kahlân. (See Note *, p. 26.) The Persian Satraps resided at el-Hîrah; but after the reduction of 'Irâk by the Muslims, the latter people built el-Kûfah at about three miles' distance from el-Hîrah, and from thenceforth el-Kûfah became the capital of the province and the seat of government.

Sáad-ibn-Abi-Wakkâs was one of the first who, following the example of Abu-Bekr, professed el-Islám. According to el-Jannâby, it was through Sáad that 'Omar-ibn-el-Khattâb was diverted from a design, which before his conversion he entertained, of assassinating the Prophet; though Abu'l-Fedâ says it was through Náîm-ibn-'Abd Allâh, el-Khâm. Sáad was one of the most successful and celebrated generals ever possessed by the Muslims. He fought valiantly for the Prophet at the battle of Ohod (A.H. 3), and was afterwards invested with a command under Osâma-ibn-Zeid, whom the Prophet just before his death appointed general of the army destined to act against the Greeks in Syria. In A.H. 14, Sáad was constituted Commander-in-Chief of the Muslim army which 'Omar, the reigning Khalîfah, desired to send into 'Irâk. In the year 15, he completely routed the Persian army at the famous battle of el-Kâdisiyyah (see Translator's Note, p. 24), and pursued his successes until the whole of 'Irâk was sub- dued.

In A.H. 23, the Khalîfah 'Omar was assassinated, and as soon as it was known that his wounds were mortal, he was called upon to nominate his successor. Sâad was one of those named to him ; but 'Omar considered that his disposi- tion was too fierce and untractable. He was, however, among the six persons appointed by 'Omar to deliberate upon the choice of a new Khalîfah, and was afterwards one of 'Othmân's ('Omar's successor) governors of provinces. He died between the years 50 and 58 A.H., at his castle in Akîk, a town about ten miles from el-Medînah, and was buried in el-Bâkiya.

A STORY is told of the people of el-Kûfah, that they one day presented themselves before 'Omar-ibn-el-Khattâb, in order to complain of their governor, Sâad-ibn-abi-Wakkâs. And when 'Omar had heard them, he said, " Who will deliver me from these people of el-Kûfah ? If I appoint a virtuous man for their ruler, they think that he is weak ; and if I appoint a man of determination, they accuse him of impiety."

Then el-Mughîrah, the son of Shúabah,* said to

* el-Mughîrah, son of Shúabah, of the tribe of Thakîf, professed el-Islâm in A.H. 6. He was one of two emissaries who, three years later, were sent back with the deputies of his own tribe (which had then determined to submit to Muhammad), with orders to destroy their idol Lath. He was one of 'Omar's

him, "O Commander of the Faithful! verily if a pious man be weak, his piety is for himself and his weakness for you ; and as surely if an impious man be strong, is his strength for you and his impiety for himself."

Then said 'Omar, " Thou hast spoken the truth. Therefore, thou strong sinner, go thou and rule over them."

So el-Mughîrah ruled over them all the days of 'Omar, and the days of 'Othmân, and until he died in the reign of Mûâwiyah.

generals in 'Irâk, and was for a short time governor of Básrah, and general of the Muslim forces in Persia.   It was his Persian slave, Abi-Lŭlŭah, el-Fayruz (see Translator's Note, p. 6) who murdered 'Omar.   el-Mughîrah died of the plague at el-Kûfah, in A.H. 50 (A.D. 670), during the Khalîfate of Mûâwiyah.

'AMR-IBN-MAÅDY-KÁRIB'S STORY.

TRANSLATOR'S PREFATORY NOTE.

In the tenth year of the Hijrah, many of the pagan tribes of Arabs sent deputies to Muhammad tendering their submission. Amongst these deputies was 'Amr-ibn-Maådy-Kárib, chief of the ez-Zabîdîn. But considering himself to have been slighted by the Prophet, he joined himself the following year to el-Aswad, one of three false prophets who arose simultaneously against Muhammad. For some time he was successful in his rebellion ; but during the reign of Abu-Bekr was taken prisoner and brought before the Khalífah, who, however, on receiving his oath of allegiance, pardoned and released him. From henceforth he fought nobly for el-Islám, and is celebrated in history as one of the bravest of warriors, his worth in battle being, according to the figure of speech used by the Arabs, equal to a thousand men. When the Kalífah 'Omar sent him and another to join Såad-ibn-Abi-Wakkâs, in 'Irâk, he wrote to Sáad, saying, " I send to thee two thousand men, Tulaiha-ibn-Khuwailid and 'Amr-ibn-Maådy Kárib." He died of paralysis during the reign of 'Omar, at a very advanced age—according to some historians more than a hundred years.

IT is said that upon one occasion when 'Amr-ibn-Maådy-Kárib, ez-Zabidy, was visiting 'Omar-ibn-el-Khattâb, the latter said to him, "Tell me of the most

cowardly man you have ever met with; and of the
most crafty; and of the most courageous." To this
'Amr replied, "Willingly, O Commander of the
Faithful!" and began as follows:

"I went out once in quest of spoil; and as I
journeyed, lo! I came upon a horse fully caparisoned,
and a spear planted in the earth. And behold! a
man, girt about with belts for bearing his sword, and
looking like the mightiest of men, was sitting on the
ground close by. So I cried to him, ' Beware! for I
am about to slay thee;' upon which he inquired,
'And who art thou?' 'I am 'Amr-ibn-Maàdy-
Kárib, ez-Zabìdy,' I replied. Then he sobbed one
sob and died. And he, O Commander of the Faithful! was the most cowardly man I have ever seen.

"And I went out once again, until I arrived at a
certain place, when lo! I found a horse caparisoned,
and a spear planted in the ground. And behold! the
master of the horse was in a hollow hard by. So I
cried out to him, 'Beware! for I am going to slay thee.'
Then he asked, 'And who art thou?' so I informed
him concerning myself. And he said, ' O father of a
Bull,* thou actest unjustly towards me! Thou art

* The surname by which 'Amr was known amongst the Arabs.

upon horseback, and I upon the ground. Give me thy word that thou wilt not kill me until I shall have mounted my horse.' So I gave him my word. Then he came forth from the place where he was, and accoutred himself with his sword-belts, and sat down on the ground. Upon which I exclaimed, ' What is this ?' And he said, ' I am not mounted on my horse, and I will not fight with thee ; and if thou breakest thy plighted word, thou knowest what happens to the man who breaks his faith.' So I left him, and passed on. And he, O Commander of the Faithful ! was the most crafty man I have ever seen.

"And I went out yet once again, until I came to a place about the roads of which I lay in wait to rob. But I saw no one. So I galloped my horse right and left, and lo ! I perceived a horseman. And when he came near to me, behold ! he was a comely youth. The hair on his cheeks grew in greater beauty than I had ever seen among even the handsomest of young men. And verily he came from the direction of el-Yemâmah.* And as he approached he saluted me, and I returned his salutation, and asked, 'Who art

* Two or three days' journey south-east of ed-Diriyyah, the present Wahhâby capital.

thou, young man ?' He replied, 'Hârith the son of Sáad, a horseman of Shabhá.' Then I cried, 'Beware! for verily I am about to slay thee.' But he retorted, 'Woe be to thee! And who art thou ?' I said, ''Amr-ibn-Maády-Kárib, ez-Zabîdy.' 'The despicable! the vile!' he exclaimed, 'by Allâh! only thy contemptible estate prevents my killing thee!'

"Then, O Commander of the Faithful! I appeared mean in my own eyes, and he who was before me appeared mighty. But I said to him, 'Leave off talking, and defend thyself, for I will fight thee, and by Allâh! but one of us shall quit this spot.' Then he cried, 'Go! may thy mother be bereft of thee! Verily we are of a family of which a horseman has never deprived us of a member.' I replied, 'It will be he whom thou hearest.' Whereupon he said, 'Choose for thyself whether thou shalt charge me, or whether I shall charge thee.'

"So I took advantage of him, and said to him, 'Go thou to a distance from me.' And when he had this done, I bore down upon him, and thought to thrust my spear through his shoulders ; but lo! he had bent himself down as were he the girth of his horse. Then he leant over towards me, and placed his spear as a veil over my head, and cried, 'Take this to thyself as one, O 'Amr! And but that I abhor the slaughter of such as thee, surely I had slain thee.'

"Then, O Commander of the Faithful! I appeared despicable unto myself, and death was dearer to me than what I had experienced. And I cried to him, 'By Allâh! only one of us shall quit this spot.' And he repeated to me his former speech. So I said to him, 'Place thyself at a distance from me.' And he retired. Then I thought I had him in my power, and I pursued him until I imagined I had thrust my spear between his shoulders. But lo! he had bent himself down like the breast-band of his horse, and then leant towards me, and again veiled my head with his spear, and cried, 'Take this, the second, O 'Amr!'

"So I despised myself exceedingly, and said, 'By Allâh! only one of us shall quit this spot.' Then he retired from me again, and I thought that I could thrust my spear between his shoulders. But he sprang from his horse, and lo! he was upon the ground, and I missed my aim. Then he vaulted on to his horse, and pursued me, until once more he veiled my head with his spear, and cried, 'Take this, the third, O 'Amr! And but for my abhorrence of killing such as thee, surely I had slain thee.'

"Then I said, 'Slay me. I would rather die than that this should be reported amongst the Arab horsemen.' To which he replied, 'O 'Amr! Pardon can only be granted three times. If I had thee in my power a fourth time, I should certainly kill thee.' And he recited, and said,

> I affirm by the most solemn of faiths,
> That hadst thou, O 'Amr! returned to the combat,
> Verily thou hadst felt the fire of the lance,
> Or I am not of the sons of Shîbân.*

"Then I feared him with exceeding fear; and I said to him, 'Truly there is one thing I crave of thee.' He asked, 'And what is that?' I replied, 'That I may become thy friend.' He said, 'My friends are not such as thee.' And that answer was even harder upon me, and more terrible to bear, than his victory over me. And I did not cease entreating for his friendship until at length he said, 'Unhappy man! knowest thou whither I purpose?' I replied, 'No,

---

* Fehr, surnamed Kuraish, (see Note *, p. 79,) had three sons, from one of whom, Muhârib, sprang the Benu-Muhârib, also called Benu-Shîbân.

by Allâh !'   He said, 'I seek Red Death, its very self.'*
To which I replied, 'I desire death with thee.'   So
he said, 'Go with us.'   And we journeyed the whole
of that day until night closed upon us.   And half of it
had passed when we arrived at an encampment of
the encampments of the Arabs.   And he said to me,
'Red Death is within this encampment, O 'Amr!
Wilt thou then hold my horse whilst I go, and return
with what I want ; or wilt thou go whilst I hold thy
horse, and bring me what I desire ?'

"So I replied, 'It is well that thou shouldst go,
for thou knowest better than I what thou wantest.'
Then he flung to me his horse's bridle, and I was
willing, by Allâh ! O Commander of the Faithful, to
be Sâyis‡ to him !

" Then he passed into a tent, and brought out of it
a damsel, than whom my eyes have never beheld one
excelling in beauty and grace.   And he mounted her

---

* " Red Death," *i.e.*, which takes place through the shedding
of blood.   Amongst the mystics, the resistance of man to his
passions.   " White Death," *i.e.*, natural death.   Amongst the
mystics, hunger.   "Black Death," *i.e.*, death by strangulation.
" Green Death," *i.e.*, clothing oneself in rags or patched garments, after the manner of dervishes.

‡ Sâyis, groom or horsekeeper.

upon a camel, and said, 'Ho! 'Amr.' I replied, 'At your service.' He asked, 'Wilt thou guard me whilst I lead the camel, or shall I guard thee whilst thou leadest her?' I replied, 'No; I will lead her, and thou shalt defend me.'

"So he threw me the camel's halter, and we journeyed until, behold! day dawned upon us. Then he said again, 'Ho! 'Amr.' I replied, 'What is thy will?' He said, 'Turn round and look whether thou seest any one.' So I turned round, and I saw something like camels. And I said, 'I see camels.' He said, 'Quicken thy pace.' Presently he added, 'Ho! 'Amr. Look again; and if they are few, courage and strength! for it will be Red Death, but if they are many there is nothing to fear.'

"So I turned round, and said, 'They are four or five.' Upon hearing which he said, 'Slacken thy pace.' And I did so. Then he stopped and listened, and heard the footfall of the horses* already near. And he said, 'Wait thou at the right-hand side of the road, O 'Amr! and turn the heads of our animals towards the road.' And I did so. And

* In the dim light of early dawn, the mirage on the desert horizon would allow of horses being easily mistaken for camels.

I stood on the right of the camel, and he stood on her left.

"And the people approached us, and behold! they were three persons, two young men, and one very old man. And the latter was the father of the damsel, and the two young men were her brethren. And they saluted us, and we returned the salutation.

"Then said the old man, 'Give up the girl, O son of my brother!' But Hârith replied, 'I will not give her up; nor was it for this that I took her away.'

"Then said the old man to one of his sons, 'Do battle with him.' And he went out towards him dragging his spear. But Hârith bore down upon him, and said:

> Ere gaining that thou seekest, shall be dyed the spear
> In blood from a horseman, visored, trained to combat.
> He belongs to Shibân, the noblest of the tribes of Wâil,
> And journeys not thitherwards in vain.

"Then with his spear he struck the old man's son a violent blow, which pierced his spine, and he fell dead.

"Then said the old man to his other son, 'Do battle with him, for there is no worth in life with ignominy.'

" But Hârith approached, and said :

> Of a truth thou hast seen how struck my lance,
> And the blow was for a warrior mighty of prowess.
> Death is better than separation from my beloved,
> And my death this day, but not my disgrace.

" Then he struck the old man's son a mighty blow with his spear, and he fell from it, dead.

" Then said the old man to him, ' Give up her who is seated on the camel, O son of my brother ! For I am not like these whom thou hast overcome.'

" But Hârith said, ' I will not give her up. Nor was it for this that I sought her.'

" Then said the old man, ' O son of my brother ! choose for thyself. Wilt thou that I fight thee on foot, or that I charge thee on horseback ?'

" So the young man took advantage of the choice and dismounted. And the old man also dismounted, and recited this poem :

> I will not quail at the end of my life;
> I hold my ninety years as a single month ;
> Warriors have feared me through all time ; '
> While the sword endures backs shall be cleft.

" Then Hârith approached, and he also recited, saying :

Distant has been my course, and lengthened my journey,
Until I have conquered and rejoiced my bosom;
And death is better than the garment of perfidy
And shame I present to the tribe of Bekr.*

"Then he approached. And the old man asked him, 'O son of my brother! wilt thou that I strike thee, and if I leave life in thee that thou return the blow; or wilt thou that thou strikest me, and if thou leavest life in me that I return the blow?'

"So the young man seized the opportunity, and cried, 'I will begin.'

"'Come on,' said the old man.

"Then Hârith raised his hand holding his sword. And when the old man saw that he was certainly aiming it at his head, he thrust his spear into Hârith's stomach, and his entrails protruded. And the young man's blow descending upon his uncle's head, they both fell down dead.

"And so I, O Commander of the Faithful! seized upon the four horses and the four swords, and then approaching the camel, the girl said to me, 'Whither? O 'Amr! For I am no friend of thine, and thou art no friend of mine; nor am I like these whom thou has seen.' So I said to her, 'Calm thyself.' But

* Probably the name of the old man's tribe.

she continued : 'If thou art my friend, give me a
sword or a spear; and if thou conquerest me I am
thine ; but if I conquer thee I will slay thee.'

"I replied, 'I will not give you either of them,
for truly I was acquainted with thy family, and knew
the bravery and courage of thy people.' And at
these words she threw herself from her camel, and
came forwards, and recited, saying :

> After my father, and then after my brethren,
> Can pleasure or delight survive in my life?
> Shall I consort with one who is not brave?
> Shall not rather than that be my death?

"Then she rushed towards a spear, and forced it out
of my hand. And when I saw her do this, I feared
that she might succeed in killing me, and so I killed
her.

"And Hârith, O Commander of the Faithful! was
the most courageous man I have ever seen."

THE FAITHFUL ARAB AND HIS LOVING WIFE.

TRANSLATOR'S PREFATORY NOTE.

Abu-Sufyân commanded the Kuraish against the Muslims at the battles of Bedr, and Ohod, and also at the siege of el-Medînah.   He was at that time one of the Prophet's bitterest enemies ; but after his conversion to el-Islâm, which occurred in A.H. 8, and was, it would seem, the result of policy rather than conviction, he became one of Muhammad's most zealous adherents.   Abu'l-Fedâ relates that after his conversion, Abu-Sufyân demanded three things of the Prophet.   First : That he was to be made Commander-in-Chief of all forces that were to act against the infidels.   Secondly : That the Prophet would appoint as his Secretary Abu-Sufyân's son, Múâwiyah.   Thirdly : That the Prophet would marry his daughter, Gazah.   The two first petitions Muhammad granted, but refused to comply with the third.   He was already married to Umm-Habîba. another of Abu-Sufyân's daughters.

In the last year of the first Khalîfah, Abu-Bekr's reign, A.H. 13, Múâwiyah was sent in command of a large force, to the assistance of his half-brother Yezid, at that time Commander-in-Chief of the Muslim army then invading Syria. After the reduction of that province, which took place six years later, during the reign of 'Omar, the second Khalîfah. Múâwiyah was appointed prefect of Syria.   In A.H. 24, during the reign of 'Othmán, the third Khalîfah, Múâwiyah gained many advantages over the imperial forces, took several towns, and reduced the islands of Cyprus, Aradus, and Ancyra, exacting from their inhabitants a yearly tribute which amounted to a considerable sum. After the assassination of 'Othmân, A.H. 35, Mùâwiyah disputed the succession with 'Aly son of Abu-Tâlib ; and so powerful was the faction in his favour, that, during the reign of 'Aly, the Khalîfate was in fact divided, 'Aly reigning over Arabia and the Persian provinces, and Mùâwiyah reigning over Syria and Egypt. 'Aly was murdered A.H. 40, and his son Hásan, a pious but weak man, was nominated his successor, and was urged to prosecute the war against Mùâwiyah. He therefore led his army towards Syria, but after the first engagement some of his troops mutinied, and he himself nearly lost his life ; which so dispirited him, that in spite of his brother Husein's remonstrances, he wrote a letter to Mùâwiyah, offering upon certain terms to resign the Khalîfate. Thus did Mùâwiyah become sole Khalîfah six months after the death of 'Aly, and according to Abu-Jaáfar, et-Tábary, he reigned from the time of Hásan's resignation, 19 years, 3 months, and 5 days. Historians do not agree with regard to his age, which is variously given as from seventy to eighty-five years at the time of his decease. He held rule in Syria, first as Prefect, then as Khalîfah, for about forty years. He was buried at Damascus, which he made the residence of the Khalîfahs ; and so long as his descendants or the Khalîfahs of the house of 'Omeyyah held the Muslim throne, that city enjoyed this prerogative.

THE first from among the Benu-'Omeyyah who reigned over the Khalîfate, was Mùâwiyah, son of Abu-Sufyân.

One day Mùâwiyah was sitting in council at Damascus, and the chamber was open on the four sides ; the breeze could enter it from all quarters. But the

day was extremely hot, there was no wind, and it was
the middle of the day, and verily the noontide was
blazing.   And it so happened that he looked out
in a certain direction, and observed a man coming
towards him, who was being scorched by the heat of
the ground, and limped in his barefoot walk. And
Mùâwiyah, after regarding him attentively, said to
those about him, " Has God (may He be praised
and exalted !) created a more miserable being than he
who is forced to walk about in such weather and at
such an hour as this ? "   Then answered one of them,
" Perhaps, Commander of the Faithful, he brings a
petition."   Said Mùâwiyah, "By Allâh ! if he seeks
anything from me, I will certainly give it him, and
take upon myself his affair ; or be he oppressed, I will
surely help him.   Ho, slave ! stand at the door, and
if this Arab asks for me, do not deny him access
to me."   So the youth went out and met him, and
asked, "What seekest thou ? "   He replied, " The
Commander of the Faithful."   " Enter," said the slave.
Then Mùâwiyah asked him : " Whence art thou ? "
" From Tamîm," * said he.   " What is it that has

---

* The Benu-Tamim, one of the most considerable tribes of
Arabia, were dispersed over the north-east of Nejd from the
Syrian desert to the borders of el-Yamâmah.

brought thee at such a time as this?" asked Múâwiyah. He answered, "I have come to thee lamenting, and seeking through thee redress." Múâwiyah asked, "From whom?" He said, "From Marwân-ibn-el-Hákam,* your vicegerent." And he recited, saying:

* Marwân-ibn-el-Hákam was Secretary of State to 'Othmân, the third Khalîfah, and was highly favoured by him, so much so that the large sums squandered by the Khalîfah upon Marwân, and one or two others, gave great offence to the people. But nevertheless it was chiefly through the treachery of Marwân that the intrigues of Aishah (the Prophet's widow), Talhah and Zubair (two of the Associates), and Muhammad, son of Abu-Bekr, were successful, and ended in the assassination of 'Othmân, the traitor's master and benefactor. In A.H. 54, Marwân was appointed governor of el-Medînah by Múâwiyah, and in A.H. 64 (A.D. 684) was chosen Khalîfah of Syria upon the abdication of Múâwiyah the Second, the son of Yezîd, the son of Múâwiyah. The Khalîfate was now again divided, 'Abd-Allâh-ibn-Zubair having been appointed Khalîfah in Arabia after the death of Yezîd. But Marwân's election was upon condition that Khaled, a younger son of Yezîd, should succeed on Marwân's death, his own children being excluded. And to show his sincerity in this matter, Marwân married Yezîd's widow, the mother of Khaled. Afterwards, however, he caused his own eldest son, 'Abd-el-Mâlik, to be proclaimed his successor, which so angered Khaled that he reviled his step-father in public, who, being incensed at his reproaches, grossly aspersed the character of Khaled's mother. News of the affront being carried to her by the child, she vowed vengeance, and in consequence soon afterwards poisoned her husband, as is stated by some of the Arab historians. Others assert that she laid a pillow on his face while he slept, and sat upon it till he was smothered. Abu-Jaäfar-et-

O generous and indulgent and munificent Muâwiyah !
And O liberal and wise and uncorrupt and powerful !
I came to thee when my pathway on earth was narrowed ;
Then, mighty one ! refuse not my prayer for justice.
But vouchsafe me judgment 'gainst the oppressor, who
Has injured me in suchwise ; 'twere better had he slain me.
He forced from me Saida, and my suit hath wasted me :
And he tyrannized, and acted not justly, but tore from me my
    wife ;
And he thought to kill me, but my time was not yet
Accomplished, nor ended the term of my daily sustenance.

Then when Muâwiyah heard his words, and the fire
that burnt within him, he said to him, "Gently, O
brother of the Arabs ! Tell your tale, and let me judge
of your affair."

" So he began : " O Commander of the Faithful ! I
had a wife. I was enamoured of her and fascinated
by her. Through her my eye was refreshed and my
heart was glad. And I had a camel foal to which I
looked for the maintenance of my condition and the
support of my beloved. But a year of misfortune
fell upon us : I lost even to socks and slippers, and
there remained to me of my possessions, nothing.
And when that which I had held was diminished, and
my wealth was gone, and my state impoverished, I

Tábary, however, intimates that Marwân died of the plague, nor
does Abu'l-Fáraj say anything of his wife's being accessory to
his death. He reigned less than a year.

became grievously despised by those who knew me, and he who had sought my neighbourhood avoided me, and he absented himself who did not wish to visit me. And when her father heard how ill was my condition, and how poor my estate, he took her from me, and renounced me, and drove me away, and used hard language to me. So I came to your vicegerent, Marwân-ibn-el-Hákam, hoping that he would help me. But when her father appeared before him, and Marwân asked him about my position, he replied, 'I know nothing whatever of him.' Then I exclaimed, 'God save the Prince! May it please thee that she be summoned and questioned concerning her father's speech?' So he agreed, and sent and fetched her. But when she appeared before him, he was seized with admiration of her, and became my enemy, and renounced me, and showed hatred towards me, and sent me to the prison. And it was as though I had fallen from heaven and been borne of the wind to a far distant spot. Then he said to her father, 'Wilt thou marry her to me for a thousand dinârs, and ten thousand dirhems, and I will be surety for her release from this Arab?' Now her father coveted the gift, so he agreed to this. And when he had received the sum, he sent to me and had me brought into his presence, and behaved towards me like a raging lion. And he cried, 'Divorce Saida!' But I cried, 'No!' So he gave harsh orders about me to a troop of slaves, who seized me and tortured me with various kinds of torture. And there was no help for it but by divorcing her, so I did it. Then he sent me back to the prison, and I remained there until the legal period of her seclusion* had elapsed. Then Marwân married her and released me. And verily I have come to thee in hope, and seeking redress through thee, and craving protection from thee." And he recited, saying :

> There is desire in my heart,
>   It is consumed by the fire therein,
> And my body is pierced by an arrow,
>   By which the physician is baffled.
> And in my breast are living coals,
> And in the living coals are sparks.
> And my eye sheds tears,
> And the tears flow in torrents.
> And only through my Lord
> And through the Amîr is help.

* There is no one word in English, as there is in Arabic, which expresses this period. In the case of a *divorcée* three months, and of a widow four months and ten days, during which it is unlawful for her to marry again.

Then he was agitated, and his throat became dry, and he fell swooning, and writhed like a serpent. And when Muâwiyah heard his words and his recital, he said, "The son of el-Hákam has exceeded the limits of prudence, and has been unjust, and has dared to do what is unlawful amongst Muslims :"—and then added, "Of a truth, O Arab! even in tradition I never heard the like of what thou hast brought before me." And he sent for an inkstand and paper, and wrote a letter to Marwân-ibn-el-Hákam, in which he said :

"Verily what I have heard concerning thee is, that thou hast overstepped the limits of prudence in dealing with thy subjects. And it is imperative that he who holds rule should, concerning his passions, be as one who is blind, and should turn his back upon his desires." Then after this he wrote a long epistle [I have abridged it], and recited, saying :

Thou didst reign over a mighty province, but thou wert not
    capable ;
Therefore ask pardon from God for thine adulterous deed.
And verily the miserable youth came weeping to us,
And laid before us his trouble and his sorrows.
I swear an inviolable oath to Heaven,
Yea, and else may I be excluded from my religion and my
    faith,

> That dost thou disobey me in what I have written
> I will surely make of thee meat for eagles.
> Divorce Saida, and send her equipped instantly,
> With el-Kamît and Nasr son of Dzabyân.

Then he folded the letter and sealed it, and summoned el-Kamît and Nasr son of Dzabyân, and entrusted this important matter to their care.

So they took the letter and journeyed until they arrived at el-Medînah. Then they went to Marwân son of el-Hákam, and saluted him, and presented the letter to him, and intimated to him the state of affairs. And Marwân read the letter, and he wept. Then he went to Saida and told her. And not daring to disobey Muâwiyah, he divorced her in presence of el-Kamît, and Nasr son of Dzabyân. And he equipped them, and Saida accompanied them. And Marwân wrote a letter, saying the following lines :

> Be not hasty, Commander of the Faithful. For verily
> Thy vow shall be redeemed in private and in public.
> Though overcome by admiration, I acted not unlawfully,
> For how could I bear the titles oppressor, adulterer?
> Hold me excused, for surely, hadst thou seen her,
> My passion had been thine, by nature's inevitable law.
> This Sun will soon approach thee ; there is not her peer
> Within the realms of men or of genii.

Then he sealed the letter and made it over to the

messengers. And they journeyed until they came to Múâwiyah, to whom they presented the letter. And he read it, and said: "Verily he has obeyed well, and has been particular in his mention of the woman." Then he commanded that she should be brought before him. And when he saw her, he found her appearance admirable. He had never seen one more lovely than she, nor equalling her in beauty, and grace, and stature, and symmetry. Then he addressed her, and found her eloquent of speech, happy in expression. And he said, "Bring the Arab to me." So they brought him; and he was in extremity through the change in his condition. Then cried Múâwiyah, "O Arab! art thou to be consoled for her? And wilt thou take in exchange for her three full-grown virgin slaves like moons, and with each slave a thousand dinârs, besides what will suffice thee and will enrich thee, which I shall apportion to thee every year from the Treasury?"

And when the Arab heard Múâwiyah's words, he sobbed chokingly—Múâwiyah thought he had died. So he asked him, "What evil has come over thee that thou art in this sad plight?" The Arab replied, "I sought protection through thy justice against the tyranny of the son of el-Hákam ; but to whom shall I turn from thy oppression ?" And he recited, saying :

> May the king live for ever ! Do not cause me to be
> Like him who from burning sand takes refuge in the fire.
> Restore Saida to one whom grief has distracted.
> At eve and at morn he finds himself remembering and sad.
> Covet her not from me, but loosen the bonds ;
> For doest thou this, verily I am not without gratitude.

Then he said, "By Allâh ! O Commander of the Faithful ! wert thou to offer me the Khalífate, I would not take it without Saida." And he recited, saying :

> Excepting Saida, my heart refuses to love; and hateful
> To me is womankind. I am guileless on their account.

Then said Muâwiyah to him, "But thou hast confessed that thou didst divorce her, and Marwán confessed that he divorced her, and we wish to give her the choice. If she choose other than thee, we ourselves will marry her : but if she choose thee, we will give her up to thee." He said, "Let it be done." So Muâwiyah cried, "Speak, Saida ! which is dearest to thee, the Commander of the Faithful with his power, and his rank, and his palaces, and his empire, and his wealth, and all that thou hast seen around him ; or Marwân son of el-Hákam, with his tyranny and his injustice ; or this Arab, with his hunger and his poverty ? "

So she recited, saying :

> This one.   And even in hunger and want
> He were dearer to me than my kin and my friends,
> And the wearer of the crown, or his vicegerent, Marwân.
> And for me all are possessed of dirhems and dinârs.

Then she continued : " By Allâh ! O Commander of the Faithful ! I am not going to forsake him because times have changed, nor because the days are darkened.   Neither let it be forgotten that I have been his companion from the first, and our love is not worn out.   And it is right that I should be the one to bear patiently with him in adversity, who have with him been happy in brighter days."

Then Mùâwiyah marvelled at her wisdom, and her affection for the Arab, and her fidelity to him.   And he gave her ten thousand dirhems, and gave the same sum to the Arab, who took her and departed.

HOW HÁSAN-IBN-'ALY BY HIS ELOQUENCE DISCOMFITED HIS ADVERSARIES.

From " Thamarât-el-Aurâk, or Speaking Leaves," concerning
the eloquent and pungent replies of Háshim.

TRANSLATOR'S PREFATORY NOTE.

'Amru-ibn-el-'As, son of 'Omeyyah of the tribe of Kuraish, was
one of three Mekkan poets whose satires caused so much
vexation to the Prophet that he engaged three poets of the
tribe of el-Kházraj to answer them.   One of the latter
was Hásan son of Thâbit, of whom mention is made in
the story of Jábalah (see page 34).   'Amru fought against
Muhammad under Abu-Sufyân at the battles of Bedr and
Ohod.   He professed el-Islám in the eighth year of el-Hijrah,
and was sent by the Prophet to destroy Sâwah, the idol
worshipped by the tribe of Hudhail at Rohat, a place about
three miles from Mekkah.   He was also sent on an embassy
inviting to el-Islám two princes of the tribe of el-Azd, who
were reigning at 'Omân.   In the reign of Abu-Bekr he was
sent into Lower Palestine in command of a large force, and
in that Khalîfah's last year, A.H. 13, 'Amru laid siege to and
took Gaza, and Theophanes asserts that he forced the inhabitants of the whole tract from Gaza to Mount Sinai and
the borders of the desert, to submit to the Khalîfah.   He
was one of the generals who this same year, under the
supreme command of Khâlid son of el-Walid, sat down
before Damascus and reduced it.   On Abu-Bekr's death

and the accession of 'Omar, Khâlid was deposed, and Abu-'Obaidah appointed in his stead. Under him 'Amru held command at the siege of Jerusalem. In A.H. 16, that city surrendered to the Khalîfah in person (see Note *, page 11) ; after which 'Omar despatched 'Amru to invade Egypt. He was, however, delayed in Syria, in order to reduce certain towns and fortresses which still held out ; and it was not until A.H. 18 that he entered Egypt.* Having conquered that country, he was made its governor, but was, in A.H. 24, dis-

* Now that the energy and indomitable perseverance of Mons. de Lesseps has accomplished the great work of cutting the Suez Canal, it is interesting to note that rather more than twelve centuries ago a design to cut a channel through the present Isthmus of Suez, and thereby open a communication between the Arabian Gulf and the Mediterranean Sea, was formed by 'Amru-ibn-el-'As. It did not, however, meet with the Khalîfah's approval, for he considered that the execution of it would facilitate the entrance of Christians into Arabia.

It was 'Amru who, by the order of 'Omar, destroyed the noble and most valuable library at Alexandria. It was in the Serapœum and suburb Rhacotis, and was called the daughter of that founded by Ptolemy Philadelphus. The latter was burnt, and the four hundred thousand volumes it contained entirely consumed, in the time of Julius Cæsar ; and the former, which contained when the other perished at least five hundred thousand MSS., and was afterwards greatly increased, was destroyed, as stated, by 'Amru-ibn-el-'As, in accordance with 'Omar's fanatical order which said that if these books agreed in all points with the Book of God (el-Kurân), the latter would still be perfect without them, and they would therefore be superfluous ; but that if they contained anything repugnant to the doctrine of that book, they ought to be condemned as pernicious, and destroyed. And thus was caused an irreparable loss to science, philosophy, and history.

missed from that post by 'Othmân, 'Omar's successor. He then retired into Palestine, and led a private life until after the murder of 'Othmân the dissensions arose betwixt 'Aly and Mùâwiyah. 'Amru joined himself to the latter under the promise of being returned to the lieutenancy of Egypt, and he it was who, when the dispute between 'Aly and Mùâwiyah was to be decided by two persons nominated by either party, was chosen as Mùâwiyah's advocate. In A.H. 40, a conspiracy was formed to assassinate on the same day 'Aly at el-Medînah, Mùâwiyah at Damascus, and 'Amru in Egypt ; but it was successful only in the case of 'Aly. 'Amru died A.H. 43. He was justly esteemed one of the greatest men amongst the Arabs of the age in which he lived. The Prophet is reported to have said, " There is no truer a Muslim, nor any one more steadfast in the faith, than 'Amru."

THE following is one of the best among them.

There assembled before Mùâwiyah, 'Amru-ibn-el-'As, and Walîd-ibn-'Ukbah,* and 'Utbah-ibn-Abu-Sufyân, and el-Mughîrah-ibn-esh-Shùabah,† who said to him, " O Commander of the Faithful! send to Hásan son of 'Aly, ‡ and let him appear before us."

" And why ?" asked Mùâwiyah.

" In order," they replied, " that we may reprove him, and inform him that his father killed 'Othmân."

* See Note †, p. 72.
† See Note *, p. 38.
‡ See Prefatory Note, pp. 52, 53.

"But," said Múâwiyah, "you cannot cope with him, and you will get nothing out of him ; nor can you say anything to him without his giving you the lie ; and if he makes use of his eloquence against you, all his hearers will be convinced."

But they persisted, saying, " Send for him, for we are certainly a match for him."

So Múâwiyah sent a message to Hásan, and when the latter appeared, Múâwiyah said to him, " O Hásan ! I did not wish to send for thee ; but nevertheless these others would have thee brought. Hearken therefore to their words."

Then Hásan replied, " Let them speak, and we will give heed."

So 'Amru-ibn-el-'As arose, and having praised and glorified God, said : " O Hásan ! art thou aware that thy father was the first who incited to insurrection, and aimed at the sovereign power ? * And what didst thou think of the judgment of the Most High ? "

Then rose el-Walîd-ibn-'Ukbah, and praised and glorified God, and then said : " O ye sons of Háshim ! ye were of kin to 'Othmân-ibn-'Affân, and thanks

* See Note *, p. 75.

to that kinship ye were brought into connection with
the Apostle of God, whereby ye greatly benefited,
and were fulfilled with good.*   But ye rebelled
against him, and slew him.   And of a truth we
sought your father's death ; but God delivered us
from the fear of him ; though, had we slain him, it
had been no sin in the sight of God."

Then 'Utbah-ibn-Abu-Sufyân rose up, and said,
" O Hásan ! because thy father transgressed against
'Othmân, and killed him, coveting the kingdom and
things of this world, God snatched both away from
him.   And verily we desired thy father's death, until
he was slain by the Most High."

Then el-Mughîrah-ibn-esh-Shuabah stood up, and
uttered blameful words concerning 'Aly, and lauda-
tory concerning 'Othmân.

And when they had all spoken, Hásan rose ; and he
gave praise and glory to God, and then said : " With

* El-Walîd apparently chose to overlook the fact that 'Aly's
blood-relationship to the Prophet was much nearer than 'Othmân's.   The latter, it is true, married two of Muhammad's
daughters, but 'Aly was also married to his best-beloved, and,
according to Abu'l-Fedâ, eldest, daughter, Fâtimah.   The
common ancestor of the Prophet and 'Othmân was 'Abd
Manâf, from whom Muhammad and 'Aly were descended in
the fourth, and 'Othmân in the fifth generation.

thee, O Múâwiyah ! will I begin, for such as these others cannot insult me. But thou dost insult me, by thy hatred, and enmity, and opposition to my maternal grandfather the Prophet of God." Then he turned to the people, and said : " God is my witness before you, that he whom these men have insulted was without doubt my father. And he was the first who believed in God, and prayed at the two Kiblahs.* Whilst thou, O Múâwiyah ! wert an infidel

* According to Abu'l-Fedâ, the second year of the Hijrah was ushered in by a change in the Kiblah, or the part to which Muhammadans are to turn their faces in prayer. At first the Prophet and his followers observed no particular rite in turning their faces towards any certain place when they prayed. But when he fled to el-Medînah, he directed them to turn towards the temple of Jerusalem (probably to ingratiate himself with the Jews) ; this continued to be their Kiblah for seventeen or eighteen months. Afterwards, either finding the Jews too intractable, or despairing of otherwise gaining the pagan Arabs, who could not forget their respect to the temple of Mekkah,* he ordered that prayers should for the future be towards that place. It would consequently be proof of having been one of the earliest converts to el-Islâm to have prayed towards both Kiblahs.

* The genuine antiquity of the Ka'abah ascends beyond the Christian era. In describing the coast of the Red Sea, the Greek historian Diodorus has remarked, between the Thamudites and the Sabœans, a famous temple, whose superior sanctity was revered by *all* the Arabians. The linen or silken veil, which is annually renewed by the Turkish emperor, was first offered by a pious king of the Homerites, who reigned 700 years before the time of Muhammad. Muslims believe that Adam, after his expulsion from Paradise, implored of God that he

and an idolater. And on the day of Bedr,* my
father bore the standard of the Prophet, whilst the
standard of the idolaters was borne by Mûâwiyah !
And the Most High is my witness before you, that
Mûâwiyah was scribe to my maternal grandfather,†
who one day sent for him, but the messenger returned
and said, ' He is eating.' And he sent the messenger
to him three times, and every time he said, ' He is
eating.' Then cried the Prophet, ' May Allâh never
appease the craving of thy belly ! . . . Dost thou

* The first great battle gained by Muhammad, which vastly
helped his cause. Fought A.H. 2.

† See Prefatory Note, p. 52.

might erect a building like what he had seen there, called Bait-el-
Mamûr, or the Frequented House, towards which he might direct his
prayers, and which he might compass as the angels do the celestial
mansion. In compliance with this request, God exhibited a representa-
tion of that house in curtains of light, and set it in Mekkah perpen-
dicularly under its original, ordering Adam to turn towards it when he
prayed, and to compass it by way of devotion. After Adam's death,
his son Seth built a house in the same form of stones and clay, which
being destroyed by the deluge, was rebuilt by Abraham and Ishmael, at
God's command, in the same place and after the same model, they being
directed by revelation. Abu-Horeira affirms that this model, or the
celestial building from whence it was taken, was a thousand years older
than Adam, and that the angels began to form that heavenly edifice the
same number of years before the creation of the world.

The Kuraish rebuilt the Ka'abah after the birth of Muhammad ; it
was afterwards repaired by Abd 'Allah-ibn-Zubair (See Note *, p. 55),
Khalifah of Mekkah ; and el-Hajjâj (see Notes, p. 126, and p. 151), in
A.H. 74 (A.D. 694-5), put it in the form in which it now remains.

acknowledge this of thy gluttony or not, O Múâwiyah?" Then Hásan continued: "And I call God to witness before you whether you are not aware that Múâwiyah was leading a camel on which his father was riding, while his brother here present was driving her. And the Prophet of God said what he said.* And thou, thou knowest this! So much for thee, O Múâwiyah!—As for thee, O 'Amru! five of the Kuraish were disputing with thee, and one of them got the better of thee, like el-Aiham.* He was the meanest of them in estimation, and of lower degree than the others. Then thou didst rise in the midst of the Kuraish, and saidst: 'I have ridiculed Muhammad in a poem of thirty lines.' And when the Prophet heard this, he cried, 'O Allâh! I am no poet. O Allâh! do thou for every line curse 'Amru-ibn-el-'As with a curse!' Then thou didst depart with thy poem to the en-Najâshy,† and didst tell him

---

* The circumstances here alluded to were probably well known at the time; but I have failed to discover further particulars about them.

† The king of Ethiopia, from whom some of the earliest converts to el-Islâm sought protection when persecuted by the Kuraish. He received them kindly, and refused to give them up to those whom the Kuraish sent to demand them.

about it.   And he gave thee the lie, and drove thee
away in disgrace.   So thou hast shown thyself an
enemy to the sons of Hâshim both as an infidel and
as a Muslim.—I do not blame thee for thy hatred at
the present time, O thou son of Abu-Maît!* and

* Abu-Maît was grandfather to el-Walîd, the son of 'Ukbah.
It is supposed by some that a denunciatory passage in the 25th
chapter of the Kurân particularly relates to 'Ukbah son of
Abu-Maît.   El-Beidhâwy relates that 'Ukbah used to be much
in the Prophet's company, and having once invited him to an
entertainment at his house, the Prophet refused to taste of his
meat unless he would profess el-Islâm.   He did so, but soon
after, meeting an intimate friend, and being reproached by him
for changing his religion, 'Ukbah assured him that he had only
pronounced the profession of faith because he could not for
shame allow the Prophet to leave his house without eating.   His
friend, however, declared that he should not be convinced unless
'Ukbah went to Muhammad, set his foot on his neck, and spat
in his face.   He did this in the public hall where the Prophet
was sitting ; whereupon the latter told him that if ever he met
him out of Mekkah he would cut off his head.   And he was as
good as his word, for when 'Ukbah was taken prisoner at Bedr,
the Prophet immediately condemned him to death.   El-Aghâny
states that his executioner was Asím son of Thâbit, and not
'Aly.   'Ukbah's children obtained the surname of *Sibyât-en-Nâr*
(Children of the Fire, or of Hell-fire,) in consequence of the
Prophet's answer to their father's question at the time of his
execution.   El-Walîd ('Ukbah's son) was one of Abu-Bekr's
generals in Upper Palestine, and was nominated governor of
that province before its conquest.   In an engagement before
Damascus, he was, however, seized with panic, and with his
troops fled before the enemy, for which conduct he was deposed.

indeed how can I reproach thee for thy invectives against my father, when of a truth he lashed thee with eighty lashes for drinking wine? And by command of my maternal grandfather he killed thy father who had been taken and bound, and my maternal grandfather killed him by command of my Lord God? And when thy father stood before the executioner, he said, 'Be gracious unto my young sons after me, O Muhammad!' But my maternal grandfather replied, 'Hell-fire is their portion.' For with him there could be no place for them excepting hell-fire, and with my father there could be nothing for them excepting the lash and the sword.—And as for thee, O 'Utbah! how canst thou reproach any one for murder? For why didst thou slay him whom thou didst discover with thy wife, though taking her back again after that she had sinned?—And as for thee, O thou one-eyed Thakífy!* for what reason dost thou

* Mughîrah is generally believed to have lost one of his eyes at the battle of Yermûk, though some historians say that the loss was occasioned by watching an eclipse. At the battle of Yermûk, fought A.H. 15 (A.D. 636), between the army of the Emperor Heraclius and the Muslims, (see Note ‡, p. 28,) the Christian archers are said to have done such execution that seven hundred of the Arabs lost either one or both of their eyes.

revile 'Aly? Is it because his relationship to the Messenger of God was so very distant? or because of the injustice of his administration towards his subjects in this world? For if thou sayest any such thing, thou dost lie, and men will belie thee. And if thou sayest 'Aly killed 'Othmân, verily thou dost lie, and men belie thee. And, moreover, such as thou resemble the gnat which settled on the palm-tree in the fable. The gnat cried out to the tree, 'Hold fast, for I am going to fly off!' The palm-tree replied to her, 'I was not even aware of thy presence, so how could thy taking flight harm me?' And how, O thou one-eyed Thakify! could thy blame hurt us?"

Then Hásan shook his garments and went out. And Múâwiyah said to them, "Did I not tell you that you could do nothing with him? And, by Allâh! verily the house was dark unto me until he departed." *

* The religious discord of the friends and enemies of 'Aly has been renewed in every age of the Hijrah, and is still maintained in the immortal hatred of the Persians and Turks. The former, who are branded with the appellation of Shiahs, or *Sectaries*, have enriched the Muslim creed with a new article of faith, viz., that if Muhammad be the Apostle, his companion 'Aly is the Vicar of God. In their private converse, in their public

worship, they bitterly execrate the three usurpers (Abu-Bekr, 'Omar, and 'Othmân), who intercepted his indefeasible right to the dignity of Imâm and Khalîfah. Even the sanctity of the Prophet's burial-place is no safeguard against riot and bloodshed, which have often been occasioned by the attempts of Persian pilgrims to pollute the tombs of Abu-Bekr and 'Omar (which are in close proximity to that of the Prophet), by throwing upon them some unclean substance wrapt in a handsome shawl or turban. In the language of the Shîahs, the name of 'Omar expresses the perfect accomplishment of wickedness and impiety.

There appears no reason to suppose that 'Aly was personally connected with the rebellion in which 'Othmân was slain. But though he did not directly join the Khalîfah's enemies, yet he did not help him with that vigour and activity which his relation and sovereign might naturally have expected of him ; and this want of zeal was made the most of and exaggerated by 'Aly's enemies.

THE DISPUTE CONCERNING THE SUPERIORITY OF THE KURAISH AND THE YÉMENITES.

IT is related that Múâwiyah was one day seated amid his companions, when lo! two caravans from the desert approached. And he said to some of those who were with him, "Observe these people, and bring me word concerning them." So they went, and returned and said, "O Commander of the Faithful! one caravan comes from el-Yémen, and the other from Kuraish." Then he said, "Go again to them, and bid the Kuraish that they come to us. But as for those of el-Yémen, let them remain in their place unless we desire their admittance."

And when the Kuraish entered, Múâwiyah saluted them, and went near and asked them, "Do ye know, O people of Kuraish! why I left the people of el-Yémen behind, and caused you to draw near?"

They made answer, " No, by Allâh ! O Commander of the Faithful !"

He said, " Because they never cease from vain-glorious boasting over us, in matters wherein they are incompetent. And to-morrow when they come in, and take their places in the assembly, I desire to rise amongst them as a devotee, and propose to them questions whereby I shall lessen their self-esteem, and lower their dignity. Therefore when they come in and take their seats in the assembly, and ask questions about anything, let no one but me answer them."

Now the chief of the party from el-Yémen was a man called et-Tarammâh-ibn-el-Hákam, el Bâhily. And he went to his friends and said to them, " Do ye know, O people of el-Yémen ! why the son of Hind * has left you outside, and has ordered the Kuraish into his presence ?"

And when they replied that they did not, he con-

---

* Hind, the mother of Múâwiyah, was an Amazon notorious for the cruel and revolting indignities which she practised upon the corpse of Hámzah, the Prophet's uncle, at the battle of Ohod, where she headed a band of women, who like herself took part in the combat.

tinued : " In order that to-morrow morning he may rise amongst you as a devotee, and propose to you certain questions whereby he may lessen your self-esteem and lower your dignity. Therefore when you enter his presence, and take your places in the assembly, if he ask you concerning anything, let no one reply to him excepting me."

And when the morrow came, and they had been admitted into Mûâwiyah's presence, and had taken their places, he rose from his seat, and standing erect, cried, " O ye people! who spoke Arabic before the Arabs ; and to whom was the Arabic language revealed ?"

Then et-Tarammâh rose, and answered, " To us, O Mûâwiyah!" not adding, " O Commander of the Faithful !"

" How is that ?" asked Mûâwiyah.

" Because," replied et-Tarammâh, " when the Arabs came down to Bâbel, and all mankind spake the Hebrew language, the Most High inspired the tongue of Yaárab-ibn-Kahtân, el Bâhily, with Arabic. And he was our ancestor, and spoke Arabic ; and his descendants after him handed it down from one to another until this our day. And we, O Mûâwiyah!

are Arabs by lineage, whilst you are Arabs by education only." *

* The Arabians are distinguished by their own writers into two classes, viz., the old lost Arabians, and the present inhabitants of Arabia. The former were very numerous, and divided into several tribes which are now all destroyed, or else lost and swallowed up among the other tribes ; nor are any certain memoirs or records extant concerning them, though the memory of some very remarkable events, and the catastrophe of some tribes, have been preserved by tradition, and since confirmed by the authority of the Kurân. The present Arabians, according to their own historians, are sprung from two stocks, Kahtân the same with Joctan the son of Eber (see Genesis x. 25), and 'Adnân, descended in a direct line from Ismael the son of Abraham and Hagar. The posterity of the former they call *el-'Arâb el-'Aribah*, *i. e.*, the genuine or pure Arabs ; and that of the latter *el-'Arâb-el-Must'ârabah*, *i. e.*, naturalized Arabs. (Some writers, though this is contrary to the general opinion of Oriental historians, make Kahtân also a descendant of Ismael, and call his posterity *Mut'arâb*, which signifies insititious or grafted Arabs, though in a nearer degree than *Must'arâb*.) The posterity of Ismael have no claim to be admitted as pure Arabs, their ancestor being by origin and language a Hebrew, but making an alliance with the Jorhamites by marriage. The descents between Ismael and 'Adnân being uncertain, the Arabs seldom trace their genealogies higher than 'Adnân, whom they acknowledge as father of their tribes, the descents from him downwards being pretty certain and uncontroverted. Between Adnân and Fehr, who went among the Arabs by the surname of Kuraish, and from whom the whole tribe of Kuraish deduced their name, were ten generations. The Arabs suppose Fehr to have been denominated *Kuraish* from his undaunted bravery and resolution : he may be considered as the root of the politest

And this silenced Mŭâwiyah for a time; but in a little while he raised his head, and cried, "O ye people! which tribe among the Arabs first professed el-Islám; and by whom is witness thereof borne?"

Et-Tarammâh answered, "We, O Mŭâwiyah!"

"How so?" asked the latter.

"Because," replied et-Tarammâh, "God sent Muhammad, and you accused him of falsehood, and pronounced him a fool, and deemed him mad. But we received him and succoured him. And God has re-

and most celebrated tribe of the Arabs. Kozaïy, his descendant in the sixth generation, wrested the guardianship of the Ka'abah out of the hands of the Benu-Khuzâ'ah, and with the custody of that building assumed the title of King. Kozaïy's grandson, Hâshim, raised the glory of his people to the highest pitch, and his memory is held in such veneration by the Muslims, that from him the kindred of the Prophet amongst them are called Hâshimites, and he who presides over Mekkah and el-Medînah, who must always be of the race of Muhammad, has the title of el Imâm el Hâshim, *i. e.*, The prince or chief of the Hâshimites, even to this day. Muhammad was the great-grandson of Hâshim, and when he became famous, the Kuraish, who were at first his most violent opponents, added pride in his renown to their former arrogance of birth and culture. The Arabians were for some centuries under the government of the descendants of Kahtân (the progenitor of the 'Arâb-el-'Aribah). Ya:rab (see text), one of his sons, founding the kingdom of el-Yémen, and Jorham, another son (with a descendant of whom Ismael intermarried), founding the kingdom of el-Hijâz.

vealed—those who received and succoured, they, they
are the true believers.* And the Prophet was merciful
to us in consequence, and overlooked our evil deeds.
And why did you not the same, but did, on the
contrary, oppose the Apostle of God?"

And Muâwiyah reflected upon this question; but
after a time, raising his head, he asked, "O ye men!
who among the Arabs has the most eloquent tongue,
and who has borne witness thereof?"

Et-Tarammâh answered, "We, O Muâwiyah!"

"How is that?" asked the latter.

"Because," replied et-Tarammâh, "Imru'l-Kîs, son
of Hájar-el-Kándy, was of us. He says in one of his
poems:

> In years of scarcity
> They feed mankind at times
> From platters large as cisterns
> And cauldrons immovably fixed.

And verily he quoted from the Kurân before it was

* Kurân, Sur. 8, v. 75, alluding to the persecution undergone
by the Prophet and his followers in the early days of Muhammadism at the hands of the Kuraish, and his reception by the
inhabitants of Yathreb, afterwards called el-Medînah. (See
Note *, p. 13.)

revealed. And the Prophet of God himself witnesses the same concerning him."

And for the third time Mùâwiyah was silenced. But once more he asked, "O ye men! who is greatest in courage and renown among the Arabs, and who bears witness thereof?"

Et-Tarammâh made answer, "We, O Mùâwiyah!"

"And how so?" he asked.

"Because 'Amr-ibn-Ma'ady-Kárib, ez-Zabídy,* was of us," replied et-Tarammâh. "He was a warrior in the times of paganism, and a warrior in the times of el-Islám, of which the Prophet is his witness."

"And where wert thou?" asked Mùâwiyah, "for verily he was brought bound in iron."

"Who brought him?" asked et-Tarammâh.

And when Mùâwiyah replied, "'Aly," he continued: "By Allâh! hadst thou known his power, of a truth thou wouldst have submitted the Khalîfate to him, and not have sought it for thyself." Whereupon Mùâwiyah exclaimed, "Dost thou argue with me, thou old woman of el-Yémen?"

"Yes," replied he, "I do argue with thee, thou old woman of Múdhar! Because the old woman of el-

* See Prefatory Note, p. 40.

Yémen was Balkîs,* who believed in God, and married His Prophet Sulaimân, the son of David—Peace be upon them both! But the old woman of Múdhar was thy ancestress, of whom God said concerning her —' and his wife is a *Hamâlat-el-Hátab;* round her neck is a fibre rope.'†

The historian adds: "And Múâwiyah pondered over this, and then, raising his head, said, ' May Allâh recompense thee with friends, and increase thy wisdom, and have mercy upon thy forefathers !' And he bestowed gifts upon him, and treated him kindly."

* Said to be the same as the Queen of Sheba, of our Scripture. See sequel to this tale.

† *Hamâlat-el-Hátab*—Bearer of wood. A surname given by Muhammad to Umm-Jamîl, the sister of Abu-Sufyân, and wife of Abu-Láhab, the Prophet's uncle and bitter enemy. The 111th chapter of the Kurân is as follows :

Intitled Abu-Láhab—Revealed at el-Mekkah.
In the name of the most merciful God.

The hands of Abu-Láhab shall perish, and he shall perish. His riches shall not profit him, neither that which he hath gained. He shall go down to be burned into flaming fire : and his wife also, bearing wood,* having on her neck a cord of twisted fibres of a palm-tree.

* For fuel in hell ; because she fomented the hatred which her husband bore to Muhammad ; or, bearing a bundle of thorns and brambles, because she carried such and strewed them by night in the Prophet's way.—*Sale's Kurân.*

THE MARRIAGE OF QUEEN BARKÎS WITH KING SOLOMON SON OF DAVID.

The reign of Queen Balkîs very nearly coincided with the commencement of the Christian era. She was, according to Abu'l-Fedâ, the twenty-second sovereign of the family of Kahtân, and the eighteenth in the descent from Himyar the son of Sába, the founder of the Himyarite dynasty. The existence of this princess has given rise to numerous fables, amongst others that she was the Queen of Sheba who was contemporary with and married Solomon. The following account of her marriage with that monarch I translated from a copiously annotated Kurân belonging to my sheikh. The real name. of Balkîs was Balkáma or Yalkáma, and Caussin de Perceval states that she was the daughter of Hodhád, or of el-Israh the son of Zhu-Jadán, not of Sharahíl, as stated in the text. The same author also states that she killed her husband by means of poison.

GOD taught King Solomon, son of David, the language of all created things. And over all created things He gave him power—men and genii, and the beasts of the earth, and the fowls of the air, and the fishes of the water. And the armies of King Solomon covered three hundred miles of ground. And when he travelled, it was upon a carpet of silk and gold, which had been woven by a jinn. And his throne was placed in the midst of the carpet, and he sat upon the throne. And around him were six hundred thousand chairs of gold and silver. And prophets sat upon the golden chairs, and wise men upon those of silver, whilst others stood around. And genii and devils surrounded the men, and wild beasts surrounded the genii. And the birds hovered in a flock over the carpet, to screen King Solomon from the rays of the Sun. And there was a racecourse on the carpet, and jars of provisions, and each jar was a load for ten camels. And when King Solomon desired to move, a strong wind raised the carpet, and a gentle breeze bore it along, whithersoever he commanded. And he journeyed for a month without pause. Then God said to him, " Verily, I have increased thy dominion, and should any one from afar desire to speak with thee, the wind will bear to thee his words."

And as the King journeyed, he passed over a ploughman, who said, "Of a truth Allâh has endowed King Solomon with a vast dominion." And the wind brought these words to the King's ears ; and he alighted from his carpet, and went to the plough-man, and said, "If I say, 'Praise be to God,' and God accepts my praise, verily it is of more value than the whole of my kingdom." Then he again mounted the carpet and continued his journey. And he passed by el-Medînah, and prophesied, saying, "This is the town of the last of all the prophets; and they who believe in this prophet, of a truth their place is in Paradise." And when he reached Mekkah, behold! graven images stood around the Ka'abah, and people were worshipping the graven images. And he passed on in silence. And the Ka'abah wept. And when God saw the Ka'abah weeping, He sent an angel, which said to the Ka'abah, "Why weepest thou?" The Ka'abah replied, "Because a great prophet has passed, and wise men with him, and they have not stopped nor blessed me." And God said, "Do not weep, for in the latter days I will send to thee much people, and the last of the prophets shall come from thee. And I will turn the hearts of men to thee as the heart of a mother to her son. But the prophet whom I will send will break in pieces all these images."

And when King Solomon had passed by the

Ka'abah, he entered the Valley of Ants, which is near et-Tâyif. And the chief of the Ants said to his fellows, "Go into your houses, for fear lest these people should tread on you and kill you." And the wind brought the words to King Solomon, who laughed, and stayed the carpet until all the ants had taken refuge in their houses. Then he continued his journey. And presently he descried a flowery land, exceeding beautiful, where he desired to stop that he might pray and eat. And when he had descended from the carpet, the Hud-hud * said to himself, "Our master has work to do, and will not miss me. I will fly up and see the length and breadth of the land." So he rose into the air and looked to the right and to the left. Then he perceived in the distance the gardens of Balkîs, and longed to go thither. And when he arrived, he met another Hud-hud, who asked, "Whence comest thou, and what seekest thou?" "I have come from Damascus," he replied, "with our lord Solomon, the son of David." "And who is Solomon?" asked the other. "He is," replied the Hud-hud, "the king over men, and genii, and devils, and birds, and beasts, and winds. And whence art

* The Hoopooe.

thou ?" he asked. " I am of this country," the other made answer. " And who is the ruler thereof ?" continued the Hud-hud. " A woman whose name is Balkîs," replied the other. " And she is queen of the whole land of el-Yémen, and under her are twelve thousand chiefs, and under command of every chief a hundred thousand horsemen. Dost thou desire to see her kingdom for thyself ?" he added. The Hud-hud replied, " I fear lest King Solomon should discover my absence, and be wroth with me." " Your lord Solomon would desire that thou shouldst see this kingdom and tell him about it," said the other. So they set off together, and saw the kingdom, and the Hud-hud remained until the evening.

And when King Solomon had descended from his carpet in the flowery land which he had espied, and the hour of prayer had arrived, behold there was no water for his ablutions. So he asked of men and genii and devils, " Where is water to be found ?" But not one of them could inform him. Then he sent for the Hud-hud, and was told, " He is not here."

Now it was the business of the Hud-hud to discover water for his master ; for with him was the power to perceive water as in a basin, even though it lay many feet below the surface of the ground.

So King Solomon called for the Eagle who was chief over the birds, and asked him where the Hud-hud was. The Eagle replied, " I know not." Then was the King angry, and cried, " When he returns I will certainly punish him, or cut his throat. And thou must bring him immediately."

Then the Eagle soared heavenward until the world appeared unto him as a plate. And he looked to the right and to the left, and beheld the Hud-hud re-turning from the land of el-Yémen. Then he sought to seize him, but the Hud-hud exclaimed, " By the truth of Allâh ! leave me alone, for I have done no wrong." " Thou wretch ! " cried the Eagle; " verily the Prophet of Allâh intends to kill or to punish thee unless thou hast an excuse."

Then they flew down together to King Solomon, who was seated upon his throne. And the Eagle said, " Lo ! I have brought him." And the Hud-hud settled on the ground, and raised his head and drooped his wings and tail to salute King Solomon. And the King asked him, " Where wert thou ? for verily I intend to punish thee." The Hud-hud re-

plied, "O! Prophet of Allâh! at the Day of Judgment thou wilt stand before Allâh, as I now stand
before thee : therefore have mercy upon me." And
when King Solomon heard these words, he trembled,
and pardoned him. Then he asked again, "Where
wert thou ?" The Hud-hud replied, "I have brought
news of things which thou knowest not." And the
Most High taught the Hud-hud these words in order
that the King might not grow boastful. "I went to
the land of Sába," said the Hud-hud, "and found the
ruler thereof a woman."

(Now this woman was Balkîs, the daughter of
Sharahîl, who was a mighty king, and the ruler over
the whole of el-Yémen. And he said to the other
kings of the world, "I am greater than you ; I cannot marry from among your daughters." So he chose
a woman from among the genii whose name was
Rihânah, and he married her. And of her was born
Balkîs, and they had no other child. And when her
father was dead, Balkis desired the kingdom. So she
assembled the people and asked their consent. And
some of them consented, and some of them refused.
And the latter chose for themselves a king, and the
land of el-Yémen was divided. But the king whom

they had chosen oppressed them ; and in his tyranny
he took the wives of his subjects, and brought them
into his harîm, and made them his wives. And then
the people wished to take from him the kingdom, but
they could not. And Balkîs saw his tyranny. So she
wrote a letter to him offering him marriage. And he
consented, and said, " Verily of a long while have I
desired this thing, but I feared to ask it lest thou
shouldst refuse me." So they were married. But
the same night she made him drunk with wine, and
when he was unconscious she cut off his head, and
returned to her own house. And when day dawned
the people found the King killed, and his head hanging before the door of the palace of Balkîs. So they
understood that she had offered him marriage through
craft, and in order to compass his death. And they
all assembled before her and said, " The whole kingdom is thine of right." So she became Queen of the
entire country of el-Yémen.)

And the Hud-hud continued : " And she has great
possessions, and a bed whereof the length is eighty
yards, and the breadth forty yards, and the height
thirty yards. And it is formed entirely of gold and
silver, encrusted with jewels : and it is placed within

seven doors. And she and her people are worshippers of the Sun."

Then said King Solomon, " I shall inquire, and find out whether thou hast spoken truth or falsehood." And he added, " Take this letter and go with it to her. And when thou hast delivered it, retire to a short distance, and listen to what she and her people say."

So the Hud-hud took the letter, and went to Balkìs. And he found her at a place called Ma'arab, between which and the capital of el-Yémen was three days' journey. And Balkìs was in her palace, and all the doors were locked : for when she would sleep she locked the doors and placed the keys beneath her pillow. And the window was so made that when the Sun rose his first ray might fall upon the Queen. But the Hud-hud settled upon the window and shaded it with his wings. So the Sun rose, but did not as usual enter the room. And when Balkìs awoke, she marvelled at not seeing the Sun ; and she arose and went to the window to discover the cause. Then the Hud-hud threw the letter down before her. And she took it, and when she saw the seal she trembled, and became weak, and knew that he who had sent the letter was greater than she. Then the Hud-hud retired to a little distance, and Balkis read the letter. After which she seated herself upon her throne, and assembled her councillors—a hundred thousand wazîrs. And when they were seated she said to them, "Verily a letter has come to me from King Solomon. In it he says—You must profess el-Islám. Now, therefore, what shall we do?" They replied, "We have wealth, and men, and great courage in war. If thou bid us fight, we will fight." But she informed them that it was of no avail to fight against King Solomon. "It is better," said she, "that we send him a present. If he accept it, he is but a king like myself, and then we will make war with him. But if he refuse it, he is a prophet, and will be content with nothing save our religion." So they prepared a gift—a hundred Mamlûk slaves and two hundred slave-girls, all clad alike; four bricks of pure gold, wrapt in silken handkerchiefs; a jewelled crown; musk and ambergris; and a casket of priceless jewels unpierced. There were also other precious stones which were pierced, but they were pierced crooked. Then she summoned the noblest of her subjects, whose name was Mundzir, and placed wise men under his command. And she

wrote a letter by them, enumerating the presents,
and saying, "If thou art indeed a prophet, declare
which among the slaves are youths, and which are
girls; and without opening the casket make known
its contents, and pierce the jewels, and thread the
stones without the help of men or of genii." And
she said to the Mamlûks, "If King Solomon speak
to you, answer him gently like women." And she
commanded the women to speak like men. Then she
said to Mundzîr, "If King Solomon receive you with
anger, fear not, for then he is but a man, and I am as
strong as he. But if he receive you graciously, he is
a prophet, and you must hearken to his words."

So Mundzîr set forth with the gift, and the Hud-
hud flew swiftly to King Solomon and told him all
that had taken place.

Then King Solomon ordered genii to make bricks
of gold and silver, and to pave a road with them for
twenty-seven miles from where he was, and to build
a wall on either side of the road, having the upper
part and the edge of gold and silver. Then he
inquired of his people, "Where are the most extraordinary creatures to be found?" They replied, "In
such and such a sea there are fish spotted with divers

colours, and possessed of wings and crests." He said, "Bring them at once." So they brought them. And he commanded, saying, "Place them on either side of the road, and put their food before them on the gold and silver." Then he said to the genii, "Bring your children." And they brought many. And he ordered them to be ranged on the right hand and on the left on either side of the road. Then King Solomon seated himself on his throne in the midst of his councillors. And around him were chairs — four thousand on his right and four thousand on his left. Then he said to the genii, " Place yourselves in array, and let each row be three miles long." And he ordered men the same, and beasts and wild beasts the same.

Then Mundzîr arrived. And when he saw the road, and strange animals which he had never before beheld, eating off the ground and soiling the gold and silver, he grew little in his own sight. Then he observed four empty spaces left amongst the golden bricks of the road ; so he placed therein the four golden bricks from Balkîs. And when he beheld the genii, he was afraid. But they said to him, " Fear not ; proceed." So he passed between them until he reached King Solomon, who looked upon him kindly, and said to him, "What wilt thou?" So Mundzir informed him the reason wherefore he had come, and presented to him the letter from Balkis. And King Solomen read the letter, and asked, "Where is the casket?" and he took it from Mundzîr and shook it. Then the angel Gabriel came to him and told him what it contained. And he said to Mundzir, "This casket contains precious stones unpierced, and other stones pierced crooked." "Thou art right," said Mundzîr; "but thou must pierce the jewels, and string the other stones upon a thread." So King Solomon demanded of men and of genii, "Who knows how to pierce these jewels?" But not one among them could tell him. Then he asked the devils. And they answered, "Send to the worm called 'Iradah. So he sent, and the 'Iradah came, and took a hair in its mouth, and worked through each jewel until it came out on the other side. Then King Solomon asked the worm, "What thing dost thou desire?" "To live always in trees," it replied. "Thy wish is granted," said the King (and the tree-worm lives unto this day). Then he asked, "Who can thread these stones?" A white maggot answered, "I will pass the thread through them, O Messenger of Allâh!" And it took the thread in its mouth, and went into the stones, and worked through them until it came out on the other side. Then King Solomon asked, "What is thy wish?" "To live always in fruit," replied the maggot. "Thy wish is granted," said King Solomon (and the maggot lives in fruit unto this day). Then he called for the slaves, and ordered them to wash their hands and their faces. And the women took the water first in one hand and then in the other, and rubbed it over their faces; but the men took the water in both hands at once and dashed it into their faces. And the women washed their arms from the elbow down to the wrist, while the men washed theirs from the wrist up to the elbow. And thus did King Solomon distinguish the men from the women. Then he refused to accept what had been sent him, and said, "I do not demand worldly wealth or gifts—I desire the true faith. And God has created me a prophet, and has given me dominions which are greater than this gift. To you He has given worldly goods without religion, but to me He has given both. And because you are without the true faith, worldly possessions please you, but they do not satisfy me."

Then he said to Mundzir, " Take away your gift, and when you have departed I shall send an army to make war upon you, and to seize your people and your country."

Then when her messengers returned unto Balkís, she said unto them, " By Alláh! I knew of a truth that he was more than a king—even a prophet—and we can do nought against him." So she sent a message to King Solomon, saying, " I am coming to thee, I and my people, to see what this thing is that thou desirest." Then she took her jewelled bed, and placed it within seven rooms, and outside the seven rooms were seven palaces. And she locked the doors, and placed a guard at every door. Then she said to one whom she nominated captain over them, " Guard the bed, and rule the kingdom, until my return." Then she wrote a proclamation for the people who were to journey with her, saying, " Prepare for a journey." And twelve thousand Wazîrs travelled with her, and under each Wazîr were thousands of people.

And King Solomon sat upon his throne amid his councillors, and he beheld people approaching, and asked, " What is this?" They replied, " It is Balkís."

And at three miles' distance she descended from her animal and approached on foot. And King Solomon said to his soldiers, "Who will bring me her bed before she has arrived here and professed el-Islám?" (And this he said, because after that she had professed el-Islám he could not seize her possessions, and also that he might show her his miraculous power.) Then said an 'Afrît,* "I will bring it to thee, O King! ere thou hast risen from council" (now the council sat from dawn until noon); "and I am courageous and faithful." "It must be sooner than that," said King Solomon. Then said el-'Asîf, the King's scribe, "I will bring it before thou canst close thine eyes." And he added, "Look towards el-Yémen." So the King turned his head in that direction, and el-Asif inwardly prayed to Allâh, and Allâh sent an angel who brought the bed through the ground in an instant. And the ground sank in front of King Solomon, and lo! the bed rose therefrom. And when he saw that it was the bed, he said to his people, "Change the position of

* The term *'Afrit* is generally used to designate an evil or malicious jinn. But the ghosts of dead persons are also called *'Afrits*.

the jewels in it, that I may test her intellect as she did mine, and also because a jinn has brought me a report that her mind is weak, and that her feet are like the feet of a donkey." (For the genii knew of the beauty of Balkîs, and were aware that when King Solomon should see her he would desire her for his wife. And as the mother of Balkîs was a jinn, and King Solomon possessed power over the genii, they feared lest his children should for ever lord it over the children of genii; therefore the jinn brought him this false report.) So when Balkis arrived, King Solomon asked her, saying, "Is thy bed like this one?" And she recognized her bed, and said neither "no" nor "yes," but said, " It is it." Then King Solomon commanded to make a house with a floor of glass, and to put water under the glass, and in the water fish and frogs. And he sat on his throne at the end of the house, and called to Balkís to come in. And when she saw the water and the fish and the frogs, she knew not of the glass, and drew up her garments and exposed her feet ; and the King saw that the jinn had lied. Then he commanded her to renounce the worship of the Sun, and invited her to profess el-Islám. And she did so, she and her people. Then King Solomon married her. And he loved her exceedingly, and made her Queen again over the land of el-Yémen. And he commanded the genii to build for her three fortresses to protect the kingdom. And every month until the day of his death he visited her, and remained with her three days.

And when King Solomon was dead, there came a jinn into the midst of the land of el-Yémen, and cried with a loud voice, "O nation of genii, verily King Solomon is dead; fear nothing any longer." So the genii all departed from el-Yémen, and since that time have become invisible.

HOW SAUDAH DAUGHTER OF 'AMMÁRAH OBTAINED REDRESS FROM MÚÁWIYAH.

TRANSLATOR'S PREFATORY NOTE.

'Ammâr-ibn-Yasîr, surnamed el-Asad, was one of the first to profess el-Islám, and was held in high esteem among the Associates of the Prophet. It is said that, being taken prisoner and condemned to be burnt on account of his religion by the idolatrous Mekkans, a miracle was wrought on his behalf by Muhammad, who, passing by the place of execution, stretched out his hand and commanded the fire " to become for him a refreshment, as it had been to Abraham in the furnace of Nimrod."* 'Ammâr attached himself to 'Aly's faction, and fell in the engagement which took place between 'Aly and Múâwiyah at Siffîn, a tract of

---

* It is evident that Muhammad was indebted to the Jews for many of the stories and traditions contained in the Kurân. The following is a condensed account of the tale alluded to in the above note, as given by the Commentators on the Kurân. The Ka'abah was given to Abraham by God as a place of religious worship ; so one day when the Chaldeans were abroad in the fields celebrating a great festival, Abraham broke all the idols then set up in the Ka'abah, except the biggest of them, round the neck of which he hung his axe, that the people might lay the blame upon the idol. When Terah (Abraham's father) returned, finding that he could not insist upon the impossibility of Abraham's story without confessing the impotence of his gods,

land situated on the Syrian side of the Euphrates, A.H. 37, aged 93 years. A mosque containing the tombs of 'Ammâr and the other Associates who fell in this action, was erected at Siffîn.

ESH-SHI'ABY relates that Saudah, daughter of 'Ammârah-ibn-el-Asad, demanded an audience of Mûâwiyah-ibn-Abu-Sufyân, who granted it, but said to her as soon as she entered his presence, " O daughter of el-Asad! wert not thou the reciter of this poem ?

> Gird thee like thy sire, O son of 'Ammârah !
> On the day of battle when warriors meet.
> 'Aly, Husein, and their people support,
> But look upon Hind and her son with contempt.*
> The Imâm is of kin to the prophet Muhammad,
> The Standard of Truth, and Steeple of Faith !
> Be in front of the banners ! Lead on in advance !
> Cleave thro' with the sharp-cutting sword and the lance !"

> * Mûâwiyah himself and his mother.

he fell into a violent passion, and carried him for punishment to Nimrod. By order of the latter, a large space was enclosed at el-Kuthah, and filled with wood, which, being set on fire, burnt so fiercely that none dared venture near it. Then they bound Abraham, and putting him into an engine (invented some say by the devil), shot him into the midst of the fire, from which he was preserved by the angel Gabriel, the fire burning only the cords with which he was bound. They add, that the fire having miraculously lost its heat in respect to Abraham, became an odoriferous air, while the pile changed to a pleasant meadow. But otherwise the fire raged so furiously that some maintain about two thousand of the idolaters to have been consumed by it.

"Yes, O Muâwiyah!" she replied. "But one should be held excused who only did as I did for the sake of right."

"But what moved thee to it?" he asked. And upon her answering, "Love for 'Aly, and following after truth," he exclaimed, "By Allâh! thou dost not appear to have received much favour from 'Aly." Whereupon she cried, "God be my witness before thee, O Muâwiyah! Do not recall days gone by."

"Go to!" said Muâwiyah, "I suffered nothing at the hands of thy brother, for it was impossible for such as thou, or one in his position, to harm me."

"Thou speakest truly, O Muâwiyah," she replied; "yet was my brother's estate neither mean nor blush-worthy. And, by Allâh! he resembles that saying of el-Khansâ,

> Sakhrâ is a beacon to the leaders of caravans,
> As were he a mountain crowned with fire.*

And I crave pardon, O Muâwiyah, if I have done anything requiring forgiveness."

---

* That is, that his hospitality attracted strangers to him from all quarters.

el-Khansâ was a celebrated poetess of the tribe of Sulaim. Sakhrâ was her brother, in whose praise she composed many poems. She professed el-Islâm in the early days of Muhammadism, and was much esteemed by the Prophet.

"Verily I have granted it," he said. "And now what is it thou dost want?"

"O Muâwiyah!" she cried, "surely thou hast risen as a ruler over men, and as a governor to give them laws. And thou must answer to God concerning our affairs, and what He has imposed upon you with regard to our rights. Yet thou dost continually appoint over us one who deceives thee, and who commits violence in the name of the Sultân. And he mows us down like as the harvest is mown, and causes his roller to pass over us even as cardamums are rolled, and he subjects us to degradation, and lays violent hands upon our cattle. This is the son of 'Urtah! He came down upon us, slew my men and seized my goods; and, but for Obedience' sake, in good truth there is amongst us both strength and power. Now, if thou wilt depose him, we will show thee our gratitude; but if thou maintainest him in his post, verily thou shalt know what we are."

"Dost thou mean to threaten me by these words?" asked Muâwiyah. "I am minded to bind thee upon the pack of a vicious camel, and send thee to him that he may do what he pleases with thee!"

At this she cast down her eyes and wept, and recited, saying :

> May Allâh save the soul of him who is entombed,
> For with him has justice been laid in the grave.
> He allied himself with right, accepting nought in its
> stead ;
> And with right and with religion one has he grown.

"Whom dost thou mean by that ?" asked Mùâwiyah.

She replied, "The Commander of the Faithful, 'Aly, son of Abu-Tâlib [may God make gracious his countenance]."

"And wherefore dost thou praise him ?" he asked.

"I brought before 'Aly," she replied, "a man whom he had made ruler over us ; and betwixt whom and us there was no more difference than between the lean and the fat (of meat). And I found 'Aly standing praying. But when he saw me he ceased from his devotions, and asked gently and kindly, 'What dost thou want ?' And when I told him, he wept. And he cried, 'O Allâh ! be witness between me and them ! I do not govern thy creatures tyrannously, nor rule over them contrary to thy law.' Then he drew from his pocket a piece of leather, shaped like the side of a travelling bag ; and he wrote thereon, ' In the name of God the Most Merciful, the Compassionate. * Verily an admonition from your Lord has been brought unto you. Be faithful in measure and in weight, and deprive no man of his due, and sow not the seeds of wickedness upon the earth. Obedience to God will bring its reward to you if ye be true believers, but I am not your keeper.*   When thou hast read this my epistle thou shalt hold what is in thine hand until one shall appear who will take over charge from thee. Farewell.'—So I took the letter from him, and brought it to the governor, and he obeyed and acted according to what was written therein."

Then said Múâwiyah to his scribes, " Write, ordering the restoration of her goods, and compensation for what she has suffered."   And when she asked, " Will that be for myself alone, or for me and my people ? " he replied, " Certainly for thee alone."

" Then," she exclaimed, " if justice is not for every one, and if I am not to be like the rest of my people, by Allâh ! it is an abomination and a disgrace ! "

Then said Múâwiyah, " Write for her what she wants, both for herself and for her people."

* to * Quotation from the Kurán, Sur. vi., V. 153.

ANECDOTE OF MÎSÛN.

MÎSÛN, the daughter of Báhdal,* was married to Múâwiyah, and he brought her from amongst the wandering Arabs into Damascus. But she sorrowed exceedingly for her people, and at the remembrance of her home; and one day, whilst he was listening to her, he heard her reciting, and saying :

> A hut that the winds make tremble
>   Is dearer to me than a noble palace ;
> And a dish of crumbs on the floor of my home
>   Is dearer to me than a varied feast ;
> And the soughing of the breeze thro' every crevice
>   Is dearer to me than the beating of drums ;
> And a camel's-wool Abâh † which gladdens my eye
>   Is dearer to me than filmy robes ;
> And a dog barking around my path
>   Is dearer to me than a coaxing cat ;

* I think Báhdal is a mistake. I find that other authorities speak of Mîsûn as the daughter of *Yáhdak*, of the tribe of Kalb. She had an excellent genius for poetry; and at Múâwiyah's command took her son Yezid (Múâwiyah's successor, with her into the desert, among her own relations, in order to inspire him with poetic sentiments.

† The long loose cloak of camel's wool which is to this day worn by the Bedawîn Arabs.

> And a restive young camel, following the litter,
>   Is dearer to me than a pacing mule ;
> And a feeble boor from 'midst my cousinhood
>   Is dearer to me than a rampant ass.

And upon hearing these lines, Mùâwiyah exclaimed, "The daughter of Báhdal was not satisfied until she had likened me to a rampant ass!" And he ordered her to be packed off again to her family in the desert.

"A WONDERFUL TALE OF ANOTHER PERIOD."

I T is said that when Bahrâm* succeeded to the kingdom of Persia after his father, he gave no heed to his government or his subjects, but devoted himself to amusement, and enjoyment, and pleasure, and sport ; until at length the towns threw off his yoke and fell into ruin, and cultivation diminished, and the treasuries became empty.

And one moonlight night, he was riding out towards Seleucia and Ctesiphon, where he had certain pleasure and hunting-grounds. And he sent for the Maubadz—who is amongst the Magians as the High-priest amongst the Jews, and the Bishop amongst the

---

* "Bahrâm the son of Bahrâm" was the third of that name among the kings of Persia. He was the fifth of the dynasty of the Sassanidæ, and was only the adopted son of his predecessor. Ibn-Batrîk says that this prince was a contemporary of the Emperors Gordian and Gallienus, which would bring his reign somewhere between A.D. 237 and A.D. 268, or somewhat less than four hundred years before the time of Muhammad.

Christians—to talk over his affairs with him. And as they journeyed they passed through the ruins of a large town which had fallen into decay during his reign. There was no living creature to be found therein excepting owls. And one of the owls was screeching, and his mate was answering him from amidst the ruins.

Then Bahrâm asked his companion, "Hast thou ever known amongst men one who understood the language of this bird which screams through the darkness of the night?"

The Maubadz answered, "I, O King! am of those whom God has thus endowed."

"Then tell me," said Bahrâm, "what each of these birds is saying."

"This male owl," said the Maubadz, "is courting the hen bird, and he has said to her, 'Mate with me that we may bring up children who will praise God, and that there may remain of us in this world a posterity to invoke abundant blessings upon us.' And the hen owl has answered, 'In this which you demand there is great happiness and good fortune for me, both in this present life and in the future. But I must impose one condition upon you ; if you accept it,

I will agree to what you wish.' Then the male bird asked her, 'What is your demand?' She replied, 'That out of the ruins belonging to this large town, you will bestow upon me twenty of those villages which have fallen into decay during the reign of the present fortunate prince.'"

Then the King asked the Maubadz, "And what did the male owl say to her?"

"His reply to her," answered the Maubadz, "was, 'If the days of this fortunate prince endure, I will bestow upon you a thousand of these villages. But what will you do with them?' And she made answer, 'Through our union our race will become famous, and our memory great ; and we will give one village from amid these ruins to every son amongst our children.' And he said to her, 'This is a light task that you have demanded of me, and I will fulfil it if this King lives.'"

Then when Bahrám heard the words of the Maubadz, his soul was moved within him, and he awoke from his sleep, and pondered over what had been told him. And he alighted at once, and his attendants followed his example. Then he and the Maubadz went aside, and the King cried, "O thou supporter of the laws of religion, and wise counsellor of the King, and his admonisher of neglect of the duties of his government and the misery of his country and his subjects! what are these words in which thou hast spoken to me? For verily thou hast troubled in me that which was at rest."

So the Maubadz made answer, "I found that this was the time to obtain help from the fortunate prince for the wretched people and the towns. Therefore made I a fable of my words, and an admonition in the language of birds, in order that the King might ask me that which he did ask me."

"O wise counsellor!" said the King; "recount to me the aim thou hadst in view."

The Maubadz replied, "O King! surely the empire is not secure except by obedience to the Divine law and unswerving obedience to God. And the Divine law cannot be maintained except by the King. And the King has no strength except by men. And there is no supporting men except by wealth. And there is no road to wealth except by the cultivation of the soil. And there is no road to cultivation except by justice. And justice is—upright dealing betwixt the creatures created by God, the Glorious, the Most

High. And He has appointed for Himself a deputy, who is—the King.

" Then said the King, " Certainly what thou hast described is true. But explain to me what thou dost mean by it, and enlighten me fully."

He replied, " Willingly, O King! Verily thou hast caused suffering to the villages by bestowing them upon retainers and idle persons, who took for themselves the first-fruits of the crops, and forestalled the harvest, and neglected cultivation, and the consideration of consequences, and of what would profit the villages. And they themselves being exempt from taxation on account of their relationship to the King, the burden fell upon the subjects and the tillers of the village lands. Then these deserted their homes, and wealth decreased, and both soldiers and labourers dwindled. And the country of Persia was coveted greedily by the neighbouring kings and peoples, for in their opinion the means whereby the pillars of the State were supported had been destroyed."

Then when the King heard this he remained where he was for three days. And he sent for the wazirs, and secretaries, and members of the diwáns. And he wrested the villages from the hands of his minions

and adherents, and restored them to their owners.
And they resumed their former habits, and applied
themselves to tillage ; and those of them who had
become weak, again grew strong, and thus the ground
was cultivated and waxed fertile. And the farmers
increased in substance, and the armies became powerful, and the growth of enmity ceased. And the King
set himself earnestly to business, and his conduct was
praised, and his kingdom was so well governed that
after him his reign was known as—The happy days
of him who extended bounty to all men, and over-
shadowed them with justice,

"ANOTHER WONDERFUL STORY."

EL-ASMAÏY * is said to have related the following wonderful tale.

At the time that Khâlid,† the son of 'Abd-Allâh,

---

* El-Asmaïy was a celebrated philologer, a complete master of the Arabic language, an able grammarian, and the most eminent of all those persons who transmitted orally historical narrations, singular anecdotes, amusing stories, and rare expressions of the language. He was heard to say that he knew by heart sixteen thousand pieces of verse composed in the measure called *rajaz*, and it was observed of him that he never professed to know a branch of science without its being discovered that none knew it better than he. His works consisted of treatises upon every variety of subject. Doubtful points of literature were sent to him to be resolved, and it was said that none ever explained better than he the idiom of the desert Arabs. He was born A.H. 122 or 123 (A.D. 740). and died at el-Bâsrah, of which place he was a native, or. as some say, at Marw, A.H. 214, 216, or 217, according to different authorities.

† Khâlid-ibn-'Abd-Allâh, el Kúsary, was appointed governor of Arabian and Persian 'Irâk by Hishâm-ibn-'Abd-el-Mâlik. Before that, in A.H. 89, he was governor of Mekkah. His mother was a Christian, and his grandfather Yezid was one of the Associates of the Prophet. Khâlid was considered as one

el Kúsary, was governor of el-Básrah, I went to that place seeking the Bedawîn of the Benu-Saàd. And one day when I went into Khâlid's presence, I found people surrounding a young man of prepossessing appearance, and evidently possessed of elegance and polite manners. He was well made, and of a graceful figure; his odour was fragrant, his countenance striking, and his mien calm and dignified. And Khâlid inquired his history of those who had brought him in. Whereupon they affirmed, "This is a robber whom we found yesterday in our abode."

So Khâlid looked at him; and the comeliness of his appearance, and his cleanliness, astonished him. And he said to the people, "Loose him." Then he caused him to be brought near, and asked him concerning his story; to which the young man replied, "Verily it occurred as they have said; and the affair took place as they have related."

of the most elegant and correct pulpit orators of the Arabian nation; he was also very beneficent, and generous to profusion in his donations. Doubts were cast on the sincerity of his religious belief, as he had built a church for his mother to pray in. In A.H. 125 or 126 (A.D. 743) he was deposed from the government of 'Irâk, and put to death with cruel tortures at el-Hirah (see Prefatory Note, p. 37) by his successor Yûsuf-ibn-'Omar-eth-Thakify.

"What possessed one so well-conditioned, and of so pleasing an aspect as thine, to do such a thing?" asked Khâlid.

"The wickedness of the world overcame me," he answered, "and God [may He be praised and exalted] is judge of the same."

"May thy mother be bereft of thee!" cried Khâlid. "Hadst not thou with a good countenance, and a sound mind, and excellent manners, a conscience to preserve thee from theft?"

He replied, "Let that pass, O Prince! and make known the command of the Most High concerning that upon which my hands laid hold, for God is not unjust to His slaves."

Then was Khâlid silent awhile, pondering over the affair of the young man. Presently he caused him to approach, and said to him, "Although thou hast confessed before the face of witnesses, verily I am in doubt, for I do not believe thee to be a thief. If therefore thou hast a story other than that of the robbery, make it known to me."

"O Prince!" said the young man, "do not imagine that there is anything but what I have confessed to thee; neither have I anything further to say than that I did enter the house of these people, and stole therefrom of their property; and they followed me, took it from me, and brought me before thee."

So Khâlid ordered him to prison, and commanded the herald to proclaim in el-Básrah:—Let all who desire to witness the punishment of So-and-so the robber, and the cutting off of his hand,* be present to-morrow.

And when the young man had been cast into prison with fetters fastened to his feet, he sighed deeply, and recited, saying:

> Khâlid threatens the loss of my hand
> If I reveal not to him her story;
> But I said, " Far be it from me to disclose
> What the heart has received from its mistress !
> To lose my hand for what I have confessed
> Is less grievous to the heart than her shame.

And the gaolers happening to overhear him, came and reported the same to Khâlid. And when night fell, the latter ordered him into his presence, and when he was brought in, entered into conversation

---

* " If a man or a woman steal, cut off their hands, in retribution for that which they have committed ; this is an exemplary punishment appointed by God ; and God is mighty and wise."— *El Kurán*, Sur. v., V. 42.

with him ; and found him so well-bred, sensible intelligent, and refined, that he was astonished at him. Then Khâlid ordered some food to be brought, and when they had eaten and talked together for some time, said to him, " Of a truth, I felt convinced that thou hadst some other tale besides that of the theft. Therefore, to-morrow, when the people and the judges are present, and I ask of thee concerning the robbery, if thou dost deny it and throw doubt upon it, thou wilt save thyself from mutilation. For verily the Prophet of God has said, ' Doubts invalidate penal sentences.' " Then he ordered him back to the prison.

And when the morning dawned upon the world, there was left in el-Básrah neither man nor woman who abstained from coming to witness the punishment of that young man. And Khâlid was enthroned, and with him were the chief people of el-Básrah, besides others. And he sent for the judges, and desired the young man to be brought, who came hobbling in his chains ; and there was not a woman but wept for him, crying aloud and bewailing him. But silence was imposed upon the people, and then Khâlid said to the young man, " Verily these people assert that thou didst enter their house and didst steal their goods. What sayest thou ?"

He replied, "They speak the truth, O Prince! I did enter their house, and did steal of their possessions."

"Perhaps," said Khâlid, "it was something of no great value that thou stolest ?"*

"On the contrary," said he, "I stole their goods of greatest worth."

"Then it may be," said Khâlid, "that it was not in its proper place when thou didst lay hands upon it ?"†

"Not so," he answered, "it was placed in security."

"But it may chance that thou wert partner with these people in a portion of it," suggested Khâlid.

"No," said he, "the whole of it was theirs; I had no right whatsoever to it."

Then Khâlid grew furious, and went up and struck

* According to the *Sunnah*, or Traditions of the Prophet, the punishment of mutilation was not to be carried out if the value of the stolen property was less than a quarter of a dinâr. In Sale's translation of the Kurân the sum in question is erroneously stated as four dinârs.

† To render a thief liable to the punishment of mutilation, it it was held necessary that the stolen property should have been taken from a place to which he had not easy access.

him in the face with his whip, and cried, " It verifies
the lines,

> Man desires that his wish may be granted,
> But God denies except what He thinks good."

And then he sent for the executioner to cut off the
culprit's hand. So he came, and drew forth his knife,
and stretched out the young man's hand. But a girl,
bedraggled with mud, rushed from the midst of the
women, and shrieking aloud threw herself upon him.
Then she cast aside her veil, and revealed a face
resembling the moon in its fullest beauty. And a
great confusion arose amongst the people, one would
almost have thought it to be a riot. Then she cried
with a loud voice, " I adjure thee in the name of
Allâh, O Prince! that thou delay the mutilation until
thou hast read this petition"—and she presented a
paper to him.

So Khâlid broke the seal, and lo! within it were
written the following lines:

Ah, Khâlid! This fellow is mad through love, is enslaved thereby.
His eye has been wounded by an arrow from my bow.
A dart from 'neath my eyelids deafened him.   And his heart
Is as a flaming fire.   His state is like one void of reason.
He has confessed to a crime which he did not commit, holding
That better than the dishonour of his beloved.
Therefore deal gently with the sad lover ; for he
Is of a noble disposition, by nature not a thief.

And when Khâlid had read the lines, he turned away, and withdrew from the people, and caused the woman to be brought before him, and inquired her history. So she informed him that this young man loved her as she loved him; and that he wished to come and see her; and in order to let her know where he was he threw a stone into the house. And her father and her brothers heard the noise made by the stone, and went towards him. And when he saw them coming he collected all the things belonging to the house and made them up into a bundle. So they seized upon him, and said, " This is a thief." " And they brought him," said she, "to thee. And he confessed the theft and persisted in it, in order to save me from getting into trouble amongst my brethren. And the loss of his hand was a light thing for him to bear, provided he screened me, and I was not disgraced. And all this by reason of his extreme generosity and the nobility of his soul."

Then said Khâlid, " He is worthy through this deed." And he called the young man to him, and kissed him on the forehead, and commanded to fetch the father of the girl, and said to him, " O Sheikh ! verily we had determined upon executing the law of mutilation upon this young man. But God, the Glorious and Most High, has preserved us from so doing. And verily I have ordered for him ten thousand dirhems as a compensation for his hand, and a reward for his care of thy and thy daughter's reputation, and for preserving the honour of you both. And verily I have ordered another ten thousand dirhems for thy daughter, and I pray thee to grant me permission to unite her in marriage with him."

Then said the old man, "Certainly I grant permission for that, O Prince!"

So Khâlid praised and magnified God, and preached a beautiful sermon; and said to the young man, "Verily I have united thee to this girl, Such-an-one, here present, by her consent and wish, and by the consent of her father, for this dowry, of which the sum is ten thousand dirhems."

And the young man said, "I accept this marriage at thy hands."

Then Khâlid ordered that the money should be carried on trays in procession to the young man's house. And the people dispersed rejoicing. And there was not one in the market of el-Básrah but threw almonds and sugar upon the pair, until they entered their dwelling happy and contented.

el-Asmaïy adds : "And I never saw a more wonderful day than that : the beginning of it weeping and mourning, the end of it joy and gladness."

THE SAD FATE OF THE LOVERS WHO DIED OF LOVE.

TRANSLATOR'S PREFATORY NOTE.

'Abd-el-Málik, the son of Marwân (for whom see Note *, p. 55), was the fifth Khalîfah of the 'Omeyyah dynasty. He obtained the surname *Rashi-el-Hájar*, Sweat of a stone, or as we should paraphrase it Skin-flint, on account of his extreme avarice. The anecdote here given does not, however, answer to that character of him. In power he surpassed all his predecessors, and it was in his reign that the Muslim arms made conquests in India in the east, and in Spain in the west. He began his reign A.H. 65 (A.D. 684), and died A.H. 86. He was succeeded by his son el-Walîd. the eldest of sixteen sons, of whom three besides el-Walîd reigned over the Khalîfate.

El-Hajjâj, son of Yûsuf, was governor of 'Irâk and Khorassân for 'Abd-el-Málik, son of Marwân. For a further account of him see Note *, p. 151.

THE first who was called 'Abd-el-Málik in el-Islám, was the son of Marwân ; and his surname was Rashi-el-Hájar. The following tale is told of him in the Hayât-el-Haiwân, and is also mentioned by Muhammad-ibn-Wâsi 'l Haity.

'Abd-el-Málik-ibn-Marwân sent the following letter to el-Hajjâj-ibn-Yûsuf:—"In the name of God the Compassionate, the Merciful, to el-Hajjâj-ibn-Yûsuf. When this my letter reaches thee, and thou hast read it, send to me three foreign slave-girls, full-grown, virgins. They must possess the very perfection of beauty. And write to me a description of each one of them, and the amount of her value in money."

So when el-Hajjâj had read the letter, he sent for the Nakhkhâsîn, that is, the slave-merchants, and laid upon them the commands which he had received from the Commander of the Faithful, ordering them at the same time to search through the towns until they should attain their end. So they went from town to town and from country to country, until having found what they sought, they returned to el-Hajjâj with three foreign full-grown virgin slave-girls, whose like was nowhere to be found. And el-Hajjâj was loud in his praise, and set himself to examine each one of them, and to estimate her money value. And he found that they were priceless, and that each one of them was worth the cost of them all.

Then he wrote a letter to 'Abd-el-Málik, the son of Marwân, in which, after the customary salutation, he said : " The letter of the Commander of the Faithful [may God prolong his days to me] wherein he commands me to buy for him three full-grown foreign virgin slave-girls, and to write him a description of each one of them, and her value, has reached me. Concerning the first girl—may Allâh lengthen the days of the Commander of the Faithful! for her throat is slender, her back broad, her eyes black as antimony, her cheeks sweet ; verily her bosom is rounded, and the flesh of her limbs is like gold mingled with silver, and she resembles that which is said :

> The ornament of her who is fair is the blackness of her eye,
> As if she were silver well mingled with gold.

And her price, O Commander of the Faithful! is thirty thousand dirhems.   And with regard to the second girl.   Verily she is superbly beautiful, of just stature and perfect proportion.   So gentle is her speech, that hearing it, the sick would recover health. And her price, O Commander of the Faithful! is thirty thousand dirhems.   And as to the third girl. Truly her glance is languishing, her hand exquisite, her form faultless ; she is grateful for little, obedient to her friend ; her elegance is astonishing, as though she were descended from a gazelle. And her price, O Commander of the Faithful! is eighty thousand dirhems." Then he added thanks and praise to the Commander of the Faithful, and folded and sealed the letter.

And he sent for the slave-merchants, and said, " Prepare to journey with these girls to the Commander of the Faithful."

But one of them cried, " May Allâh strengthen the Prince! I am an old man and too feeble for travelling; yet I have a son who can take my place: have I permission to equip him ?"

El-Hajjâj replied, " Yes." So they made ready and set forth.

And in the course of their journey they stopped at certain places to rest; and the slave-girls slept. And on one occasion the wind blew, and lifted the veil of one amongst them, and the dazzling light of her beauty appeared. And she was a Kûfite, and her name Maktûm. And the son of the slave-merchant saw her, and in one moment was overcome by love. Now he was a comely youth; and profiting by the inattention of his masters, he went towards her and began reciting :

Ah ! Maktûm, my eye with weeping wearies not,
And my heart by grievous darts is pierced !
Ah ! Maktûm, how many lovers has love destroyed ?
My heart is captive, how can I hide my passion ?

Then she answered him, saying :

If these thy words be true, why didst thou not seek us
At night, when closed were the eyes of envy?

So when night fell, the son of the slave-merchant
girt on his sword, and came to the girl, and found
her standing up awaiting his approach. And he
took her and hoped to make his escape with her.
But his masters became aware of it, and seized him,
and bound him with cords, and loaded him with
irons. And he was kept as a prisoner amongst
them until they stood before 'Abd-el-Málik.

And when they presented themselves to him with
the slave-girls, he took the letter and opened it and
read it. And he found that two of the girls answered
to the descriptions, but that the third did not, and
she was the girl from el-Kûfah. And perceiving
that her face was wan, he said to the slave-merchants, " What ails this girl ? She does not answer
to the description given of her by el-Hajjâj in his
letter. And what means this pallor and wasting
away ? "

Then they made answer, "O Commander of the Faithful! we will tell thee, and we put ourselves under thy protection."

"If you speak the truth," said he, "you may trust in me; but if you lie, you shall perish."

So one of the slave-merchants went out, and brought in the young man bound with chains. And when they stood before the Commander of the Faithful, the young man wept bitter tears, and made certain of punishment. Then he composed these lines, and recited them:

> Commander of the Faithful! I am brought, humbled to the dust,
> And, verily, my hand is bound unto my neck.
> I confess the wicked act, and my evil deed;
> And am not guiltless of that whereof I am accused.
> Dost thou kill me, my crime merits worse than death;
> Dost thou pardon, 'twill be thro' generosity towards me.

Then said 'Abd-el-Málik to him, "O young man! how could such a thing have entered thy mind? Was it through scorn of us, or for love of the girl?"

He replied, "By thy truth, O Commander of the Faithful! and by the greatness of thy power, it was solely for love of the girl."

Then said the Commander of the Faithful, "She is thine, with all that had been prepared for her."

So the young man took the girl, with all the ornaments and pearls that the Commander of the Faithful had made ready for her. And he journeyed with her happy and contented, until at a certain road they stopped to halt for the night.

And when day dawned and their people wished to continue the journey, they came to rouse them, and found them clasped in each other's arms, both dead !

And they wept over them, and buried them by the roadside, and sent news of them to the Commander of the Faithful, 'Abd-el-Málik, the son of Marwân. And he wept for them, and marvelled at it.

ANOTHER PITIFUL TALE OF LOVE

AND here is a similar love story.

It is said that 'Abd-Allâh-ibn-Mùàmr, el-Kîsy, used to tell the following tale :—

I one year made the pilgrimage to the Sacred House of God ; and when my pilgrimage was ended, I determined to visit the tomb of the Prophet.* And one night while I was sitting between the tomb and the Ráwdat,† lo, I heard some one sighing

---

* Muhammadans hold the pilgrimage to Mekkah to be so necessary to salvation, that, according to a tradition of their Prophet, he who dies without performing it may as well die a Jew or a Christian. To the Ka'abah, therefore, every Muslim who has health and means sufficient, ought once at least in his life to go on pilgrimage. A visit to the tomb of the Prophet at el-Medînah is constantly the sequel to the pilgrimage to Mekkah, from which place el-Medînah lies 200 miles to the north-west. It is considered a pious custom, and beneficial to him who observes it, but not indispensable to salvation.

† The following is the account of the Ráwdat given in Burton's " Pilgrimage to El Medînah and Mecca ":—" Arrived at the western small door in the dwarf wall, we entered the celebrated spot called El Rauzah, or the Garden, after a saying

aloud, and groaning heavily. So I listened silently, and, behold, he was reciting these lines :

> Does it grieve thee, the plaining of doves in the lote,*
> And awaken bitter grief in thy breast ?

---

of the Prophet's—'Between my tomb and my pulpit is a garden of the gardens of Paradise.'"—Vol. ii., p. 64.

"The 'Garden' is the most elaborate part of the mosque. Little can be said in its praise by day, when it bears the same relation to a second-rate church in Rome as an English chapel-of-ease to Westminster Abbey. It is a space of about eighty feet in length, tawdrily decorated so as to resemble a garden. The carpets are flowered, and the pediments of the columns are cased with bright green tiles, and adorned to the height of a man with gaudy and unnatural vegetation in arabesque. It is disfigured by handsome branched candelabras of cut crystal, the work, I believe, of a London house, and presented to the shrine by the late Abbas Pacha of Egypt. The only admirable feature of the view is the light cast by the windows of stained glass in the southern wall. Its peculiar background, the railing of the tomb, a splendid filigreework of green and polished brass, gilt, or made to resemble gold, looks more picturesque near than at a distance, when it suggests the idea of a gigantic birdcage. But at night the eye, dazzled by oil-lamps suspended from the roof, by huge wax candles, and by smaller illuminations falling upon crowds of visitors in handsome attire, with the rich and the noblest of the city sitting in congregation when service is performed, becomes less critical. Still the scene must be viewed with a Moslem's spirit, and until a man is thoroughly imbued with the East, the last place the Rauzah will remind him of is that which the architect primarily intended it to resemble—a garden."—Vol. ii., p. 68.

* The Sidr, or Lotus Tree. *Rhamnus Lotus*, Linnæus and Reichart. *Zizyphus Lotus*, Lamarck, Willdenow, Des fon-

Has sleep fled thee through musing on the fair ?—
She has bestowed upon thee instead crazing meditation.
O Night ! thou hast been long to the sick one ;
He suffers through desire and loss of patience.
Thou hast delivered the lover to burning flames :
He is consumed as living coals consume.
The moon bears witness that I love—
That love for one fair as herself has subdued me.
I thought not of suffering on her account,
Nor recked I of it ere it smote me.

'Abd-Allâh continues : Then the voice broke, and
I knew not whence it had come to me. So I remained motionless, when, lo ! verily the weeping and

taines. *Zizyphus Sylvestris*, Shaw. *Rhamnus Napeca*, Forskal.
This tree bears a small round fruit of much the same size,
shape, and colour as a Siberian crab-apple. It is highly astringent, but is considered a delicious fruit by the Bedawîn, to
whom its acidity is doubtless a pleasant change from their ordi-
narily dry food. A decoction of its leaves is used for washing
dead bodies. This is one of the traditions called "*hukmat
taàbbud*," *i.e.*, a precept of worship to be obeyed, but for which
no reason has been assigned ; in contradistinction to the " *hukmat màanahu zàhir*," *i.e.*, an order for which the reason is
apparent. Of the latter class is the order that corpses should
be washed in salt water, the reason being that they might
thereby be longer preserved from turning to dust. Probably
the astringent properties of the lotus were known to the Prophet,
who was skilled in chemistry, and he ordered the decoction from
these leaves to be used in places inland, where salt water was
not procurable.

groaning again began, and the man recited these lines, saying :

> The fleeting vision of Riyâ has grieved thee,
> And the night is dark as the blackest tresses.
> The foundation of love was laid by thine eye ;
> But the brilliant vision has fled from thy gaze.
> I called to the Night—and the darkness was
> Like an ocean with rolling billows beating ;
> Whilst the moon traversed the heavens
> As a journeying Monarch with the stars his armies.—
> " O Night ! thou hast been weary to the lover,
> Only with the Dawn is his aid and succour."
> But Night answered me, " Die thy natural death ! and know
> That love is the self-contempt of the lover."

And at the beginning of his verses I rose in order to find the voice, and he had not ended them before I was with him. And I found him a youth with the down yet on his face, and with tears flowing in torrents over his cheeks. So I said to him, " Good morrow, young man." He replied, " And to thee— who art thou ? " I answered, " 'Abd-Allâh-ibn-M'âmr, el-Kîsy."

He asked, " Seekest thou aught ? "

I replied, " I was sitting in the Ráwdat, and nothing troubled me this night excepting thy voice. Now my life is at thy service ; what is it thou requirest ? "

"Sit down," said he. And when I had done so, he continued: "I am 'Utbah-ibn-Khabâb-ibn-el-Mundzir-ibn-el-Jamûh, el-Ansâry.* At dawn I repaired to the el-Ahzâb mosque, and remained awhile kneeling and prostrating. Then I withdrew to a distance, and, behold! I came upon women progressing like moons, and having in their midst a girl of marvellous beauty and perfect grace, who advanced towards me, and said, 'O 'Utbah! what sayst thou to an union with one who seeks union with thee?' Then she left me and departed, and I could hear no news nor find any trace of her. And verily, I, beside myself, am speeding from place to place, seeking her."

Then he cried aloud, and swooned lifeless on the ground; and though he presently recovered consciousness, his face was as if it had been dyed with saffron. Then he recited, uttering these verses:

---

* When the Prophet fled from Mekkah to el-Medînah, then called Yathreb, and whose inhabitants consisted chiefly of the tribe of El-Aus and the Jewish tribe of Kházraj, he was received and sheltered by some of the chief men of the city; in remembrance whereof they and their descendants adopted the name of el-Ansâry (*i.e.*, helpers, supporters), and greatly glorified themselves on account of this appellation.

> My heart beholds thee in thy distant land ;
> Does thy heart likewise see me from afar ?
> My soul and my eye yearn after thee ;
> With thee is my spirit, thy memory with me.
> Even were I in the eternity of Paradise or Heaven,
> Pleasureless would be life till again I beheld thee.

The narrator continues: Then I cried to him, "O son of my brother! repent of thy sin, and return unto thy Lord, for verily the terrors of the Judgment Day await thee."*

But he exclaimed, "Get thee hence! I shall not know fear until the Kárazhan returns."†

Nevertheless, I did not cease importuning him until the morning star rose, when I said, "Let us to the Ahzâb mosque."‡

* He feared for the young man on account of the blasphemy contained in the two last lines of his verses.

+ A man of the tribe of the el-Anêzah went to gather the fruit, called Káraz, of an acacia, and never returned ; whence the proverb, " Till the return of the Kárazhan."

‡ The Ahzâb mosque lies without the city of el-Medînah. There it is said the Prophet prayed for three days during the Battle of the Ditch (A.H. 5). the last fought with the infidel Kuraish under Abu-Sufyân. After this three days' prayer, say some of the Arab writers. God sent a piercing cold east wind, which benumbed the limbs of the infidels, blew dust in their eyes, overturned their tents. put their horses in disorder, and gave the victory to the Muslims. The Prophet's prayer. therefore, having been granted. Muslims believe that no petition raised at the Ahzâb mosque is neglected by Allâh.

So we went thither, and sat down until we had performed our midday devotions—when, behold! of a truth the women approached, but the girl was not with them. And they cried, " O 'Utbah! what thinkest thou hast become of her who sought union with thee, and revealed to thee the love that was in thee ?"

" What has happened to her ? " he asked.

" Her father," they replied, " has taken her and packed her off to es-Samâwah." *

Then I questioned them concerning the girl, and they told me, " She is Riyâ, the daughter of el-Ghatrif, es-Sálamy." And the young man raised his head, and composed, saying :

> My friend ! verily Riyâ has sped away with the dawn,
> And her camel has borne her to the land of es-Samâwah.
> My friend ! verily I swooned through weeping,
> But were another possessed of tears I would borrow from
> him.

Then I addressed him : " O 'Utbah ! I brought here with me much wealth lest worthy persons should stand in need of it ; and verily I make a free gift of it to thee, until thou shalt have attained thy desire,

---

* es-Samâwah lies between Sûk-esh-Shiyukh and Hillah, on the right bank of the Euphrates.

and more than thy desire. Let us come to the mosque of the el-Ansâry."*

So we went on until we were close to the people belonging to it, whom I saluted; and when they had answered courteously, I said, "O ye people! what have ye to say concerning 'Utbah and his father?"

They replied, "They are among the chief of the Arabs."

I said, "He has been wondrously smitten of love, and I seek help from you to reach es-Samâwah."

They replied, "We hear and obey."

So we mounted, and the people rode with us until we looked down upon the abode of the Benu-Salim.† And the chief was made aware of our presence, and he came out in haste, and met us, and cried, "Long life to ye! ye great ones!" We replied, "And to thee long life! Verily we have come as thy guests."

* This is also called the Masjid en Nábi, or Prophet's Mosque. It is erected around the spot where the Prophet's camel, on his flight from Mekkah, knelt down by the order of Heaven. It was built by the Ansâry and Muhajerin (see Note *, p. 154), who were assisted in their labours by the Prophet himself.

† The Benu-Salim was a branch of the important tribe of el-Kházraj, which was spread over the country surrounding el-Medînah.

He said, "You have arrived at a most liberal dwelling. Ho, slaves! come hither." And the slaves came forward, and spread out the Intâ'a,* and placed the cushions, and slaughtered of the flocks and the herds.

But we said, "We will not taste thy food until thou hast granted us what we desire."

"And what *is* your request?" he asked.

"We seek," we replied, "thy honoured daughter in marriage for 'Utbah-ibn-Khabâb-ibn-el-Múndzîr, the noble, the illustrious, the well-descended." Whereupon he remarked, "O my brother! verily this is her business whom thou demandest, and I shall go and acquaint her of it." And he rose up wrathfully, and went out to Riyâ."

And she asked, "What is this anger, O my father! which I perceive on thy brow?"

He answered, "Some of the el-Ansâry people have arrived here seeking thee in marriage from me."

"They are illustrious chiefs," said she; "may the

* *Intâ'a,* or *Nitâ'a,* a piece of leather which is spread on the ground, and upon which the dishes are placed at a feast. It is also used when corporal punishment is to be inflicted upon criminals, and when they are brought out for public execution.

Prophet intercede for them! But which amongst them seeks me to wife?"

"The young man who is known as 'Utbah-ibn-Khabâb," he replied.

"'I have heard," said she, "of this 'Utbah, that he is one who performs what he promises, and follows what he seeks."

Then cried her father, "I have sworn that I will never marry thee to him, for of a truth a certain tale concerning thee and him has reached me."

"It was not true," she said.

"Nevertheless," he responded, "I have sworn that I will not wed thee with him."

"Yet be courteous to them," she said. "For indeed the el-Ansâry do not associate with people of low degree. An excuse is better than flat refusal."

"What kind of excuse?" he asked.

"Be exacting with them in the matter of dowry," she replied, "and they will withdraw."

"What thou hast spoken is good," said he. Then he went out quickly, and said to the people, "The daughter of the tribe has made answer. But nevertheless I must demand that her dowry be equal to her rank. Say, who is guarantee for the same?"

So I, Abk-Allâh, said, " I am."

Then the old man continued, " I require for her a thousand bracelets of red gold, and five thousand dirhems of the best stamped silver money, and a hundred garments of striped and damasked stuffs, and five skins of ambergris."

I said, " You shall have it. But what was her answer ?"

He replied, " Yes, assuredly." On hearing which, I sent off men of the el-Ansâry to el-Medînah-el-Munáwwarah,* and they brought the whole of what had been promised. Then they killed of the flocks and

* Medînah means in the abstract, city or town. But when the inhabitants of Yathreb received Muhammad, and acknowledged his mission, they changed this name to el-Medînah—*the* city *par excellence*. It has, however, many affixes—such as, Medînah-en-Náby, the City of the Prophet; el-Medînah-el-Munáw-warah, the Enlightened or Illuminated City. This latter title is said by Muslims to have been given for the following reason : above the chamber in which are the tombs of the Prophet and his successors, Abu-Bekr and 'Omar, is a green dome, surmounted by a gilt crescent springing from a series of globes. They believe (according to Mr. Burton) that a pillar of heavenly light crowns this crescent, and can be seen by the pilgrims at three days' distance. My sheikh, however, who at my request made inquiries upon this subject amongst those most lately arrived from el-Medînah, brought back word that the light resembles the morning star, and can be seen from afar, but not at the distance of three days' journey.

the herds, and people assembled to partake of the feast, which lasted for forty days. Then the father said, " Take your damsel." So we mounted her in a litter, and loaded thirty camels with her goods, and set off and departed. And we travelled until there remained between us and el-Medînah-el-Munáwwarah but one day's journey, when lo ! horsemen in search of plunder came out against us, and I believe that they were of the Benu-Salim. And 'Utbah-ibn-Khabâb charged them, and slew many of the men, and turned to withdraw. But he had received a spear-thrust, and fell to the ground. And help came to us from the inhabitants of that part of the country, who drove the horsemen away. But verily the days of 'Utbah were accomplished, and we cried, " Alas, O 'Utbah !"

Then we heard the girl exclaim, " Alas, O 'Utbah!" and she flung herself from the top of her camel, and threw herself upon his body, and began wailing aloud, and reciting passionately these lines :

I feigned patience, but in impatience. And that my soul
Has no right to live after thee is its one consolation.
Had it rightly acted, truly 'twould have died
With those who have preceded, before thy death.
After us will none be found who thus share friendship,
    Nor among souls, a responsive soul.

Then she sobbed one sob, and her spirit passed away. And we dug a single grave for them both, and covered them with earth, and I returned to the land of my people, where I remained seven years. Then I made up my mind to go again to the el-Hijâz, and as I had determined to visit el-Medinah-el-Munáw-warah, I said, "Verily I will go again and look at 'Utbah's grave." So I went to the tomb, and lo! I found a tree with streamers, red and yellow and green, upon it. And I asked the people living thereabouts, "What is the history of this tree?"

And they answered, "It is the tree of the betrothed lovers."

And I stayed a day and a night at the tomb, and then departed; and that was the last I saw of it.

ANOTHER SAD LOVE STORY.

AND resembling the foregoing tale concerning love and the concealment of passion, together with the plain proof of its discovery, is the following story, which a certain person of those who are well-to-do used to relate.

One day while sitting in my house, behold! a servant came in bringing a letter, and said, "A man at the door gave me this." So I opened it, and behold! it contained the following lines :

> Grief is far from thee, and thou hast attained happiness,
> And the King of all has withdrawn thee from sorrows.
> And in thy hands, wouldst thou bestow it, is the balm
> For my soul, and members sick through wounds.

So I exclaimed, " A lover, by Allâh !" and said to the servant, " Go out and bring him to me." And he went out, but saw no one : and this behaviour astonished me.

So I summoned all the slave-girls, both those who

went out of doors and those who stayed at home, and questioned them about it. But as they all vowed that they knew nothing whatever of the history of the letter, I said, " I am not making this inquiry through jealousy of him who loves one amongst you ; but that she who knows anything of his case may be a gift from me to him, with all that she has and a hundred dinârs." Then I wrote an answer, thanking the writer for his letter, and begging his acceptance of his beloved, which letter I placed beside the house with a hundred dinârs. And I proclaimed, " Whoso knoweth aught of this, let him take it."

But the letter and the money remained for days, and no one took them away. And I was vexed about it, and said, " He has been satisfied by the sight of her whom he loves." So I forbade those of the slave-girls whose business took them abroad from leaving the house.

And only a day or so had passed, when lo! the servant came to me bringing with him a letter. And he said, " This has been sent to you by one of your friends." So I said, " Go out, and bring him in to me;" and he went out, but found no one. Then I opened the letter, and behold! it contained these lines :

What is this thou hast wrought on a departing soul?
A soul whereon the Angel of Death attends.*
Thy tyranny forced his presence, and in journeying
They wrestled till the soul burst its bonds.
And, by Alláh! wer't said to me, Commit iniquity,
And the world and what it holds shall reward thee;
Surely I had said, No, for I fear retribution;
And, No, wer't to bring me the same twice-told.
But for bashfulness I had shown who filled that dwelling—
My heart; and had discovered the wishes of the beloved.

And I was grieved at his conduct, and said to the servant, " Let no one who brings another letter to you escape from your hands."

Now the time for the pilgrimage was near, and whilst I was descending from Mount Arafat,† behold!

* Muhammadans believe that a tree grows in Heaven upon every leaf of which a man's name is written. When death is at hand, the leaf on which the dying man's name is inscribed falls to the ground, and is picked up by Azrael, the Angel of Death, who then proceeds to the abode of the sick man and awaits the parting of soul and body. The soul is supposed to come from the feet, upwards : the last spot where it rests, ere making its final exit through the mouth, being the clavicular bones. The words which I have rendered respectively " departing soul " and " burst its bonds " are, literally. " soul hanging upon the clavicle," and " broke " or " burst away from the clavicle."

When the soul leaves the body and is taken by Azrael, if it has belonged to a good man the Angel takes it in his hand up to Heaven ; but if to a bad man, he receives it upon the point of his spear.

† One of the ceremonies observed by those performing the pilgrimage to Mekkah, is a visit to Arafat, a mountain near

a young man, of whom but a shadow remained, rode
at my side on a dromedary. And he saluted me, and
I returned his salutation and welcomed him. Then
he asked, "Dost thou know me?" And upon my
replying, "It was not through ill-will that I failed to
recognize thee," he said, "I am the writer of those
two letters."

So I bowed myself before him, and said, "O my
brother! verily thy behaviour has distressed me, and
thy concealment of thyself has disquieted me, for I
would have given thee thy desire and a hundred
dinârs."

"May God recompense thee!" he cried. "Verily
I am come to thee confessing the sight. My look
was contrary to the laws of the Book and of tradition." *

the city. Muslims have a great respect for this mountain, believing that when Adam and Eve were banished from Paradise
they were separated for a hundred and twenty years ; but at
last, wandering through the world seeking one another, they
met and recognized each other on the summit of Mount Arafat.

* A Muslim who looks upon the face of a woman not of kin
to him commits a grievous sin. Should the wind blow aside
her veil, or should she through coquetry or vanity remove it, he
is ordered to cast down his eyes. If the sight be forced upon
him, he must at the first opportunity confess the same to her
husband or master. If the latter forgives him, he will also obtain

"Allâh pardon both thee and the girl!" said I. "But journey with me to my house, that I may bestow her upon thee, together with a hundred dinârs, which sum thou shalt receive every year."

But he answered, "I do not want it." And though I pressed it upon him, he would not have it. Then I said to him, "If thou refusest this, at least tell me which she is amongst the slave-girls, that while I live I may deal kindly with her for thy sake."

But he replied, "I will not name her to any one," and took leave of me and departed.

And that was the last I ever saw of him.

forgiveness when after his death he appears before Allâh. But should he die suddenly, or should he postpone asking pardon, he and the man he has wronged will at the Last Judgment be confronted, and sentence upon him will be passed according to the forgiveness or otherwise of the injured man.

THE ACCOUNT OF HOW EL-HAJJÂJ BECAME GOVERNOR OF 'IRÂK.

LET us now return to the account of what happened in the days of 'Abd-el-Málik-ibn-Marwân. El-Hajjâj* was appointed ruler over the two sacred

* El-Hajjâj-ibn-Yûsuf of the tribe of Thakîf, and Farigha daughter of el-Hamâm, appears by all accounts to have been one of the most tyrannical and bloodthirsty monsters that ever held the lives of others in their power. Arabian historians relate that at his birth he was deformed, and that he refused to allow either his mother or any other woman to suckle him. Then the devil took upon himself the form of el-Hárith-ibn-Kaldah, a celebrated Arab physician, who died soon after the promulgation of el-Islám, and came to the parents of el-Hajjâj in their distress and perplexity, and prescribed for the child as follows : " Slay for him a black goat, and let him lick its blood. Then slay for him a black serpent, and let him lap its blood, and also anoint his face with it for three days." On the fourth day, they say the child accepted his natural food. But the consequence of this treatment was that he could not refrain from blood-shedding. He even said of himself, that his greatest enjoyment was to kill and to commit actions which no other could. He died after for fifteen days suffering agonies from an internal cancer, in A. H. 95, at the age of fifty-three or fifty-four. He was buried at el-Wâsit, a city which he had built between el-Básrah and el-Kûfah, and wherein he had died ; but his tomb was afterwards levelled to

M

and holy cities, Mekkah and el-Medînah ; and it is said that he held in high esteem a certain man named Ibrahim-ibn-Muhammad-ibn-Talhah, by whom he was accompanied to Damascus, on his return thither to visit 'Abd-el-Málik, and of whom he said to the Amir, " I have brought thee, O Commander of the Faithful! a noble, well-born, learned, and humane man from the Hijáz, with his knowledge of the divine laws and excellence in counsel. And by Allâh! there is not his equal in the Hijáz. And upon thy head be it, O Commander of the Faithful! if thou dealest not with him according to his merit."

" Who is he ? O Abu-Muhammad !" inquired 'Abd-el-Málik. And when el-Hajjáj told him, " Ibrahim-ibn-Muhammad-ibn-Talhah," he exclaimed, " O Abu-Muhammad! of a truth thou hast recalled to our mind an imperative duty. Give him leave to enter."

And when he came in, the Amir commanded him to sit down in the most honourable place in the Council, and said to him, " Verily, el-Hajjáj has

the ground, and a current of water turned over it. One historian states that el-Hásan, el-Básry, on hearing of the death of el-Hajjáj, made a prostration in thanksgiving to God, saying, " O my God ! Thou hast caused him to die ; let also his example die from among us."

reminded us of what we already knew concerning the greatness of thy benevolence and the excellence of thy advice. Now, therefore, let no desire have place in thy breast without making it known to us, that we may accomplish it for thee, and that el-Hajjâj-abu-Muhammad's praise of thee may not have been in vain."

So Ibrahîm answered, "O Commander of the Faithful! I will make known what I desire for the well-pleasing of the Most High, and union with the Prophet at the Day of Judgment, and sincere advising of the Commander of the Faithful."

"Speak," said the Amîr.

"I cannot reveal it," answered Ibrahîm, "if there be present another beside thee and me."

"Not even thy friend el-Hajjâj?" asked 'Abd-el-Málik.

"No," said Ibrahîm.

"Leave us," said 'Abd-el-Málik to el-Hajjâj. And the latter went out, reddening with anger, and not knowing whither he walked. And when he was gone 'Abd-el-Málik said, "Declare thy advice."

Then Ibrahîm began: "O Commander of the Faithful! Thou—knowing of his tyranny, and cruelty, and oppression, and neglect of right and following after wrong—hast appointed el-Hajjâj as ruler over the two sacred and holy cities; and dwelling therein, as thou art aware, are certain of the children of the Muhajarîn, and of the Ansâry,* and the Associates† of the Prophet of Allâh. And el-Hajjáj subjects them to degradation, and through his cruelty causes them to desert their country. And would to God I knew what reply thou couldst make to the Messenger of Allâh when in the Halls of Judgment he has asked thee concerning this. And by Allâh! O Commander of the Faithful! upon thy head be it, if thou deposest him not, nor layest up for thyself proximity to the Most High."

* The Muhajarîn, or *refugees*, were those Mekkans who in the early days of el-Islâm fled from their home on account of their religion. The Ansâry, or *assistants*, (see Note*, p. 137) were those who received the Prophet at el-Medînah. At the end of the first year of the Hijrah, the Prophet, in order to attach both these bodies more closely to his interests, and also to prevent rivalry as to priority of belief, and consequent consideration, between them, established a fraternity among them, the principal maxim of which society was that they should not only treat one another like brethren, but also most cordially love and cherish one another to the utmost of their power. And lest even this should prove an insufficient bond, he also coupled in a loving union the individuals of either party.

† See Note †, Author's Preface, p. 3.

Then said 'Abd-el-Málik, "Verily el-Hajjâj thought well of thee without thy deserving it." And a moment afterwards he added, " Rise, O Ibrahîm !"

So I, Ibrahîm, rose with a troubled mind and left the council-chamber, and verily the world appeared black in my sight. And the Chamberlain followed me and laid hold of my elbow, and sat down with me in the entrance. Then 'Abd-el-Málik sent for el-Hajjâj, who went in and remained a long while. And I had no doubt but that they were plotting my death between themselves. Presently the Amîr summoned me. So I got up, and as I went in I met el-Hajjâj coming away, who embraced me and cried, " May Allâh reward thee on my account by reason of this advice ! Surely, by Allâh ! if I live I will indeed increase thy power." Then he turned from me and went out. And I entered, saying to myself, " He is mocking me, and with good reason." And I stood before 'Abd-el-Málik, who made me sit in the place I had occupied before, and then said to me :

" Verily I have discovered thy sincerity, and I have deposed him from governing the two holy cities, and have appointed him ruler over 'Irâk,* giving him to

* For 'Irâk, see Prefatory Note, p. 31.

understand that thou deemedst the Hijáz too small for him, and didst demand 'Irâk for him, and that the increase of his government was thy wish. And he believes that his appointment as ruler of 'Irâk is thy doing, and verily this thought has made his countenance radiant with joy. Journey therefore with him wherever he may go. May good attend thee! and do not deprive us of thy advice."

ALLÂH IS ALL-KNOWING! *

* These words are used when the narrator does not vouch for the truth of a tale, but relates it as he has heard it.

ANECDOTE OF THE PLAIN-SPOKEN ARAB.

IT is said, that one day el-Hajjâj separated himself from his guards, and falling in with an Arab, asked him, "O chief of the Arabs! what about el-Hajjâj?" To which the man replied, "He is tyrannical and capricious." "Have you complained of him to 'Abd-el-Málik-ibn-Marwân?" asked el-Hajjâj. "He is more tyrannical and more capricious," replied the Arab. "May the curse of Allâh be upon them both!"

Now whilst this was going on, behold, the soldiers rejoined him. Then, the Arab becoming aware that it was el-Hajjâj himself, cried out, "O Prince! divulge the secret which is between me and thee to none save Allâh." Whereupon el-Hajjâj laughed, and on departing gave liberally to him.

THE STORY OF THE YOUNG MAN WHO WAS DEEMED MAD.

HISTORIANS relate that 'el-Hajjâj-ibn-Yûsuf, es-Thákify, was keeping watch one night with his councillors, Khâlid-ibn-'Urfutah being amongst them, to whom el-Hajjâj said, "O Khâlid! bring me a tale-teller from the mosque." [For in those days it was thought necessary that there should be some one continually in attendance at the mosques.] And Khâlid went out and found a young man standing up praying. He therefore sat down until the latter had said, " Peace be upon you !"* and then said to him, " Come to the Amîr."

" Did the Amir send expressly for me?" asked the young man. And when Khâlid replied, " Yes," he went with him, until, on arriving at the door, Khâlid asked him, " What canst thou narrate to the Amir ?"

* At the end of a Muslim's prayers he says, " Peace be upon you." first over the right shoulder and then over the left, to the recording angels who have their posts there.

" He shall find in me whatever he desires, in-shäa-Allâh ! " * replied the young man.

And when he appeared before el-Hajjâj, the latter asked him, " Hast thou read the Kurân ?" " I have," he replied ; "and have, moreover, committed it to memory."

" And dost thou know any poetry?" asked el-Hajjâj.

" There is not one of the poets that I have not studied," he answered.

" And art thou acquainted with the pedigrees † of the Arabs, and their adventures ?" continued el-Hajjâj.

" Of all that, nothing is forgotten by me," the young man made answer. And he continued narrating whatever the Amîr desired, until the latter thought of

---

* *In-shäa-Allâh*—If it please God. Nothing is ever proposed to be done by a Muslim without his adding these words.

† The Arabs used to value themselves excessively on account of the nobility of their families ; and so many disputes occurred upon that subject that it is no wonder if they took great pains in settling their descents. A knowledge of the genealogies and history of their tribes was one of the three sciences chiefly cultivated by them before the time of Muhammad. The others were, a knowledge of the stars sufficient to foretell the changes of weather, and the power of interpreting dreams.

retiring, when he said, " O Khâlid! make over to the young man a mule, and a slave boy and girl, and four thousand dirhems." Whereupon the young man exclaimed, " God save the Prince! the prettiest and most wonderful of my tales yet remains."

So el-Hajjâj resumed his seat, saying, " Relate it." The young man began : " God save the Amîr! My father perished when I was a child of tender years, and I was therefore brought up under the care of my paternal uncle, who had a beautiful daughter. And even in childhood we loved one another, and our love grew most wonderfully until the time came that we both learnt that matchmakers were eagerly seeking her, and offering to dower her with great wealth on account of her beauty and accomplishments. And when I saw this, sickness took possession of me, and I became weak and was laid upon my bed. Then I made ready a huge jar, which I filled with sand and stones, and sealing its mouth, I buried it under my bed. And after the fulfilment of certain days, I went to my uncle, and said, ' O uncle! of a truth I had determined upon travelling; but I have lighted upon a vast treasure, and was afraid lest I might die without any one knowing about it. If therefore my end should come, bring it forth; and liberate ten slaves for me; and send somebody ten times on the pilgrimage for me; and equip for me ten men with horses and weapons; and bestow a thousand dinârs for me in alms. And be not uneasy about it, O uncle! for verily the treasure is considerable.' And when my uncle had heard my words, he went to his wife and made the same known to her. Then nothing could exceed the hurry with which she and her slave-girls set off to come to me. And she laid her hand on my head and said, 'By Allâh! O son of my brother! I did not know of thy illness nor of what had happened to thee until the father of So-and-so told me about it this moment.' And she talked to me coaxingly, and doctored me with medicines, and overpowered me with kindness, and drove the suitors away from her daughter. And when I saw this, I was upon my guard. After a while I sent to my uncle, and said, 'O my uncle! truly God, the Glorious and Most High, has been gracious unto me and restored me to health. Seek out for me, therefore, a girl with such and such beauty and accomplishments and qualities; and let nothing be demanded from thee that thou dost not grant.' So he asked,

'O son of my brother! what hinders thee from choosing the daughter of thy uncle?' I made answer, 'She is to me the dearest of beings created by the Most High; but, verily, when ere now I sought her thou didst refuse me.' He said, 'On the contrary, the refusal was on the part of her mother; and now she is quite reconciled to it and pleased at it.' So I said, 'Do as thou wilt.' Then he returned to his wife and made my words known to her. And she assembled her kindred, and married me to the very girl. After which, I said, 'Hasten as thou wilt to bring me the daughter of my uncle; afterwards I will show thee the jar.' So she was brought to my house, and her mother did not omit anything that is customary amongst the most noble ladies; but led her daughter to me in procession, and provided her with everything that came in her way. And my uncle bought ten thousand dirhems' worth of goods from the merchants. And every morning for some time there came to us gifts and offerings on the part of her relations. But when some days had gone by, my uncle came to me and said, 'O son of my brother! verily I bought from the merchants ten thousand dirhems' worth of goods; and they are

impatient at the delay in payment.' I said, ' The
jar is thine whenever thou pleaseth.' So he went off
in haste, and returned with men and ropes. And
they dragged it forth, and carried it away quickly to
his dwelling. But when he had turned it upside-
down, there was only what I had put into it. Then
not a moment was lost before the mother came with
her slave-girls. And there was nothing great or
small in my house which she did not carry off, leaving
me as a beggar upon the bare ground, and treating
me with every sort of unkindness. And this, God
save the Amîr! is my condition; and in my trouble
and anguish of heart I have taken refuge in the
mosques."

Then said el-Hajjâj, "O Khâlid! make over to the
young man rich garments, and Armenian carpets, and
a slave boy and girl, and a mule, and ten thousand
dirhems." And he added, "O young man! come to
Khâlid to-morrow morning, and thou shalt receive all
the goods from him."

So the young man went out from el-Hajjâj. He
says: And when I reached the door of my house, I
overheard the daughter of my uncle saying, " Would
to God I knew what has delayed the son of my uncle!

Has he been slain, or has he died, or can wild beasts
have devoured him!" He continues: So I entered,
and cried, "O daughter of my uncle! rejoice, and let
thine eye be refreshed! For verily I was taken before
el-Hajjâj, and so-and-so occurred." And I related to
her what had been my occupation. Then when the
young woman heard my words, she smote her face
and screamed aloud. And her father and her mother
and her brethren heard her cries, and came in and
asked her, "What aileth thee?" And she answered
her father, "May Allâh show no mercy to thee,
neither reward thee with good on my account, nor on
account of the son of thy brother! Thou hast been
cruel to him and hast despoiled him until thou hast
brought madness upon him, and his reason has departed. Listen to his words!" Then said my uncle,
"O son of my brother! what has happened to
thee?" I answered, "By Allâh! there is nothing
amiss with me, only I was taken into the presence
of el-Hajjâj."

And he related what he had been about, and that
el-Hajjâj had ordered for him great riches. And
when the uncle had heard his tale, he said, "This
fellow is smitten with violent jaundice," and they re-

mained watching him all that night. And at day-break they sent him to the insane-doctor, who began treating him, and injected medicine through his nose, and otherwise prescribed for him. And the young man reiterated, " By Allâh! there is nothing the matter with me, only I was taken before el-Hajjâj and so-and-so occurred." But when he saw that his mention of el-Hajjâj did but increase his miseries, he left off speaking of him or of his recollection of him. So then when the doctor asked him, "What hast thou to say about el-Hajjâj ?" he replied, "I never saw him." Then the doctor went out, and said to the young man's friends, "Verily the malady has departed from him. Nevertheless, be not hasty in removing his chains." So he was kept fettered, and with his hand chained to his neck.

And after some days el-Hajjâj remembered him, and said, "O Khâlid! what has become of that young man ?"

"God save the Amîr!" replied Khâlid, "I have not seen him since he left the Amîr's presence."

"Then send some one to him," said el-Hajjâj.

So Khâlid despatched a soldier of the guard, who went to the young man's uncle, and asked him,

" What is the son of thy brother about ?   For verily
he is wanted by el-Hajjâj."

The uncle replied, "Of a truth the son of my
brother is otherwise occupied than with el-Hajjâj.
Verily, he has been visited by disorder in his reason."

The soldier said, " I know nothing about that, but
he must go this moment, there is no help for it."

So the uncle went and said to him, " O son of my
brother ! el-Hajjâj has really sent to seek thee.   Shall
I therefore liberate thee ?"

He answered, " No ; unless in his presence."

So they bore him upon men's backs, in his fetters
and chains, until they came before el-Hajjâj. And
he, when he beheld him afar off, welcomed him until
he reached his presence. Then the young man displayed his fetters and chains, and said, " God save
the Prince ! Verily the end of my affair is more wonderful than the beginning of it."   And he related to
him his story.   And el-Hajjâj marvelled, and said,
" O Khâlid ! make what we had ordered for the young
man double."

So he received the whole fortune, and his condition
was excellent ; and he continued to be nightly tale-
teller to el-Hajjâj until he died.

EL-HAJJÂJ AND THE ARAB.

A N Arab was once in presence of el-Hajjâj when a repast was brought in. And people ate thereof; and afterwards some sweet fruits were produced. And el-Hajjâj took no notice of the Arab until he had eaten one mouthful, but then exclaimed, "Whoever eats of the sweet fruits shall lose his head!" So all the people refused to eat any, and only the Arab was left. He looked once at el-Hajjâj, and once at the sweet fruits, and then cried, "O Prince! I willingly leave thee the legacy of my children"— and plunged his hand into the dish. Then el-Hajjâj laughed till he rolled over on the back of his head, and ordered the man a reward.

THE STORY OF THE THREE EDUCATED
YOUNG MEN.

IT is related that el-Hajjâj commanded the captain
of his guard to patrol during the night, and to
behead any one whom he might find abroad after
supper. So one night he patrolled, and found three
young men reeling about, and bearing traces of wine.
And he surrounded them, and asked, "Who are ye
that thus disobey the Amîr?"

Then answered the first,

> His son am I to whom indebted are
> All who 'midst maimed or wounded may be found
> Before him low his slaves themselves abase,
> He takes their means, he takes their blood.

And the captain of the guard, who had seized hold
of him to kill him, said, "Perhaps he is of kin to the
Commander of the Faithful."

Then said the second young man,

> I am his son whose power will never be lowered.
> Is it one day lessened?—instantly it returns.
> Thou mayst see men in crowds by the glow of his fire,
> And amongst them those who stand and those who sit.

And the captain of the guard, having seized him to kill him, said, "But perhaps he may belong to the noblest among the Arabs."

Then said the third young man,

> My sire rushed boldly into the ranks,
> And corrected with his sword until all was in order
> His feet are never parted from his stirrups,'
> E'en when in raging fight the horsemen flee.

Then the captain of the guard, who had laid hold of him to kill him, said, "But maybe he is of the Arab heroes." And early next morning he reported their affair to el-Hajjâj, who ordered them to be brought before him. And he discovered their condition, and lo! the first was the son of a barber,* and the second was a son of a bean-seller,† and the third was the son of a weaver.‡ And el-Hajjâj was astonished at their quickness, and said to those seated

* Even to the present day, barbers in the East practise phlebotomy by cupping, bleeding, leeching, and teeth-drawing, as did English barbers until recent years.

† The bean-seller cooks his beans over an open fire in his shop. And these beans being a favourite article of food among the lower orders, he rarely wants for customers, some of whom sit round his fire and eat their beans on the spot, while others carry their purchase away with them.

‡ Any one who has seen a handloom will at once recognize the applicability of the weaver's son's enigma.

with him, "Give your sons a good education,* for by
Alláh! had it not been for ready wit, they would
have been beheaded.   Then he released them, and
quoted:

> Be the son of whom you may, yet acquire knowledge;
> The glory thereof will serve thee instead of lineage.
> Verily the youth who can say—I have got,
> Is not the same as the youth who says—My father was.

* Ibn-Khalikán, on the authority of Ibn-'Abd-Rabbih, says
that el-Hajjáj and his father kept school at et-Taïf, and that
the former afterwards entered the police-guard of the Khalífah
'Abd-el-Málik.

HOW HIND, DAUGHTER OF EN-NÙAMÂN, REVENGED HERSELF UPON EL-HAJJÂJ.

IT is said that Hind, the daughter of en-Nùamân,[*] was the most beautiful woman of her time; and

[*] There appears to be some confusion here, consequent upon the possession of the same name by two women who lived about the same time, and both of whom were celebrated for beauty of person and power of mind. Ibn-Khalikân, in his Biographical Dictionary, gives a slightly different version of the lines in the text which he attributes to Hind, daughter of en-Nùamân, but states that she composed them upon her husband, Abu-Zarâa, Rûh-ibn-Zinba, whom she detested. This Abu-Zarâa was the head of the tribe of Judâm, and was appointed Governor of Palestine by the Khalîfah 'Abd-el-Málik, whose intimate and inseparable companion he became. Ibn-Khalikân says that the lines were also attributed to Humaidah, Hind's sister; and he makes no mention of Hind having been married either to el-Hajjâj or to 'Abd-el-Málik. According to the same author, the Hind who married el-Hajjâj was daughter of el-Muhállab, who when el-Hajjâj was made ruler over 'Irâk, Sijistan, and Khorassân, was appointed to administer the affairs of the last-mentioned province in the name of el-Hajjâj. On el-Muhállab's death-bed, he nominated his son Yezîd as his successor; but el-Hajjâj, having conceived a violent dislike to, and jealousy of, him, persuaded the Khalîfah to dismiss him. He then fell into the power of el-Hajjâj, who extorted money from him with tortures so cruel that he could not restrain his

her beauty being highly extolled before el-Hajjâj, he sought her in marriage, and laid out large sums upon her, and settled two hundred thousand dirhems upon her over and above the dowry. Then he married her, and she went down with him to el-Máárrah, her father's country.* And el-Hajjâj remained with her in el-Máárrah for a long while, and then set off with her for 'Irâk, where she abode with him according to the will of God.

And Hind was well-educated and eloquent; and it happened that one day as el-Hajjâj was going to see her, he heard her reciting:

> How can Hind, the perfect little Arabian mare,
> The daughter of noble blood, have mated with a mule?
> Should foal of hers prove thoroughbred—richly has Allâh
>   endowed her,
> If mulish be his nature—'tis from the mule his sire.

And when el-Hajjâj heard this, he would have

screams. His sister, Hind, who heard his cries, began to weep and lament, whereupon el-Hajjâj divorced her. Whether, however, Hind were the daughter of el-Muhállab, or of en-Núamân, she must have been a woman of great spirit and determination; for she seems to have been the only person capable of coping with such a monster of cruelty as el-Hajjâj is represented to have been.

  * Máárrat-en-Núamân lay in the territory of el-'Awâsin, a large district in Syria, having Antioch for its capital.

nothing more to say to her, but determined to divorce her, and sent 'Abd-Allâh-ibn-Tâhir to her with two hundred thousand dirhems (which were what he owed her) saying to him, "O ibn-Tâhir! divorce her in two words, and add nothing thereto."

So 'Abd-Allâh-ibn-Tâhir went to her and said, " Abu-Muhammad, el-Hajjâj, says to thee—*Kunti fabinti.** And here are the two hundred thousand dirhems which are due to thee from him." Whereupon she made answer: " Know, O ibn-Tâhir, that by Allâh! I was—(his wife) but I did not glory in it, and I am repudiated, but I do not regret it. And as for this two hundred thousand—it is thine, for bringing me the good news of my deliverance from that dog of a Thakîfy!"

And after a while, the Commander of the Faithful, 'Abd-el-Málik-ibn-Marwân, heard of her, and her beauty was greatly praised to him. So he sent to demand her in marriage for himself. But she wrote a letter to him in reply, wherein, after compliments, she said, "Know, O Commander of the Faithful! that I have already had one dog for a husband."

* " Thou wert (ellipsis for, Thou wert my wife)—and thou hast been repudiated."

And when 'Abd-el-Málik read this, he laughed at her words, and wrote to her a second time; after which it was no longer possible for her to refuse him. So she addressed another letter to him, saying —after compliments—" Know, O Commander of the Faithful! that upon one condition only will I proceed with the contract. And wert thou to ask, What is the condition? I should reply, That el-Hajjâj might lead my litter from el-Máârrah to the country whereinsoever thou mayst be. And that he should do this walking barefoot, but with the accoutrements which he always wore."

And when 'Abd-el-Málik read her letter, he laughed a hearty laugh, and sent to el-Hajjâj, ordering him the same ; and he, on reading the mandate of the Commander of the Faithful, accepted it, not daring to disobey, but acted according to the command, and sent to Hind warning her to equip.

So she made ready ; and el-Hajjâj travelled with his cavalcade until he reached el-Máârrah, Hind's country. Then she mounted her litter, and her slave-girls and servants rode around her ; but el-Hajjâj walked barefoot. And he journeyed thus with her, leading her camel by the bridle.

Then she took to mocking him, and laughing at him, with her nurse, el-Hîfâ. And by-and-by she said, "O my nurse! open me the curtains of the litter, that I may smell the perfume of the breeze." So the nurse opened them, and Hind and el-Hajjâj found themselves face to face. And she mocked him, but he recited, saying :

> Spite of thy jeering now, O Hind ! for how long a time
> Have I forsaken thee, like a thrown-off garment ?

But she answered, saying :

> It troubled me not when bereft of high estate,
> Through what I had lost of wealth and rank ;
> For wealth may be acquired and honour recalled,
> If Allâh preserve the soul from death.

And she continued deriding and laughing, until they drew nigh unto the Khalîfah's country. And when they came near the town, she dropped some dinârs out of her hand on to the ground, and then cried, "Ho, cameleer ! we have let some dirhems fall ; pick them up for us." So el-Hajjâj looked on the ground, but seeing only dinârs, said, "They are dinârs." "Not so," said she; "they are dirhems." He repeated, "They are *dinârs.*" Whereupon she exclaimed, "Allâh be praised ! Dirhems fell from our hand, and Allâh has replaced them by dinârs !"

Then was el-Hajjâj covered with confusion, and was silent, and made no answer ; but went with her into the presence of 'Abd-el-Málik-ibn-Marwân, who married her. And according to her will, so was everything.

THE MARTYRDOM OF SAÎD-IBN-JUBAIR.

THE following story is related by 'Awn-ibn-Abi-Shaddâd, el-'Abdy, in the Hayât-el-Haiwân.

When el-Hajjâj-ibn-Yûsuf was reminded of Saîd-ibn-Jubair,* he sent a man of rank called el-Mutalámmis-ibn-el-Ahwas, and twenty men with him, from Damascus, to seek Saîd. And whilst they were doing

* Abu-'Abd-Allâh (some say Abu-Muhammad) Saîd-ibn-Jubair-ibn-Hishâm, surnamed el-Asady, was an enfranchised negro, and a native of el-Kûfah. He was eminent for his religious knowledge and piety. In A.H. 79, according to Greek writers, and A.H. 82 according to Arabian historians, he joined 'Abd-er-Rahman-ibn-Ashâth in his revolt against the treachery and cruelty of el-Hajjâj. Though successful for some time, 'Abd-er-Rahman was at length defeated and slain, and Saîd upon that fled to Mekkah. Ibn-Khalikân states that he was there arrested by Khâlid-ibn-'Abd-Allâh, el-Kúsary, (see Note †, p. 116,) then governor of Mekkah, and sent by him to el-Hajjâj. The same author gives a different account of his last interview with the tyrant, and also states that after his death Ahmed-ibn-Hanbal said, "el-Hajjâj killed Saîd-ibn-Jubair, yet there was not a man on the face of the earth who did not stand in need of Saîd and his learning."

this, behold ! they passed by a Christian monk* in his

* It is difficult to assign the precise era at which Christianity was introduced into Arabia. It is the universal belief of the Eastern Churches that St. Thomas preached in Arabia Felix and Socotra on his way to India, about A.D. 50. It is also said that the Himyarites obtained their first knowledge of Christianity from St. Bartholomew. 'Abd-Kelál, the ruler of el-Yémen from A.D. 273 to 279, is said to have embraced Christianity, though from fear of his subjects he never openly professed it, nor does Christianity appear to have made any considerable progress in Arabia until the next reign, that of the Tobba* Ibn-Hásan, from A.D. 297 to A.D. 320. It is generally supposed to have been in his reign that Christianity was also established in Abyssinia, an event which in after-years seriously affected the fate of Arabia. The ruler of el-Yémen in A.D. 490 was Zhu-Nawwás, a zealous partisan of Judaism, who cruelly persecuted all the Christians within his dominions. The greater number of the inhabitants of the district called Nejrán had embraced Christianity, and upon the pretext of the murder by them of two Jews, Zhu-Nawwás besieged the city with 120,000 men. Failing to take it by force, he assured the inhabitants, upon oath, that no evil should happen to them if they opened their gates. They therefore surrendered ; but no sooner had Zhu-Nawwás entered the town than he plundered it, and gave the inhabitants their choice between Judaism and death. They preferred the latter ; accordingly large pits were dug and filled with burning fuel, and all who refused to abjure their faith, amounting it is said to 20,000, were either cast into the flames or slain by the sword. One of the few who escaped this massacre traversed Arabia, Syria, and Asia Minor, and at last reaching Constantinople, implored the Emperor Justin I. to take up the cause of the persecuted Chris-

---

* Tobba signified governor or ruler, and was a title common to the princes of the Himyarite dynasty.

chapel, from whom they made inquiries. The monk said, "Describe him to me;" and when they had

tians in el-Yémen. Unable to do so himself on account of the troubled state of his own dominions, he however wrote to the King of Abyssinia, begging him to send troops into el-Yémen for the punishment of Zhu-Nawwás. The King of Abyssinia, who was a Christian, acquiesced, and sent an army under a general named Aryát to invade Arabia; a battle ensued on the sea-coast, in which the Himyarites were entirely defeated. Aryát then penetrated into el-Yémen, and in a very short time subdued the greater part of the country. Zhu-Nawwás at the first engagement fled from the field, but being closely pursued and hemmed in by his enemies, he leaped his horse into the sea and was drowned. Thus was el-Yémen conquered by the Abyssinians, and thus terminated the Himyarite dynasty, which had ruled there for two thousand years.

The reign of Abrahá, the second Abyssinian viceroy of el-Yémen, was favourable to Christianity. A bishop, who is reckoned as Saint Gregentius in the Roman calendar, was sent there by the Patriarch of Alexandria. The unbelievers were challenged to public disputations with him in the royal hall in the city of Dzafír, the viceroy and his nobles were present, and a learned Rabbi named Herbanus was chosen to advocate the cause of Judaism. The dispute lasted three days, and resulted in the conversion of Herbanus and many of his followers to Christianity. Abrahá, who was a zealous Christian, is said to have built a church at Sanáa which was the wonder of the age. The Emperor of Rome and the King of Abyssinia supplied marble for its construction, and Nowairi states that when completed, a pearl was placed on the altar of such brilliancy that on the darkest nights objects were clearly seen by its light. Abrahá, deeply grieved to see the multitudes who still performed idol-worship in the Káabah at Mekkah, endeavoured to substitute

done so, he showed them where Sáíd was.   And they
found   him   prostrate   upon   the   ground,   praying

his church as the object of their superstitious reverence, and
issued an order that all the Arabs in the neighbourhood should
perform the pilgrimage to his church at Sanáa.   He also sent
missionaries to the Hijáz and Nejd, and wrote to the King of
Abyssinia telling him that he intended forcing the Arabs to
abandon the Káabah and substitute this temple as the object of
their pilgrimage.   This design being speedily known throughout
Arabia, excited the indignation of all the pagan tribes, especially
the custodians of the Káabah, and accordingly Abrahá's messengers were badly received in the Hijáz, and one of them was
murdered by a man of the tribe of Kinânah.   Another man of
the same tribe was bribed by the guardians of the Káabah to
defile the church at Sanáa.   He effected this during the prepa-
ration for a high festival; but Abrahá having discovered the
author of this indignity, vowed to take signal vengeance by the
total destruction of Mekkah and its Káabah.   The war which
followed is well known in Arabian history, and is called in the
Kurân "The War of the Elephant."   Abrahá was at first successful, but the Christian army was afterwards destroyed, by miraculous agency as Arabian authors maintain, though others, with
more probability, suggest that it perished either from want of
provisions, or from an epidemic disease, most probably smallpox.   Abrahá himself, with a very small remnant of his army,
reached Sanáa, where he soon after died, A.D. 570.   He was
succeeded by his son Yascoom, who reigned two years, and he
was succeeded by his brother Masrûk, under whose viceroyalty
the Arabs grew impatient of the Christian yoke, and at length
found a liberator in Saïf, the last of the old Himyarite race.
This Saïf made his way to Constantinople, and implored the
emperor to send an army to repel the Abyssinians.   The emperor being a Christian, refused to aid the Jews against those

earnestly to his Lord in a loud voice. And when they drew near, and saluted him, he raised his head,

professing his own religion. Saïf then repaired to the court of the Persian monarch, Kesra Anowshirwân, who gave him promises of assistance, but owing to other wars delayed their fulfilment. In the meanwhile Saïf died, but his son, Máady-Karib, animated by the same zeal as his father, once more sought Kesra's presence. The latter armed all the malefactors in the prisons, amounting to 3,600 men, organized them into an army, and placed them under the command of Horzád-ibn-Narsee, surnamed Wahráz, one of themselves, but superior to them by birth and education. This party, together with Máady-Karib, sailed for el-Yémen ; the courage of the native Arabs was excited by the sight of the troops, and the presence of a descendant of their ancient kings ; and those who had suffered from the persecution of Masrûk, a cruel and tyrannical prince, flocked to the standard of Máady-Karib, who soon found himself at the head of an army of 20,000 men. Masrûk prepared to oppose their advance with a force of 120,000 men, but during the battle which ensued was killed by an arrow shot by Wahráz, the Abyssinian army was thrown into the utmost confusion, and finally routed with great slaughter. Máady-Karib was, by order of Kesra, installed as viceroy of el-Yémen, agreeing to pay tribute as a vassal of the Persian monarch. These events occurred about A.D. 575, and thus was the Christian power in el-Yémen overthrown, though many Abyssinians still remained there. These, Máady-Karib began by persecuting, but afterwards changed his policy and surrounded himself with Abyssinian guards. One day, however, when he was out hunting, these guards fell upon him and slew him, and thus finally extinguished the dynasty of Himyar. An Abyssinian, whose name is not mentioned, then seized the supreme power, and el-Yémen was for some time filled with violence and bloodshed. In A.D. 595. however, Wahráz,

but completed his devotions before returning their salutation. Then they told him, "el-Hajjâj has sent to fetch thee."

"And is compliance absolutely necessary?" he asked.

"Absolutely," they replied.

So he praised and glorified God, and blessed His prophet, and then rose and walked with them until they came to the monastery of the monk, who called out, "O ye horsemen! have ye found your friend?" "Yes," they replied. "Then come up into the monastery," said he; "for of a truth lions and lionesses prowl round about it during the night. Therefore come in quickly, before dusk."

And they all did so excepting Sâid, who refused to

with an army of 4,000 men, again invaded el-Yémen, and inflicted cruel retribution upon the Abyssinians, whom to the number of about 3,000 he put to death. The Persian monarch was so much pleased with his conduct that he appointed Wahráz viceroy of the country, and then it was that el-Yémen and its dependencies became provinces of the Persian empire. The Persian rule was mild, and the three religions, Pagan, Jewish, and Christian, were equally tolerated. Christianity maintained its ground (chiefly at Nejrán, which place was at the time of the Hijrah governed by a noble Christian family named Oulad 'Abd-el-Madán-ibn-Deyyan), but rapidly declined after the promulgation of Muhammadism.

enter. Finding which, they said to him, "It appears to us that thou desirest to escape."

He replied, "Not so ; but nevertheless I will never enter a polytheistic habitation."

"But of a truth we will not leave thee," said they ; "for verily the lions will kill thee."

Said Sáîd, "If my Lord bewith me, He will turn them away from me ; and should such be the will of the Most High, He can convert them into a guard for me against all evil."

They asked, "Art thou a prophet ?"

"I am not among the prophets," he answered, "but am, on the contrary, a slave among the erring and sinful servants of God."

So they said, "Swear to us that thou wilt not flee." And he swore it. Then the monk cried out to them, "Come up into the monastery, and string your bows in readiness to scare away the lions from this pious slave. For verily the thought of your taking up your abode with me in the chapel was abhorrent to him."

So they entered the monastery, and strung their bows. And lo! they beheld a lioness approaching. But when she came near Sáîd, she rubbed herself fondling against him, and caressed him. Then she laid down near to him, and the lion came and did likewise. And having seen this, as soon as day dawned the monk went down to Sâîd, and questioned him concerning the divine laws of el-Islám, and the traditions of the prophet of Allâh. And Sâîd explained everything clearly to him, and the monk professed el-Islám, and his practice therein was admirable. And the people assembled before Sâîd, excusing themselves to him; and they kissed his hands and his feet, and collected the earth that he had trodden upon during the night, and prayed upon it. And they said, "O Sâîd! we swore to el-Hajjâj, by divorce and enfranchisement,* that if we found thee we would not leave thee until we had brought thee unto him. But now order us as thou wilt."

He said, "Fulfil your task; for there is no way to escape from the return to my Maker, nor any questioning of His decree."

So they journeyed until they reached Wâsit;† and

---

* A solemn oath, the breaking of which entailed the divorce of wives and enfranchisement of slaves.

† The town built by el-Hajjâj A.H. 83. Wâsit signifies "middle," and was so called because it stood midway between el-Básrah and el-Kûfah.

when they arrived there, Sàid said to them, "O all ye people ! I have been respected by you, and have been your companion, and I feel certain that my end draws near, and that my time is accomplished. Leave me alone, therefore, this night, that I may make provision for death, and prepare for Múnkar and Nakîr,* and reflect upon the torments of the grave, and that I must lie beneath the ground. And in the early morning I will come to any spot you may choose as a meeting-place between us."

Then said some among them, "We do not want to be following traces, having the man himself." And another one said, "And surely you would wish your desires fulfilled, and that the Amîr should deem you worthy of his favour ; therefore leave him not alone." But then another said, "I take it upon myself to restore him to you, if it be the will of God."

Then they looked at Sàîd, and tears were flowing

---

* Two angels through whom the dead, when laid in the grave, undergo a strict examination as to their past lives. There is a difference of opinion amongst Muslims as to these angels. Some hold that there are only two (Múnkar and Nakîr) by whom all human beings, whether true believers or infidels, are examined. Others maintain that these angels are four in number, Múnkar and Nakîr being for infidels, and two other angels, named Mubàshir and Bashîr, for true believers.

from his eyes, and his colour was grey, for he had neither eaten nor drank nor laughed since they had met him. So they cried with one accord, "O thou best of living men! Would to God we had never known thee, and never been sent for thee! Woe be to us! How hardly have we been dealt with! What will excuse us before our Maker at the great Day of Resurrection, and who shall answer for us to Him!"

Then he who had offered to be his surety said to Sáîd, "I ask thee by Allâh, O Sáîd! whether thou wilt not provide for us by thy prayers and thy good words? For in truth we have never met the like of thee?"

So Sáîd prayed for them; after which they left him alone. Then he bathed his head, and washed his shirt and his robe. And the people remained concealed the whole night. And when the light of dawn appeared, Sáîd-ibn-Jubair came to them, and knocked at the door. And they cried one to another, "Our friend, by the Lord of the Káabah!" And they went down to him, and wept with him a long while, and then took him before el-Hajjáj.

And el-Mutalámmis entered the presence of el-

Hajjâj, and saluted him, and announced to him the arrival of Saîd-ibn-Jubair. And when Saîd stood before him, el-Hajjâj asked, "What is thy name?"

He replied, "Saîd-ibn-Jubair."

"Thou art Shâky-ibn-Kasîr,"* said el-Hajjâj.

"No," said Saîd, "my mother knew my name better than thou dost."

"Thou art vile, and so was thy mother!" cried el-Hajjâj.

"That which is hidden is known to Another beside thee," answered Saîd.

"Of a surety I will soon change this world into hell-fire for thee," said el-Hajjâj.

"Had I known that that had been in thy power," responded Saîd, "verily I had abased myself before thee as before a god."

Then el-Hajjâj asked, "What sayest thou of Muhammad?"

"He is the Prophet of the Merciful," replied Saîd.

---

* The play upon words in this sentence cannot be rendered in English. *Shâky* means "vile," "evil," the opposite of *Saîd*, which means "good," "happy." And *Kasîr*, from *Kâsara*, "to break," is the opposite of *Jubair*, from *Jábara*, "to mend," "to heal," "to unite."

" And what dost thou say of 'Aly?" continued el-Hajjâj; " Is he in heaven or in hell?"

" Had I been in both," answered Sâîd, " and did I know the inhabitants of both, I could tell who was in both."

" And what dost thou say of the Khalîfahs?" asked el-Hajjâj.

" I am not their overseer," replied Sâîd.

" Which of them dost thou love best?" inquired el-Hajjâj.

" He among them who was the most pleasing to my Maker," answered Sâîd.

" And which of them was the most pleasing to the Creator?" said el-Hajjâj.

" That knowledge," replied Sâîd, " rests with Him who knows their inmost thoughts and secret words."

" And how is it that thou laughest not?" asked el-Hajjâj.

" How should a creature formed out of clay—clay which may be consumed in the fire—laugh?" responded Sâîd.

" And why is it that we ourselves cannot laugh?" inquired el-Hajjâj.

" The thoughts of the heart are not pure," said
Saîd.

Then el-Hajjâj ordered pearls and emeralds and
rubies to be brought in and laid before Saîd. But he
said, " If by accumulating these thou couldst ransom
thyself from the terrors of the Day of Resurrection—
well. But one of those terrors would cause a mother
to forget her sucking child ; and every worldly possession will be profitless, except what did good, and
was laid out in charity."

Then el-Hajjáj sent for pleasant music. And Saîd
wept. So el-Hajjâj cried, " Woe be to thee, O Saîd !
Choose by what kind of death I shall kill thee."

" Choose for thyself, O Hajjâj!" replied Saîd; "for
by Allâh ! whatever death thou causest me to die, by
the same will God cause thee to die at the last day."

Then asked el-Hajjâj, " Wouldst thou that I pardon
thee ?"

He replied, " Were the pardon from Allâh,—yes,
assuredly. But from thee,—no."

" Be off with him and execute him !" cried el-
Hajjâj.

Then as he was going out of the door, Saîd laughed.
And el-Hajjâj was told of this, and ordered him to

be brought back, and asked, "What causes thee to laugh ?"

" I was marvelling," answered Sâîd, "at thy provocation of Allâh, and at His long-suffering toward thee."

Then el-Hajjâj commanded to bring the *Nitâ'a.*[*] And it was spread out before him, and he cried, " Kill him !"

And Sâîd said, " I gave myself up to the worship of Him who laid out the heavens and the earth, believing in the true faith, and I am not one of the polytheists."

" Turn him away from the Kiblah !" called out el-Hajjâj.

" Wherever thou mayst turn me, there is God's countenance," said Sâîd.

" Lay him with his face on the ground," commanded el-Hajjâj.

Then Sâîd quoted, " Out of it We created you, and to it We will cause you to return, and from it We will once more cause you to come forth."

" Kill him !" again cried el-Hajjâj.

Then Sâîd said, " I bear witness that there is no

* See Note *, p. 141.

god but God, and I bear witness that Muhammad is His servant and His messenger. O Allâh! grant that after me he may have power over none other to kill him!"

Then they executed him upon the *Nitâ'a* [may God have mercy upon him!] And after his head was struck off, it uttered, "There is no god but God." And el-Hajjâj lived after this fifteen days. And this happened in the year 95. And the age of Sâîd [may God be satisfied of him!] was nine-and-forty years.*

ALLÂH IS ALL-KNOWING!

* It is said that during his last illness el-Hajjâj was tormented by the spirit of Sâîd-ibn-Jubair. The report was that whenever he fell asleep he saw Sâîd come and seize him by the girdle, saying, "Enemy of God, arise! why didst thou murder me?" On which he would awake in terror, and exclaim, "What business has Sâîd-ibn-Jubair with me?" It is also related that a person saw el-Hajjâj in a dream after his death, and that upon being asked what had been done to him, he stated that God had caused him to die the death of every man whom he had slain, but that he had suffered seventy deaths on account of his treatment of the saintly Sâîd.

THE REIGN OF EL-WALÎD-IBN-'ABD-EL-MÁLIK-IBN-MARWÂN.

IT was his custom to read through the whole Kurân every three days; during Ramadhân * he used to read it through seventeen times. Ibrahîm-ibn-'Uliah relates, "He sent me bags of dinârs to be dis-

---

* Ramadhân. "The month of Ramadhân shall ye fast. in which the Kurân was sent down from Heaven. . . . Therefore let him among you who shall be present in this month fast the same month; but he who shall be sick or on a journey shall fast the like number of other days."—*el-Kurân*, Sûr. 2., V. 181. Muslims are extremely particular in their observance of this fast, which, as their year is reckoned by lunar months, varies in the season at which it takes place, being a few days earlier every year. When Ramadhân occurs during the heat of summer, when the days are longest, the trial to bodily health and strength is excessive; for they neither eat, nor drink, nor even smoke, from early dawn till sunset, and the nights are spent in eating and drinking, visiting the mosques, and reading the Kurân or hearing it read. A true Muslim should not, however, betray weariness or languor on account of what he endures during Ramadhân; but at the same time it is a pious act on the part of those in authority to spare their servants and show them as much consideration as possible.

tributed amongst the pious." And the Hâfiz, ibn-Asâkir,* says, "The Syrians considered el-Walîd as the best of their Khalîfahs. He built the mosque at Damascus; and he set apart a sufficiency for lepers, and said to cripples and to the blind, "Do not beg from other people, and I will give to each a servant or a guide.'"

And it is recorded that the sum total of what el-Walîd laid out in building the mosque of el-'Ummawy was four hundred chests, each chest containing eight-and-forty thousand dinârs; and six hundred chains of gold for the lamps. [But the building would not have been completed had not his brother Sulaimân, when he reigned over the Khalîfate, done many good deeds, and left behind him traces of excellence.] And yet, after all this, it is recorded by 'Omar-ibn-'Abd-el-Azîz † that when el-Walîd was wrapt in his winding-sheet his hands were chained to his neck.‡

* Abu-'l-Kâsim-'Aly, commonly known by his surname of ibn-Asâkir, was the chief *Hafiz*, or Traditionist, of the age in which he lived. He was born A.H. 499, and died A.H. 571 (A.D. 1176).

† First cousin to el-Walîd and Sulaimân, and successor to the latter in the Khalîfate, A.H. 99 (A.D. 718).

‡ That is, that in spite of all his good deeds he chose to appear as a criminal at the Day of Resurrection.

NOTE TO ABOVE.

El-Walîd was proclaimed Khalîfah the same day that his
father died, A.H. 85.   He died A.H. 96 (A.D. 715), and was
buried at Damascus, having reigned nine years and eight
months.   Historians differ much in their accounts of his
character; those of Syria represent him as the greatest
prince of the house of 'Omeyyah, whereas Persian and
other Muslim writers describe him as naturally cruel and
violent, and subject to intemperate fits of passion.   He is
said to have had some skill in architecture, and expended
large sums upon public buildings.   El-Makîn's estimate
of the sum laid out upon the mosque at Damascus, is,
however, considerably less than that of the historian
quoted in the text.   The former reckons it at four hundred
chests, each containing fourteen thousand, instead of forty-
eight thousand, dinârs.

THE REIGN OF SULAIMÂN-IBN-'ABD-EL-MÁLIK-IBN-MARWÂN.

AMONG his other good deeds, it is related that a man came before him and cried, "O Commander of the Faithful! I adjure thee by Allâh, and the Izhân (notification)!" "As to 'I adjure thee by Allâh!'" said Sulaimân, "verily we understand that, but what dost thou mean by the Izhân (notification)?" The man replied, "These are the words of the Most High : 'The Muazh-zhin (crier) will proclaim amongst them that the curse of God is upon oppressors.'"[*] "What is thy wrong?" asked Sulaimân. The man answered, "Thy vicegerent So-and-so has taken Such-and-such a village away from me by force."

Then Sulaimân descended from his throne, and turned back the carpet, and laying his cheek upon the ground, said, "By Allâh! I will not lift up my

---

[*] El-Kurân, Sûr. vii., V. 42. The Muazh-zhin, or "crier," is supposed by some to allude to the angel Isrâfil.

cheek from the earth until he has been written to and ordered to restore the village." So the scribes wrote, and he remained with his cheek laid upon the ground that he might hear the words of the Lord who created him and surrounded him with good things, fearing the curse of God, and banishment from His presence.

It is said that he released from the prison of el-Hajjâj three hundred thousand souls, between men and women.* But he honoured the family of el-Hajjâj. And he chose for his wazîr and councillor 'Omar, the son of his uncle 'Abd-el-Azîz.

Ibn-Khalikán in his biography states that Sulai-mân's appetite was enormous: he ate about a hundred Syrian *ratls* every day.†

Muhammad-ibn-Sirîn ‡ says that Sulaimân opened

---

* The figures here given seem truly incredible. But it is also computed by Arabian historians, that el-Hajjâj killed a hundred and twenty thousand men, besides those who fell in war; and suffered fifty thousand men and thirty thousand women to perish in prison.

† I believe the Syrian *ratl* here mentioned was the same as the present Egyptian ratl. The latter weighs from 1 lb. 2 oz. 5¾ dwt. to about 1 lb. 2 oz. 8 dwt. Troy.

‡ Abu-Bekr-Muhammad-ibn-Sirîn was a native of el-Básrah. His father was an enfranchised slave, and he himself was one of the jurisconsults by whose opinion the people of el-Básrah were guided. He was famed for his piety, and his knowledge of the Traditions. He was born A.H. 33, and died A.H. 110 (A.D. 729).

his reign with well-doing, and sealed it with well-
doing. He opened it well by establishing the earliest
hour for prayer, and he sealed it well by appointing
'Omar-ibn-'Abd-el-Azîz as his successor.

NOTE TO ABOVE.

Sulaimân-ibn-'Abd-el-Málik-ibn-Marwân succeeded his brother
el-Walîd A.H. 96. He died at Marj-Dabek, in the district of
Kinnafrîn, A.H. 99 (A.D. 718). He possessed quick parts
and surprising eloquence, and endeared himself to his subjects by his mild and merciful disposition. They surnamed
him *Miftâh-el-Khair*, The Key of Goodness, on account
of his clemency and the multitude of prisoners whom he
released.

THE HISTORY OF THE SLAVE-GIRL ZHALFÂ.

ABU-SUWAID says: Abu-Zeid, el-Azdy, related to me the following tale.*

I went into the presence of Sulaimân-ibn-'Abd-el-Málik, who was seated in the hall paved with red marble, and carpeted with green damask, in the middle of the enclosed garden. Verily, the trees were in full bearing, and the fruit was ripe. And behind him stood female slaves each one of whom was more beautiful than her neighbour. And the sun was sinking, and winged creatures were humming around, and

* I think that el-Wajîh Abu-'Abd-Allâh Muhammad-ibn 'Aly ibn-Abi-Tâlib, generally known by the name of Ibn (not Abu)-Suwaid, must be meant here. He was a merchant of Takrit, a place on the Tigris, north of Baghdâd, in lat. 34° 33′ N., long. 43° 40′ E.

I have been unable to discover anything further concerning Abu-Zeid, and cannot therefore explain the allusion to some quarrel or disagreement with the Khalîfah contained in his address.

the winds were whispering among the trees, and rustling the leaves, and bowing the branches. And I said, "Peace be upon thee, O Prince! and the mercy of God and His blessing!" And he was lost in thought; but he raised his head on hearing my voice, and remarked, "O Abu-Zeid! art thou come at such a time as this to make thy peace with us?"

So I exclaimed, "God save the Prince! Has the Day of Resurrection arrived that thou art so pre-occupied?"

He replied, "Yes, for those who love." Then he looked down, and was silent awhile.

Presently he raised his head, and asked, "O Abu-Zeid! what would improve such an existence as this?"

"May Allâh strengthen the Prince!" I cried. "Red wine in white cups, served by one slender as a reed, but with rounded limbs. I would drink it from the palm of her hand, and wipe my lips on her cheek."

At this, Sulaimân turned away his head, and uttered no sound nor gave any response, but silent tears stole from his eyes. And when the slave-girls saw this, they retired to a distance. Then he raised his head and said, "O Abu-Zeid! thou hast reached the day

of thy death, and the conclusion of thy term, and the
end of thy life! For, by Allâh! I will sever thy neck
unless thou inform me how this picture has been
impressed upon thy heart."

"Willingly, O Prince!" I replied. "I was sitting
before the door of thy brother Sa'ad-ibn-'Abd-el-
Málik,* when lo! I beheld a damsel escaping from
the palace gate like a gazelle fleeing from the snare
of the hunter. She wore a flowing Alexandrian robe,
through which appeared the whiteness of her bosom,
and the roundness of her form, and the embroidery
of her belt. Her feet were shod in silk, and verily
the whiteness of her instep gleamed brilliantly against
the redness of her shoes. Two long tresses reached
down to her hips, and her temples resembled two
nūns.† Her eyebrows were indeed arched above her
eyes; and her eyes were full of enchantment. Her
nose was like a crystal reed, and her mouth like a

---

* This is an instance of the carelessness and inaccuracy of
Arab writers with regard to names, whereby the labour of
searching out historical facts belonging to those remote times is
much increased. It is very possible that one of 'Abd-el-Málik's
sixteen sons may have been named Sa'ad; but it is evident
from the sequel that Sulaimân's predecessor in the Khalifate is
here intended; and his name was el-Walid, not Sa'ad.

† The Arabic N, which is thus formed ﻦ.

wound with the blood welling therein. And she cried, 'Slaves of Allâh! who will bring me medicine for one that cannot be consoled, and a remedy for one that may not be named? Long has been the parting, and the traveller has tarried. But the heart takes wing, and the mind is absent, and the soul is troubled, and the spirit stolen, and sleep is imprisoned. Allâh's pity be upon those who live in suffering and die in sorrow! Had there been either strength to bear, or a road to consolation, it had been truly an excellent thing.'

"Then she was silent for a space with drooping head. When she raised it, I said, 'O thou maiden! art thou of men or of genii? a heavenly being or an earthly? For of a truth the ardour of thy mind has astonished me, and the beauty of thy language has turned my head.'

"Then she hid her face in her sleeve as though she had not perceived me, but presently said, 'Pardon its inadequacy, O Speaker! but what is more helpless than an arm deprived of its fellow, and who more injured than a forsaken lover?'

"Then she turned and departed. And by Allâh! God save the Prince! I have not since then eaten heartily without being choked by the remembrance of her; nor have I looked upon beauty without its appearing hideous in my eyes because of her beauty."

Then said Sulaimân, "O Abu-Zeid! the sadness of what I have heard has wellnigh moved me to folly, and passion has taken possession of me, and judgment has fled from me. Know, O Abu-Zeid! that this girl whom thou sawest is Zhalfâ, of whom it has been said,

> Zhalfâ resembles nought save a ruby
> Produced from the purse of a merchant.

She cost my brother ten hundred thousand dirhems; and she was in love with him who sold her. By Allâh! if he be dead, it can only be through love of her, and ne must have entered his grave solely by grief on her account, and from lacking consolation for her loss, and through fearfully anticipating death. Rise, O Abu-Zeid! Allâh have thee in His keeping. Ho, slave! lade him with a *bádrah*."*

So I took the present and departed.

And when Sulaimân succeeded to the Khalifate, Zhalfâ also became his. And he ordered tents, and

---

* A sum of from one thousand to ten thousand dirhems, according to different writers.

went out to the Ghautah plain,* and pitched in a green and luxuriant garden. It was a beautifully bright garden : the ground was covered with divers kinds of flowers, clear yellow, brilliant red, and pure white.

And Sulaimân had a musician named Sinân, whom he had admitted to his friendship, and in whom he confided. And Sulaimân had ordered him to pitch his tent beside his own. And Zhalfâ also had accompanied Sulaimân to his pleasure-ground. And he continued eating and drinking and amusing himself with perfect enjoyment, until the night was far spent, when he retired to his tent, and Sinân did likewise.

And a number of friends came to Sinân, and said to him, "Allâh preserve thee ! We want a feast."

"How would you feast ?" he asked.

And they replied, "With eating and drinking and music."

"As for eating and drinking," said he, "that is permitted you ; but with regard to music, verily ye know the jealousy of the Commander of the Faithful, and his prohibition of that excepting in his presence."

* The name given to the cultivated country around Damascus.

But they persisted, " We do not want thy food and thy drink if thou wilt not let us hear thee sing."

So he said, " Then choose a song, and I will sing it to you."

" Sing us such-and-such a song," said they.

So he began singing these lines :

> The hidden one heard my voice, and it brought her unrest,
> At the end of the night when awakens the dawn.
> When the moon is full, her companion knows not
> If 'tis her face beside him or the face of the moon.
> Nor guardian nor bolt can shut out a voice,
> And her tears overflow when at night it visits her.
> Could it be so, her feet to my side would bring her,
> But such is her tenderness, walking would wound them.

The narrator proceeds : And Zhalfâ heard Sinân's voice, and she went out into the court of the tent. And so it was, that when she heard mention of this beauty of person and elegance, she fancied that it referred entirely to her and her appearance. Then that which had been at rest in her heart was troubled, and her eyes filled with tears, and her sobs were audible.

And Sulaimân awoke ; and when he found her absent, he also went out into the court of the tent, and there he saw her in this condition. So he cried, " What means this, O Zhalfâ ?"

She replied :

> A person may inspire admiration, yet be ugly--
> May be deformed in feature and base by birth.
> Thou mayst be struck with delight at his voice,
> Yet may he doubly trace his birth to slaves.

"Have done with thy nonsense!" cried Sulaimân. "By Allâh! he seems to have taken possession of thy heart. Here, slave! bring Sinân to me."

Then Zhalfâ called her servant, and said to him, "If thou canst reach Sinân and give him warning before the messenger of the Commander of the Faithful, ten thousand dirhems are thine, and thou art free to do the will of Allâh."

So the two messengers set off, but he bearing the message of the Commander of the Faithful arrived first. And when he had returned with Sinân, Sulaimân asked, "O Sinân! have I not forbidden thee from thus acting?"

"O Commander of the Faithful!" he replied, " numbers overcame me, and I am the slave of the Commander of the Faithful, and the plant grown by his favour; therefore if it seems well unto the Commander of the Faithful to pardon me, let him do it."

So Sulaimân said, "Verily, I have forgiven thee ;

but, nevertheless, hast thou not learnt that if the horse neighs the mare will come to him, and if the he-camel brays the she-camel will follow him?   And if a man sings the heart of a woman is drawn to him. Beware of a repetition of thy fault, or thy regret will be lasting."

THE STORY OF KHUZAIMAH AND 'IKRIMAH.

IT is said that in the days of Sulaimân there lived a man called Khuzaimah-ibn-Bishr, of the sons of Asaad. His means were ample, and he was famed for generosity and goodness and kindness towards his brethren ; and this character he kept up until adversity befell him. Then he sought help from his brethren who had been enriched by him, and upon whom he had lavished favours, and for a while they helped him, but afterwards grew weary of him. And when he observed this change in their conduct, he went to his wife, who was his cousin, and said to her, "O daughter of my uncle! surely I have noted the alteration in my brethren, and am resolved to remain shut up in my house until death shall come unto me." So he locked his door and prepared to support himself upon what he had left, until all should be exhausted and he without resource.

Now 'Ikrimah-el-Fayyâdh, er-Rabiiy, the Governor of Mesopotamia, had been acquainted with him. And once whilst 'Ikrimah was seated in his council, behold, mention was made of Khuzaimah-ibn-Bishr. And 'Ikrimah-el-Fayyâdh * [who was thus named solely on account of his generosity] asked, " How is he getting on ? " They replied, " Indeed his condition is desperate. He has locked his door and remains in his house." " But," said 'Ikrimah, " can Khuzaimah-ibn-Bishr find no one to give to him or to recompense him for his benevolence ? " They answered, " No one."

And 'Ikrimah made no further remark ; but when it was night he took four thousand dinârs and put them into a bag. Then he ordered his steed to be saddled, and went out unknown to his people, and mounted, and took with him one of his slaves to carry the money. And he journeyed until he drew near Khuzaimah's door, when he took the bag from the slave and ordered him to retire to a distance, while he himself advanced towards the door and knocked at it.

---

* *el-Fayyâdh* signifies The boundlessly generous ; it is one of the titles used in speaking of the Most High, and is sometimes applied, as in this case, to an extremely generous man.

Then Khuzaimah came out to him, and 'Ikrimah held the bag towards him and said, "With this restore thy condition." And Khuzaimah took it from him, but found it heavy. So he put it out of his hand, and laid hold of the bridle of 'Ikrimah's steed, and said, "That I might be a ransom for thee! Who art thou?" 'Ikrimah replied, "O thou!* I did not come at such a time and such a season as this, desiring that thou shouldst recognize me." "But," said Khuzaimah, "I will not accept it unless thou tell me who thou art." So 'Ikrimah said, "I am Jâbir-'Atharât-el-Kirâm." † "Tell me more," said Khuzai-mah. But he answered, "No," and passed on.

* *Ya enta! Ya hazha!* O thou! O such-an-one! An exclamation importing no manner of respect to the person addressed.

† It is now I believe generally known that most, I might say all, English proper names have a meaning; though in only a few instances, *e.g.*, where the names of the cardinal or Christian virtues have been made use of as proper names, is the meaning instantly apparent. This is, however, not the case in an original language such as Arabic. In Arabic, proper names which are made use of as commonly as Mary, Elizabeth, Anne, or Susan, in English, bear their meaning as obviously as the English names Prudence, Grace, Hope, or Charity. In the instance related above, the name " Jâbir-'Atharât-el-Kirâm " would mean *the mender (or repairer) of the slips of the generous.* But such a name would awaken no suspicion of its being assumed in the mind of the person whom it was intended to deceive.

Then Khuzaimah took the bag, and went in to the
daughter of his uncle, and said to her, " Rejoice ! for
verily happiness and freedom from care have been
bestowed upon us by Allâh; and if it be but copper,
still there is plenty. Get up, and bring me a light."
But she said, " I have no means of getting a light."
So he spent the night in fingering the money, and the
stamp seemed to him like that of dinârs. And he
could not believe it.

As for 'Ikrimah, he returned to his dwelling, and
there found that his wife had discovered his absence,
and had been asking about him, and had been
informed of his riding off. And she disapproved of
it, and began to suspect him, and said to him, " The
Governor of Mesopotamia should go out in the middle
of the night unattended by his servants and unknown
to his people only to visit his wives or his slaves."
He made answer, " Know that I went not to any of
them." " Then tell me whither thou wentest," said she.
He replied, " O woman ! I did not go out at such a
time desiring that anybody should know about me."
" There is no help for it," said she, " thou must tell
me." " Wilt thou keep it secret ?" he asked. " Certainly
I will," she replied. So he told her the whole story as

it had happened, and what he had said, and the answer
he had received. And then he added, " Wouldst
thou that I swear to this?" "No," she answered.
" In good truth my heart is tranquil, and rests upon
thy word."

With regard to Khuzaimah, when day dawned he
paid off his creditors and re-established good order
in his affairs, after which he equipped himself for a
journey, desiring to visit Sulaimân-ibn-'Abd-el-Málik,
who at that time had gone down to Palestine. And
when he reached Sulaimân's door, he demanded
admittance, and the chamberlain went in and acquainted the Amír of his arrival. And Sulaimân
knew about him, for he was famous on account of
his generosity and benevolence. So he was admitted,
and when he entered he saluted the Amír as Khalîfah.
Then Sulaimân-ibn-'Abd-el-Málik asked him, " O
Khuzaimah! what has kept thee so long away from
us?" "My miserable condition," he replied. " But,"
continued Sulaimân, "what hindered thee from coming
to us?" "My weakness, O Commander of the Faithful!" he answered. "Then how hast thou been
enabled to come now?" asked Sulaimân. "O Commander of the Faithful!" he replied, "I know

nothing except that in the middle of the night, before I was aware, a man was knocking at the door, who did so-and-so." And he related the tale from beginning to end. "Didst thou recognize the man?" asked Sulaimân. "I did not, O Commander of the Faithful!" replied Khuzaimah, "and that because he was muffled up, and I only heard his voice while he said ' I am Jâbir-'Atharât-el-Kirâm.' "

The narrator proceeds: Then the heart of Sulaimân-ibn-'Abd-el-Málik burnt within him, and he lamented this want of knowledge of him, and said, "Did we but know him, verily we would recompense him his benevolence." Presently he said, "Bring me the Wand of Office." And when it had been brought, he invested the afore-named Khuzaimah-ibn-Bishr with the governorship of Mesopotamia in the room of 'Ikrimah-el-Fayyâdh.

So Khuzaimah set out for Mesopotamia. And when he drew near, 'Ikrimah and the townsfolk came forth to meet him. And they saluted one another, and journeyed together until they entered the town. And Khuzaimah dismounted at the governor's house, and commanded that the surety for 'Ikrimah should be brought, and that the accounts should be calculated. So they reckoned them, and found that he had to answer for a considerable overplus of goods. And Khuzaimah claimed from him the payment thereof. But he said, "I have no means whatsoever." "There is nothing else to be done," said Khuzaimah. But he repeated, "I have it not; therefore do thy duty."

So Khuzaimah ordered him to prison ; but afterwards sent some one to him, again demanding the money from him. But he sent the messenger back, saying, "I am not one who for the sake of concealing his wealth would lose his reputation (by imprisonment). So do with me as thou wilt." Then they loaded him with irons, and thus he remained for a month or longer, and became in consequence weak and miserable.

And the daughter of his paternal uncle heard news of this, and it distressed and disquieted her. So she summoned a freed slave who was clever and intelligent, and said to her, "Go instantly to the gate of this Amír, Khuzaimah-ibn-Bishr, and say, 'I am possessed of good advice.' And if they ask it of thee, say, 'I will not reveal it except to the Amír Khuzaimah-ibn-Bishr.' Then if thou art admitted to him, beg that thou mayst be alone with him. If he grants this, then thou shalt say to him, 'This was hardly the return which Jâbir-'Atharât-el-Kirâm deserved from thee! Thou hast recompensed him with prison, and pain, and iron.'"

So the girl did this, and when Khuzaimah had heard her words, he cried with a loud voice, "Ah! what a mischance! and is it really he?" She said, "Yes."

Then he ordered his steed immediately; and they saddled it; and he sent to fetch the chief men of the city, who assembled themselves before him, and they came with him to the gate of the prison. And it was opened, and Khuzaimah entered, and they that were with him. And they beheld 'Ikrimah sitting in the courtyard of the prison, changed in appearance, and reduced by his misfortune and suffering, and the weight of his chains and fetters. And when he saw Khuzaimah and the people with him, he blushed for shame, and hung down his head. But Khuzaimah drew near until he bent over him and kissed his brow. Then 'Ikrimah turned towards him and said, "What has given rise to this on thy part?" "Thy noble deed," said Khuzaimah, "and my ill requital." "May

God pardon both us and thee!" said 'Ikrimah. Then they fetched the gaoler, who struck off his chains. And Khuzaimah commanded that they should be put upon his own feet. But 'Ikrimah asked, "What is this thou desirest?" He replied, "I wish to experience the same misery that thou hast undergone." "I adjure thee by Allâh!" said 'Ikrimah, "do it not."

So they went out together until they reached Khuzaimah's house. Then 'Ikrimah bade him farewell, and would have departed from him, but Khuzaimah said, "Thou wilt not leave me." He asked, "What dost thou wish?" "To alter thy condition," said Khuzaimah, "for verily my shame before the daughter of thy uncle is even greater than my shame before thee." Then he ordered a bath, and every one left it, and they two went in together. And Khuzaimah took it entirely upon himself to wait on 'Ikrimah and act as his servant. And when they came out, Khuzaimah bestowed a robe of honour upon him, and put it on him, and gave him also much money. Then Khuzaimah accompanied him to his house, and begged permission to go in and ask pardon of 'Ikrimah's cousin. So he made his excuses to her, and blamed himself for what had occurred.

The narrator adds : And after this Khuzaimah begged 'Ikrimah to go with him to Sulaimân-ibn-'Abd-el-Málik, who had then taken up his abode at er-Ramlat.* And this being agreeable to him, they journeyed together until they reached Sulaimân-ibn-'Abd-el-Málik. And the chamberlain entered, and informed him of the arrival of Khuzaimah-ibn-Bishr. And Sulaimân was alarmed at this, and exclaimed, "The Governor of Mesopotamia has arrived without an order from us ! This can only be by reason of some serious tidings." And when Khuzaimah came in, before he could utter his salutation, Sulaimân cried, " What is thy news, O Khuzaimah ?" " Good, O Commander of the Faithful !" he replied. " What then has brought thee hither ? " asked Sulaimân. " I have discovered Jâbir-'Atharât-el-Kirâm," he answered, "for ever since I perceived thy vexation at losing him, and thy desire to see him, I have longed to please thee by finding him." " And who is he ? " asked Sulaimân. " 'Ikrimah-el-Fayyâdh," replied Khuzaimah.

So Sulaimân ordered him to be admitted, and when he entered he saluted Sulaimân as Khalîfah. And

* er-Ramlat in Palestine, in lat. 31° 55' N., long. 34° 52' E.

the latter welcomed him, and invited him to be seated, and said, O 'Ikrimah! thou didst good to him by harming thyself!" Then he continued, " Write all thy wishes, and everything of which thou art in need, on a piece of paper." So he did this, and Sulaimân ordered the immediate accomplishment of them, and commanded ten thousand dinârs to be given to him, and two suits of clothes. Then he sent for the Wand of Office, and invested 'Ikrimah with the government of Mesopotamia and Armenia and Azarbijân, and said to him, " Khuzaimah's fate is in thy hands, whether thou wilt retain him, or whether thou wilt depose him." " Not so," said 'Ikrimah ; " I would, O Commander of the Faithful ! that he return to his government."

After this they departed from him in company, and continued to be Sulaimân's vicegerents so long as lasted his reign.

ALLÂH IS ALL-KNOWING !

HOW YÛNUS THE SCRIBE SOLD HIS SLAVE-GIRL.

TRANSLATOR'S PREFATORY NOTE.

Abu'l-Fáraj-'Aly was a member of the tribe of Kuraish, and a descendant of Marwân-ibn-Muhammad, the last of the 'Omeyyade Kalîfahs. His family inhabited Ispahân, but he passed his early youth in Baghdâd, and became the most distinguished scholar and most eminent author of that city. His "Kitâb-el-Aghâny," whence this tale is taken, is considered as unequalled. It is said that he was fifty years in compiling it, and that when the Wazîr, Sahib-ibn-Abbâd (who was looked upon as the wonder of his age for wisdom and learning), received it, he found that he could dispense with the thirty camel-loads of books on literary subjects which he was in the habit of taking with him when travelling or changing residence ; the " Kitâb-el-Aghâny" being sufficient for him. Abu'l-Fáraj wrote many other works, and composed much poetry. He was born A.H. 284 (A.D. 897-8), and died at Baghdâd A.H. 356 (A.D. 967). Previous to his death, his fine intellect became disordered.

ABU'L-FÁRAJ-EL-ISBAHÂNY, in his Kitâb-el-Aghâny (Book of Songs), says, Yûnus the scribe relates as follows.

During the reign of Hishâm-ibn-'Abd-el-Málik, I set

set off for Syria, taking with me a slave-girl musician, to whom I had taught everything required by her art, and whose value to me I estimated at a hundred thousand dirhems. And when we drew near Syria, the caravan halted at a pool of water, by the side of which I dismounted, spread the food I had with me, and brought out a flask of wine. And whilst I was thus occupied, behold! a young man of fair countenance and form, mounted upon a chesnut horse, came by, and two attendants with him. And he saluted me, and asked, "Wilt thou receive me as thy guest?"

I replied, "Certainly;" and held his stirrup while he dismounted.

Then he said, "Give me to drink of thy wine."

So I gave him to drink, and he added, "Will it please thee to sing me a song?"

So I sang to him,

> Beauties, never before united, in her are met together;
> And for love of her, tears and sleeplessness are sweet to me.

And he praised this warmly, and begged for a repetition of it many times; and then said, "Speak to thy slave-girl, and let her sing."

So I commanded her, and she sang,

> A young girl bewilders my heart with her beauties ;
> For she is not a reed, and she is not the sun, nor is she
> the moon.

And this also pleased him greatly, and he asked several times to have it repeated. And he did not quit his position until time for our evening prayer, after which he inquired, "What brings thee to this our town ? "

" I want to sell this slave-girl," I replied.

" And how much demandest thou as her price ? " he asked.

I answered, " Enough to pay my debts and to put my affairs in good order."

" Thirty thousand ? " said he.

" By favour of Allâh, that and more," I replied.

" Will forty thousand satisfy thee ? " he asked.

" That would pay my debts," said I, " but my hands would remain empty."

Then he said, "Verily I will take her for fifty thousand dirhems ; and besides that, thou shalt have a rich robe, and the expenses of thy journey, and I will make thee a partner in my business so long as I live."

" Surely I have sold her to thee ! " I cried.

Then he asked, "If I take her with me, wilt thou trust me to send this to thee in the morning ; or shall she stay with thee until it is brought to thee to-morrow ?"

Now the wine had overpowered me, and the consequent confusion and bashfulness caused me to say, "To be sure! I will certainly trust thee. Take her, and may Allâh make thee happy with her !"

So he said to one of his young men, " Place her upon thy animal, and get up behind, and take her away." And then he himself mounted, and took leave of me, and departed.

And he had been scarcely an instant out my sight ere I was conscious of the mistake and error into which I had fallen. And I cried, "What have I done? I have parted with my slave-girl to a man with whom I have no acquaintance, nor do I even know who he is; and supposing I did know him, where is he to be found?"

So I sat down thinking over this, until the dawn prayer-hour. And my companions went into Damascus, but I remained behind, perplexed and undecided what I should do. And the sun beat down upon me, and I hated the place. And I thought of entering

Damascus, but afterwards I said, " It would not do for the messenger to come and not find me, for then verily I should have committed a second error against myself." So I sat down in the shade of a wall hard by. And when the day was far spent, behold! one of the two youths who had been with the young man drew near. And I never remember to have felt greater pleasure at anything than my pleasure that moment on seeing him.

And he said to me, " O my lord! I am late in reaching thee."

But I said not a word to him of what I had suffered.

Then he asked me, " Didst thou recognize the man ? "

I said, " No."

" He is the heir-apparent," said he, "el-Walid-ibn-Hishâm."*   Upon hearing which, I remained silent.

Then he said, " Rise, and mount."

* This is another careless misstatement of historical fact. El-Walîd was the heir-apparent, but he was the nephew, and not the son, of Hishâm ; the Khalifah, Yezîd-ibn-'Abd-el-Mâlik having nominated his brother Hishâm to succeed him, on condition that upon the death of the last-named prince, his own son, el-Walîd, should be called to the throne.

And behold! there was a riding-horse with him, and I mounted, and we journeyed together until we arrived at his master's house. And I entered, and lo! there was the slave-girl, who sprang towards me, and saluted me. And I asked, "How hast thou fared?"

She replied, "He lodged me in this little room, and ordered for me everything I required."

So I sat with her awhile, and then, behold! one of his servants came to me, and said, "Come." So I got up, and he led me into the presence of his master. And lo! he was my companion of yesterday, and was now seated upon his chair of state.

And he asked, "Who art thou?"

"Yûnus the scribe," I answered.

"Thou art welcome," said he. "By Allâh! I have indeed been desirous to see thee, for thy fame has reached me. And how didst thou pass the night?"

"Excellently, may Allâh preserve thee!" I said.

"But," he continued, "perhaps thou didst blame thyself for thy yesterday's work, and didst say, 'I have given up my slave to a man whom I do not know, with whose very name I am unacquainted, and in ignorance even of the place to which he belongs.'"

"God forbid," I cried, "that I should take blame to

myself, O Prince!   Had I even offered this slave-girl
as a gift unto the Prince, it had been one too poor
and mean and worthless."

Then he said, "By Allâh! I nevertheless blamed
myself for taking her from thee, and thought, ' Here
is a man from a strange country who does not know
me, and verily I have come upon him at unawares,
and have caused him to act foolishly by my eagerness
to take away the girl!' Now dost thou remember
what was the agreement between us?"

"Yes," said I.

"Thou didst sell the slave-girl for fifty thousand
dirhems," he said.

"It was so," I replied.

Then he said, "Ho! slave, bring the money."

So he brought it, and placed it in his master's
hands, who then said, "Bring a thousand dinârs, O
slave!"

And he brought them. And then the Prince said,
"Here, slave! bring another five hundred dinârs."
And when he came with them, the Prince said to me,
"This is the price of the slave-girl; collect it together.
And this thousand dinârs is for thy good opinion of us;
and this five hundred dinârs is for the expenses of thy

journey, and to buy something for thy family.   Art thou satisfied ?"

I replied, "I am satisfied."   And I kissed his hand, and said, "By Allâh ! thou hast filled my hand and my eye."

Presently he cried, " By Allâh ! I have not been to see her, nor appeased my craving for her singing. Bring her to me."

So she came, and he commanded her to be seated ; and when she had sat down, he said to her, "Sing." So she recited these lines :

> Of one who unites every single perfection
> How sweet the embrace, the caress !
> All beauties there may be 'mongst Arabs and strangers,
> But none blends all like thee, O my fawn !
> Reveal thee, O beautiful ! unto thy lover,
> Or by thy promise, or like a dream-vision.
> Sweet for thy sake are abasement and scorn,
> And good in my sight is my sleepless night ;
> But I am not the first through thee driven mad—
> Say, how many men ere me hast thou slain ?
> As my portion in this world, thou wouldst content me,
> For thou'rt dearer to me than my soul or my wealth.

And the Prince applauded loudly, and thanked me for her excellent training and teaching.   Then he cried, " Ho, slave ! bring a riding animal, saddled and accoutred for his mounting, and a mule to carry his baggage and his necessaries." Then he addressed me, saying, "O Yûnus! shouldst thou learn that this empire has really descended to me, return hither, and by Allâh! I will certainly fill thy hand and raise thy position, and will appoint thee for my musician so long as I live."

So I took my money and departed. And when the Khalifate came down to el-Walîd, I journeyed to him, and by Allâh! he fulfilled his promise, and increased my dignity. And my condition with him was most happy, and I was comfortable in my post, and verily my means were extended and my wealth increased. And villages and lands became mine, which are ample to support me, and will suffice those who come after me. And I remained with him until he was killed. May God pardon him!"

THE BÉDAWY WHO TAUGHT THE KHALÎFAH MANNERS.

TRANSLATOR'S PREFATORY NOTE.

Hishâm-ibn-'Abd-el-Málik was the fourth of that Khalîfah's sons who reigned over the Muslims. He succeeded his brother Yezîd A.H. 105 (A.D. 724), and died of quinsy at er-Rusâfa, A.H. 125 (A.D. 742), aged from fifty-three to fifty-six years, according to different authors. He was buried at er-Rusâfa, a town which lay opposite to er-Rákkah, at one day's journey west of the Euphrates; and which is placed by Abu'l-Fedâ in lat. 36° N. It was founded by Hishâm, who made it his summer residence, and retired there to avoid the plague which desolated Syria. Hishâm governed without any prime minister, and greatly harassed his subjects by his rapacious and covetous disposition. He was richer than any of his predecessors, but the Persian historian Khondemir says that Hishâm would not trust any person with the keys of his coffers, and that he was one of the most avaricious princes that ever lived.

IT is related, amongst other anecdotes, that Hishâm-ibn-'Abd-el-Málik was engaged one day in hunting and sport. And he saw a gazelle being pursued by the dogs. And he followed it. And it passed round the hut of an Arab who was pasturing his flocks. So

Hishâm cried, "Ho, young man! here is work for thee. Bring me that gazelle."

But the youth turned his head towards him, and said, "O ignorant of the manners of high estate ! verily thou hast looked upon me scornfully, and spoken to me disdainfully; and thy speech was the speech of a tyrant, and thy deed the deed of an ass!"

Then cried Hishâm, "Woe be to thee! O young man! Dost thou not know me?"

He replied, "I know this of thee, that thou hast been badly educated; for thou didst begin talking to me before saluting me."

"Woe upon thee!" repeated Hishâm. "I am Hishâm-ibn-'Abd-el-Málik."

Then cried the Arab, "May good be far from thy dwelling, and may thy grave be forgotten! Do not add to thy words and diminish thy dignity."

And he had scarcely ceased speaking before the soldiers gathered round them from all sides, each one of them saying, "Peace be upon thee, O Commander of the Faithful!"

"Enough of words!" said Hishâm; "secure this young man."

So they seized him; and Hishâm returned to his

palace, and seated himself in his council-hall, and said, " Bring the young Bédawy to me."

So they brought him. And when he beheld the multitude of slaves, and porters, and wazîrs, and scribes, and scions of royalty, and lords of justice, he paid no heed to them, and sought no notice from them ; but let his chin fall on his breast, and watched his own foot-steps until he reached Hishâm, and stood before him. Then the young man cast his eyes upon the ground, and stood still, and spoke no word. And one of the attendants exclaimed, "O dog of an Arab! what hinders thee from saluting the Commander of the Faithful ? "

Then he turned towards him in a fury, and cried, "O saddle of an ass ! I am prevented by the length of the approach, and the projecting steps, and other obstacles."

Then said Hishâm, and verily his anger was in-creasing, " O young man ! of a truth the day has arrived when thy death is near, and thy desires frus-trated, and thy life at an end."

The young man replied, " By Allâh ! O Hishâm ! even were the term of my life to be prolonged, thy words, whether little or big, could do me no hurt."

Then the chamberlain cried, " Has it come to this,

that one in thy position, and of thy station, O most vile Arab! should bandy words with the Commander of the Faithful?"

The young man instantly replied, "May disappointment attend thee, and woe and destruction smite thee! Hast thou never heard what saith the Most High—'At the coming day, every man will argue concerning his soul.'* Therefore, if God may be argued with, pray what is Hishâm that he is not even to be spoken to?"

Upon this Hishâm rose up in a towering rage, and cried, "Ho! executioner! bring me the head of this young man, for verily he has added to his words more than any one would believe possible."

So the executioner came forward, and laid hold of the young man, and made him kneel upon the Nitâ'a † of Blood, and unsheathed above his head the Sword of Vengeance, and cried, "O Commander of the Faithful! is it by his own act that thy wretched

* " A day is coming when every soul shall plead [or argue] for itself."—el-Kurân, Sur. xvi., V. 112. el-Beidhâwy explains: " Every soul shall be solicitous for his own salvation, not concerning himself with the condition of another." The Bédawy, however, gives it a turn to suit his purpose, and the language quite bears him out.

† See Note *, p. 141.

slave descends to his grave ? If I strike off his head, shall I be guiltless of his blood ?"

Hishâm answered, "Yes."

Then the executioner asked permission a second time, and Hishâm consented. And then he asked it a third time; and the Amîr was about to grant it, when the young man laughed until his eye-teeth were visible. Then Hishâm wondered more and more at him, and exclaimed, "O young man, it appears to me that thou must have lost thy reason. Thou knowest that thou art about to quit this world, and to end thy life, and yet thou canst laugh derisively to thyself!"

"O Commander of the Faithful!" the young man replied, "were my days to be prolonged, and were not my life to be cut short, nothing on thy part, whether great or small, could injure me. But, nevertheless, some lines occurred to me a moment ago; listen to them, for my death will not escape, and let there be great silence."

So Hishâm said, "Repeat them, and that quickly; for these moments are thy last in this world, and thy first in that which is to come."

Then the young man composed and recited these verses :

> I have heard that once a partridge, led by Fate,
> Was by a falcon seized upon ;
> Suspended from his claws the partridge hung,
> And, absorbed in him, the falcon flew away.
> Then, in bird-language, came a voice which said,
> " Yes, thou hast conquered me, and I am captive ;
> But the hunger of thy like my like cannot appease,
> For even when I'm eaten, as nothing shall I seem ! "
> At this the falcon smiled, touched by his self-abasement,
> And set that partridge free.

The historian continues : " Then Hishâm smiled, and said, ' By my relationship to the Messenger of God ! had he thus spoken at the first moment, and asked anything short of the Khalîfate, verily I would have given it to him. Here, attendant ! cram his mouth with pearls and jewels, and be liberal in compensating him, and let him go about his business.' "

HOW 'URWAH-IBN-UDZÎNAH GAINED A LIVELIHOOD.

IT is said that 'Urwah-ibn-Udzînah* presented him-self before Hishâm-ibn-'Abd-el-Málik, complaining of poverty. Hishâm asked, "Was it not thou who saidst,

> ' Verily I have discovered (tho' extravagance is not one of
>   my qualities)
> That my subsistence will come of itself to me.
> I strive for it, and the pursuit of it wearies me,
> But I sit down, and without my pains it comes to me.'

And hast thou now come from el-Hijâz to Syria to seek a livelihood ? "

He made answer, " O Commander of the Faithful! thou hast been exhorted and informed." Then he went out, and mounted his dromedary, and returned to el-Hijâz.

---

* Abu-'Aâmir 'Urwah-ibn-Udzînah, a man eminent for his learning and piety, was a member of the tribe of Laith, and a celebrated poet and traditionist. He died A.H. 118 (A.D. 736).

And when night came, Hishâm was resting on his bed, and he thought of 'Urwah, and said, " He is one of the Kuraish, and he spoke wisely ; he came to me, and I dismissed him disappointed." So as soon as daylight appeared, he sent him a thousand dinârs.

And the messenger knocked at the door of 'Urwah's house in el-Medînah, and gave him the money. Then said 'Urwah, " Salute the Commander of the Faithful from me, and say to him, ' What thinkest thou now of my words ? I worked hard, but found barren soil. When I returned home unsuccessful, and sat down in my house, my livelihood came of itself to me in my dwelling.' "

THE BEGINNING OF THE ABBASSIDE DYNASTY.

THE founder of this dynasty was Abu-Muslim, el-Khurasâny, and his name was 'Abd-er-Rahmán-ibn-Muslim.   Amongst his sayings are the following lines :

> Tho' they were reinforced, I obtained by vigilance and secrecy
>> What fell away from the Kings of the Benu-Marwân.
> I ceased not striving with might for their overthrow,
>> And the people were careless and verily the men slept.
> Never before had been such slumber.   But with the sword
>> I fell upon them, and from their slumber woke them.
> For he who sleeps while tending his flock where wild beasts
>> roam,
> Will find that the lion constitutes himself their shepherd.

The first of these Abbasside Khalîfahs was Abu-'Abd-Allâh, es-Saffâh.

TRANSLATOR'S NOTE.

Upon the death of Hishâm, A.H. 125 (A.D. 742), el-Walîd, the son of Hishâm's brother and predecessor, Yezîd, succeeded to the throne.   (See Note *, p. 222.)   But so immoral was el-Walîd's life, and so impious were his religious opinions,

that the people of Syria unanimously resolved to depose
him the following year. They accordingly chose Yezîd,
the son of el-Walîd I. (see pp. 192—194), el-Walîd's
cousin-german, for their leader, and inaugurated him
Khalîfah. He marched against el-Walîd, dispersed his
troops, besieged him in his palace, and finally slew him,
after he had reigned a year and three months. Yezîd himself died of the plague at Damascus, after he had reigned
six months, and was succeeded by his brother Ibrahîm. In
the beginning of the year 127 (A.D. 744), however, Marwân-
ibn-Muhammad-ibn-Marwân-ibn-el-Hâkim, who was the
governor of Mesopotamia and surrounding provinces, and
who had rebelled against Yezîd under pretext of avenging
the murder of el-Walîd II., marched against Ibrahîm, in-
tending to besiege Damascus, and depose the Khalîfah.
At Kinnafrin and Hems he was joined by many of the
Khalîfah's subjects, who took the oath of allegiance to him ;
but Sulaimân-ibn-Hishâm, Ibrahîm's general, marched
against him with an army of a hundred and twenty thousand
men. Sulaimân's army was, however, routed with great
slaughter, and he himself was forced to fly to Damascus.
Marwân released his many prisoners upon condition of
their taking an oath of fidelity to el-Hâkim and 'Othmân,
el-Walîd's sons, who, since the murder of their father, had
remained in prison at Damascus. But Sulaimân, being
well assured of Marwân's intention to place one of them
upon the throne, no sooner arrived at Damascus than in
concert with Ibrahîm he ordered their execution, and then
made his escape from the city. El-Hâkim and 'Othmân,
however, foreseeing what would happen, took care before
their deaths to transfer their right to Marwân, and declared,
in presence of a fellow-prisoner, that in case they should be
slain, Marwân ought to be regarded by all Muslims as the
lawful Khalîfah and Imâm. So after Sulaimân's flight, the
citizens of Damascus opened their gates to Marwân, and,

there being no other person in the empire capable of disputing his title or standing in competition with him, he was declared Khalîfah. Ibrahîm himself recognizing his authority, A.H. 127. So short indeed was Ibrahîm's reign, that many writers scarcely mention him. He died A.H. 132. But the manner of his death is uncertain: some say he was assassinated, some that he was drowned, and others that he was poisoned.

Marwân, however, though proclaimed Khalîfah, did not long enjoy peace. The very same year (A.H. 127) the people of Hems rebelled against him. The Damascenes followed their example, and also the people of el-Básrah, who had proclaimed Sulaimân-ibn-Hishâm Khalîfah at that place. And though Marwân was successful in, to a certain extent, quelling these insurrections, yet the partisans of the house of el-Abbâs were now beginning to grow powerful in some of the interior provinces of the empire. El-Abbâs was the Prophet's uncle; and the first of the family who made any considerable figure was his descendant in the third generation, Muhammad-ibn-'Aly, who flourished in the time of 'Omar-ibn-'Abd-el-Azîz. 'Omar succeeded Sulaimân-ibn-'Abd-el-Mâlik A.H. 99 (A.D. 717). Muhammad-ibn-'Aly was nominated chief or *Imâm* of the house of el-Abbâs in the hundredth year of the Hijrah. He is reported to have said to the deputation sent to him on this occasion, "I shall soon die, and my son Ibrahîm will be your leader till he shall be slain. After his death, my other son, 'Abd-Allâh, surnamed Abu-'l-'Abbâs, es-Saffâh, shall preside over you, and settle the government of the Muslims upon a solid and lasting basis." Muhammad died A.H. 125, and was succeeded in the honourable post of Imâm by his son Ibrahîm. It was Ibrahîm who two years later appointed Abu-Muslîm-'Abd-er-Rahmân-ibn-Muslim, el-Khurasâny, then a youth of nineteen, to go as his representative to Khorassân. Abu-Muslim is called in the text the *founder* or *establisher* of the

Abbasside dynasty. Ibn-Khalikân calls him the *champion
and asserter of the rights of the Abbassides to the Khalîfate.*
He was not of the house of el-Abbâs, nor do historians
seem agreed as to his birth, some even maintaining that he
was originally a slave of Kurd extraction. Be that as it
may, he attached himself to the house of el-Abbâs, and so
great were his talents as a general, that the Khalifah
Marwân's troops could make no head against him, and in
A.H. 129 all Marwân's commandants of fortresses in Khorassân were obliged either to take an oath of fidelity to
Ibrahîm, or within a limited time to quit the province. In
A.H. 131, Ibrahîm, while on his way to perform the pilgrimage to Mekkah, was seized by the troops of Marwân,
which came up with him near Harrân, carried him to that
city, and confined him in prison, where he soon after died.
His brother Abu-'Abd-Allâh, es-Saffâh, succeeded him, and
mainly owing to the exertions and ability of Abu-Muslim,
Marwân and his forces were driven from point to point until
at length he retreated to Egypt, where he was slain, A.H. 132
(A.D. 750), and es-Saffâh took possession of the Khalifate
without further resistance.

Es-Saffâh after this treated Abu-Muslim with the highest honour
for his services, and the talents he had displayed in con-
ducting this important enterprise. And from that time
he constantly repeated aloud the lines given in the text.
Ibn-Khalikân gives a slightly different version of them.

Es-Saffâh died of smallpox at el-Anbâr, or at el-Hâshimiyyah, a
city erected by him at a short distance from the former, A.H.
136, on the very day that he completed his thirty-third year.
He was succeeded by his brother Abu-Jaâfar, el-Mansûr.
But though the house of el-Abbâs owed its elevation to the
Khalifate almost entirely to Abu-Muslim, there had for
some time been a considerable misunderstanding between
that general and Abu-Jaâfar. The latter, indeed, observing
the devotion of the people of Khorassân to Abu-Muslim,

would even during his brother's lifetime have persuaded the latter to put Abu-Muslim to death. But es-Saffâh could not so far forget all sense of gratitude. Some writers assert that it was the intention of this great general to transfer the Khalîfate from the house of el-Abbâs to the descendants of 'Aly, and that that was the principal cause of his destruction. Be that as it may, he was treacherously inveigled into the palace of Abu-Jaâfar, el-Mansûr, and there, in presence and by order of the Khalîfah, was more treacherously slain, A.H. 137 (A.D. 755). He was a man of indisputable talent, though with regard to his intellectual abilities and humanity authors are not agreed, some representing him as prudent, merciful, and discreet ; while others have characterized him as of a fierce, merciless, and intractable disposition. A certain Muslim being once asked whether Abu-Muslim or el-Hajjâj (see Note *, p. 151) was the better man, replied, " I will not say that Abu-Muslim was better than any other man, but that el-Hajjâj was worse than he." Abu-Muslim is said to have killed six hundred thousand men in the various battles he fought for the house of el-Abbâs and on other occasions.

HOW ABU-DULÂMAH GAINED ALL HE WANTED.

IT is related that one day, when the poet Abu-Dulâmah * was standing in the presence of es-Saffâh, the latter said to him, " Ask of me whatever thou desirest."

" I want a sporting dog," he replied.

" Give him one," said es-Saffâh.

" And a horse upon which to hunt," he added.

" Give him a horse," said es-Saffâh.

" And a slave to lead the dog and carry the game," proceeded Abu-Dulâmah.

" Give him a slave," said es-Saffâh.

---

* Abu-Dulâmah-Zand-ibn-el-Jaun was, according to Abu-'l-Fáraj, a black slave from Abyssinia. Ibn-Khalikán records many anecdotes of his ready wit, and remarks that he was celebrated for his wit, amusing adventures, acquaintance with general literature, and talent for poetry. He died A.H. 161 (A.D. 777-8), though some say that he lived to the reign of er-Rashîd, who succeeded to the Khalifate A.H. 170.

" And a slave-girl to prepare the game, and cook it for us," continued the other.

" Give him a slave-girl," said es-Saffâh.

Then Abu-Dulâmah said, " These, O Commander of the Faithful! form a family, and without question they must have a house to live in."

" Give him a house which will hold them all," said es-Saffâh.

Presently Abu-Dulâmah added, " But though they have a house, whence are the means of living to come ?"

Es-Saffâh made answer, " Verily I bestow upon thee ten *ghamîrât* villages in the plains of the children of Israel."

" What is the meaning of *ghamîrât*, O Commander of the Faithful ?" asked Abu-Dulâmah.

" That which is uncultivated," answered es-Saffâh.

" Then," said Abu-Dulâmah, " I bestow upon thee, O Commander of the Faithful! a hundred *ghamîrât* villages in the plains of the Benu-Sa'ad."*

---

* I am unable to explain the point of this repartee. My sheikh, who was however more apt to give any answer which he thought would satisfy me than to trouble himself with research, told me that there was no such tribe as the Benu-Sa'ad ; and I therefore imagined that the answer was much as if a person in

And es-Saffâh, hearing this, laughed, and said, " I will give them all in cultivated land."

And the narrator of this tale remarks, " Observe his adroitness and cunning in asking ; how he began with the sporting dog, which it was easy to grant, and made one demand lead to another, in order and amusingly, until he had gained everything he wanted. Whereas had he asked for all at once, verily it would have been refused him. May Allâh prosper him !"

the present day were to say, " I'll give you a hundred castles in Spain." But I find that there were three different tribes of that name, though there seems to be nothing in their history or locality to give point to the expression in the tale. One of these tribes appears to have been connected with the Benu-Tamîm (see Note *, p. 54), and it may be that at the epoch referred to it would have been a difficult matter for the Khalifah to derive any benefit from the gift thus jocosely made.

THE CONCEALMENT AND FLIGHT OF IBRAHÎM-IBN-SULAIMÂN.

HÁSAN-IBN-EL-HUSEIN relates, that when the Khalîfate came into the hands of the Benu-Abbâs, amongst the numbers who concealed themselves was Ibrahîm-ibn-Sulaimân-ibn-'Abd-el-Málik. And he remained in hiding until he was weakened and exhausted by it; and then a safety-warrant was taken to him from es-Saffâh. And Ibrahîm, who was a well-educated, eloquent man, and agreeable in conversation, was highly esteemed by es-Saffâh. And the latter said to him, "Verily thou didst remain a long while in hiding; tell me therefore the most wonderful thing thou sawest during thy concealment, for of a truth those were troubled times."

He replied, "O Commander of the Faithful! was ever anything heard more marvellous than this my tale? Verily, I was hiding in a house which looked out upon the plain; and whilst there, behold! I per-

ceived a black standard * which had certainly come
from el-Kûfah, and was advancing towards el-Hîrah.†
And the idea struck me that people had come out to
seek for me. So I fled forth in disguise, and reached
el-Kûfah by another road. And, by Allâh! I was
uncertain what to do, knowing nobody there. And
lo! I found myself at the great gate of an enclosed
court ; so I entered the court, and stood near the
house. And behold! there came by a man of gracious
mien, mounted upon a horse, and with him a crowd of
friends and attendants. And he came into the court,
and saw me waiting in perplexity. So he asked me,
'What dost thou want?' I replied, 'I am a stranger
who fears lest he should be murdered.' He said,

---

* Black was the chosen colour of the Abbasside family. All
its members, and the chief officers of their empire, wore that
colour. Ibrahîm-ibn-Muhammad, when he succeeded his father
as Imâm of the house of el-Abbâs, sent to his general, Abu
Muslim, a black standard, ordering him to have it borne before
him while he proclaimed his master legal Khalîfah and Imâm,
and published the title and pretensions of the house of el-Abbâs.
The standard was called es-Sáhab, *the cloud*, and a banner sent
at the same time was called ezh-Zhill, *the shadow*, which names
he interpreted thus : that as the earth would never be uncovered
by the clouds, nor quite void of shade, so the world would never
henceforth be without a Khalîfah of the house of el-Abbâs.

† For el-Kûfah and el-Hîrah, see Prefatory Note, p. 37.

'Enter.' So I went into a small room in his house, and he said, 'This is thine.' Then he fetched for me all that it required—a bed, dishes, clothes, food and drink. And I stayed with him, and, by Allâh! he never once asked who I was, nor of whom I was afraid. And during this time he used to ride out every day, and return weary and sad, as though he sought something he had lost, but found it not. So one day I said to him, 'I observe that thou ridest out every day, and returnest tired and vexed, as though thou wert seeking something thou hast lost.' And he answered, 'Verily, Ibrahîm-ibn-Sulaimân-ibn-'Abd-el-Málik slew my father, and I have been informed that he is in hiding from es-Saffâh, and I seek him that perchance I may find him and be revenged on him.' Then, O Commander of the Faithful! I marvelled that having taken flight, a fatal chance should have led me to the abode of the very man who desired my death, and sought to take vengeance upon me. And when this misfortune overtook me, the idea of life grew hateful to me, and I prayed for death to deliver me from my misery. Then I asked the man the name of his father and the manner of his death. And he gave me an account of it which I found correct. So I cried, 'O thou! of a truth it is incumbent upon me to do thee justice, and it is thy right that I should point out to thee the murderer of thy father, and spare thy footsteps, and bring that near to thee which is afar off.' Then he exclaimed, 'Dost thou know where he is ?' I replied, 'I do.' 'Where is he ?' he asked. I said, 'By Allâh! he is I; so take thy revenge upon me.' Then he, disbelieving me, said, 'I believe that concealment has weakened thee, and that thou art tired of life.' I answered, 'No, by Allâh! I slew him on such-and-such a day.' And when he was convinced that I spoke the truth, he changed colour, and his eyes kindled, and he cast down his head for a while. Then he turned towards me and said, 'However, he will meet thee on the Resurrection morn, and will cite thee before One from whom concealment will not hide thee ; and certainly I am not the betrayer of one who is under my protection, nor a traitor to my guest. Get thee away from me, for verily I will not answer for myself concerning thee after this day.' Then, O Commander of the Faithful! he ran to a chest, and took out of it a purse containing five hundred dinârs, and said, 'Take this to help thy concealment.' But I abso-

lutely refused to take it, and went away from him.
And he was the most noble-minded man I have ever
seen."

And es-Saffâh was deeply touched, and marvelled
at the tale.

DISPUTE BETWEEN THE MÚDHARITES
AND YÉMENITES.

EL-HAITHAM-IBN-'ADIY relates that Abu-'l-'Abbâs, es-Saffâh, enjoyed the nightly gatherings and discussions among the people. And I was present, he says, one night when Ibrahîm-ibn-Makhramah, el-Kindy, and men of the sons of el-Hârith-ibn-Ka'ab* his mother's brethren, and Khâlid-ibn-Safuân*-ibn-Ibrahîm, et-Tamîmy, were assembled. And they began their tales, and were discussing among themselves the Múdharites and the Yémenites,†

---

* El - Hârith - ibn - 'Amr - ibn - Ka'ab was the grandfather of Minkar, who gave his name to a numerous tribe the members of which were surnamed el-Minkâry. This tribe produced a great number of remarkable men, amongst whom were Khâlid-ibn-Safuân, and his cousin Shabîb-ibn-Shabba. They were both noted as good orators, speaking with elegance and precision. Khâlid had frequent sittings with the Khalifah, es-Saffâh.

† See Tale, p. 76, *et seq.*

and Ibrahím said, " O Commander of the Faithful ! in good truth, the Yémenites were the Arabs to whom everything was subjected. They possessed cities, and never lacked kings and rulers, but one illustrious ancestor transmitted their might to another from the beginning to the end. The Nuámanites, the Mundhirites, the Kabusites, and the Tobbaïtes [1] came from them. And from them came he who is praised in the writings of Daûd : [2] and he who was washed by angels. [3] And from them came he whose death shook el-'Arsh. [4] And from them came he who was spoken to by the wolf. [5] And from them came he who seized all vessels by force. [6] And there was nothing of value but derived its origin from them —whether thoroughbred steeds, or trenchant blades, or impenetrable armour, or rich robes, or precious pearls. If anything were asked from them, they granted it ; but if it were demanded of right, they refused it. And if guests came to them, they feasted them. None could excel their greatness, neither could any attain superiority over them. They were the Arabs of Arab descent, and all beside them were but Arabs by nurture." *

* See Note *, p. 79.

Then Abu-'l-'Abbâs, es Saffâh, remarked, " I do not think that et-Tamîmy agrees to thy words." And he asked him, " What dost thou say, O Khâlid ? "

Khâlid replied, " If thou givest me permission to speak, I will speak."

Said es-Saffâh, " I give thee permission. Speak therefore, and fear no man."

Then said Khâlid, " He is in error, O Commander of the Faithful ! who enters into an argument without knowledge, and into a discussion without reflection. For how could it be as he states when of a truth the people have not even eloquent tongues nor a correct dialect ? And there is no good proof that the Book *
was sent down in their language, nor that the Sunnah†
were given in it. And their country is a two days' journey from our country : if they stray away from where we have authority, they are eaten ; and if they leave our kingdom, they are murdered. They have vaunted themselves above us on account of the Nuámanites, and the Mundhirites, and other things which I shall soon mention ; but we glorify ourselves above them on account of the best of men, the noblest

---

* El-Kurân.

† The traditions of the Prophet.

of the noble, Muhammad, on whom be the greatest blessing and peace! and the grace of God be upon us and upon them! Verily they were followers of him, and gained esteem from him, having been generous to him.* But the Prophet came from us, and from us came the chosen Khalîfah,† and to us belongs the Frequented House,[7] and el-Ma'asa,[8] and Zem-zem,[9] and el-Makám,[10] and el-Mimbar,[11] and er-Rukn,[12] and el-Hatîm,[13] and el-Mashâ'ir,[14] and el-Hijâbat,[15] and el-Batha'a,[16] together with all the qualities which we are known to possess.‡ And no excellent thing can be found that we cannot equal, nor can uttered words express our superiority. And from us came es-Sadîk,[17] and el-Farûk,[18] and el-Wasy,[19] and Asad-Allâh,[20] and Sâîd, esh-Shúhadah,[21] and Zhu 'l-Janahîn,[22] and Saif-Allâh.[23] These knew God, and He brought them to the True Faith. And whosoever overrides us we will override him; but whosoever shows enmity towards us we will exterminate."

---

* Alluding to the reception met with by the Prophet at el-Medinah on his flight from Mekkah. See Note *, p. 137.

† A compliment to es-Saffâh.

‡ Courage, benevolence, liberality, etc.

Then he turned towards Ibrahîm, and asked, "Art thou acquainted with the dialect of thy people?"

He replied, "Yes."

"Then what is the name of the eye?" asked Khâlid.

"The observer," said Ibrahîm.

"And what is the name of the tooth?"

"The labourer," he answered.

"And what is the name of the ear?"

"The listener," said he.

"And what is the name of the fingers?"

"The holders," answered Ibrahîm.

"And what is the name of the beard?"

"The thick hair," he replied.

"And what is the name of the wolf?"

"The avoider," he made answer.

Then Khâlid asked him, "Art thou a believer in Allâh's book?"

"I am," said Ibrahîm.

"But," continued Khâlid, "of a truth the Most High says, 'Verily We have caused to descend the Arabian Kurân, that perchance ye may be instructed.' And the Most High speaks in the plain Arabian tongue, and He says, 'We have not sent a messenger except with (knowledge of) the language of his people. Now we are Arabs, and the Kurân was sent down in our tongue. Hast thou never remarked that God says, ' An eye for an eye,' and does not say, ' An observer for an observer ; ' and He says, 'A tooth for a tooth,' and does not say, 'A labourer for a labourer ; ' and He says, ' An ear for an ear,' and does not say, 'A listener for a listener ; ' and He says, ' They shall put their fingers in their ears,' and does not say, ' Their holders ; ' and He says, ' Thou shalt not seize by the beard, neither by the head ; ' and does not say, ' By the thick hair ; ' and the Most High says, ' The wolf shall eat him,' and does not say, ' The avoider shall eat him.' And now," continued Khâlid, " I will ask of thee four things: if thou admittest them, thou art vanquished ; if thou deniest them, thou art an unbeliever."

" What are they ? " asked Ibrahîm.

" The Messenger," said Khâlid, " was he of us or of you ? "

" Of you," answered Ibrahîm.

" And the Kurân," asked Khâlid, " did it descend upon us or upon you ? "

" Upon you," said Ibrahîm.

"And the Holy House, is it ours or yours ? "

" Yours," he replied.

" And the Khalîfah, is he of us or of you ? "

" Of you," he answered.

" Then," said Khâlid, "to all excepting these four things thou art welcome."

---

[1] Nuámân, Mundhir, Koubais, and Tobbá. Four powerful kings amongst the ancient Arabian tribes who gave their names to their followers and descendants. *Tobba* was retained as a title by the princes of the Himyarite dynasty. See Note *, p. 178.

[2] The Psalms of David. I imagine this refers to "Og the king of Bashan."

[3] Hánzhalah, one of the Associates, who was killed at the battle of Ohod, A.H. 3, where Muhammad and his followers were defeated by the Kuraish under Abu-Sufyân. According to Muslim faith, those who die fighting for el-Islám are martyrs, and when their bodies are buried their souls depart at once to Paradise, where they eat and drink and sleep in bliss. Their bodies are buried unwashed, martyrdom being held in lieu of ablution, unless they were known to have entered the fight in a state of ceremonial impurity,—*i. e.*, in a state in which they could not have entered a mosque, nor performed their devotions. After the battle of Ohod, the Prophet beheld angels performing the last offices upon the body of Hánzhalah, showing thereby that he had entered the fight in a state of impurity, but raising him in the opinion of surviving Muslims to the rank of a saint. Occasionally a soul has been known to return in the form it wore while in the flesh, and wash its own lifeless corpse.

[4] It is impossible to translate this word in the meaning here intended. This is—What is above the seventh heaven, where

the Almighty dwells. The first heaven is of water, solid and hard like ice. The second of green emeralds. The third of brass. The fourth of silver. The fifth of gold. The sixth of fine steel. The seventh of red rubies. Then comes *el-'Arsh*, of which no one knows aught save God alone. But of so vast an extent is it, that, were the world and the seven heavens united and laid therein, they would appear but as a scribe's seal set in the midst of the desert. The individual alluded to in the tale was Saâd, one of the Associates, a man of extraordinary piety, as the supposed effect of his death shows. According to Muhammadan faith, when a corpse is laid in the grave, the sides of the tomb contract and crush the body: with good persons, only " like a mother pressing her child to her bosom," but in the case of sinners with such force as to drive the ribs through the opposite side of the body. When the surviving Associates found out the effect caused in el-'Arsh by the death of Saâd, they said to the Prophet, " Surely the tomb will not contract upon him ; " but the Prophet told them it would, and it did. And the only person who has ever escaped this torture was Fâtimah, daughter of el-Asad and mother of the Khalîfah 'Aly, into whose tomb the Prophet descended, and in which he slept the night before her burial.

⁵'⁶ I cannot discover anything further concerning these heroes.

⁷ The Ka'abah at Mekkah. See Note *, p. 69.

⁸ A road between two hills called Sáfah and Merwah, within the city of Mekkah. One of the rites observed by pilgrims consists in traversing this road seven times, and invoking blessings upon themselves, their families, and friends the while.

⁹ The holy well at Mekkah. Muhammadans are persuaded that this is the very spring which appeared miraculously in the desert for the relief of Ismael when he and his mother were cast out by Abraham. It is drank with particular devotion by the pilgrims, and sent in bottles to all parts of the Muslim dominions. According to a tradition derived through the Khalîfah 'Omar-ibn-el-Khattâb from the Prophet, the water

of this well is medicinal, and will heal many bodily distempers. Taken copiously, adds the same tradition, it will heal all spiritual disorders, and procure an absolute remission of sins.

[10] A stone upon which Abraham stood whilst rebuilding the Ka'abah, and which, as the walls grew higher and higher, was miraculously raised from the ground to form a platform upon which he might stand to work.

[11] The pulpit whence the Friday's sermon is preached.

[12] The Corner. Every corner in the Ka'abah has a name, but this is *par excellence* The Corner, as it contains the stone said to have been one of the precious stones of Paradise which fell to the earth with Adam, and became black on account of the iniquity of mankind. Pilgrims kiss this stone with great devotion, believing that at the end of time it will return to Paradise and bear witness to the faith of true believers.

[13] A semicircular wall built to the height of a few feet, which encloses a portion of ground belonging to the Ka'abah though not within its walls, and which the pilgrims are in duty bound to circumambulate when making the round of the building.

[14] All those places at Mekkah where any particular ceremony takes place during the pilgrimage.

[15] The hereditary right to hold the office of Guardian of the Ka'abah.

[16] The desert plain surrounding the city of Mekkah.

[17] The faithful witness. Surname given by the Prophet to Abu-Bekr.

[18] The Divider or Distinguisher. Surname given by the Prophet to 'Omar-ibn-el-Khattâb upon the following occasion. A wicked Muslim having a dispute with a Jew, appealed from the adverse decision of Muhammad to 'Omar. The latter, greatly angered that any one should dare to prefer his judgment to that of the Prophet himself, cut the Muslim in two with one blow of his scymitar. El-Farúk alludes both to the division of the pleader's body and to 'Omar's distinction between truth and falsehood.

[19] The legatee or heir—(of the Prophet). An honourable title or surname conferred by the Arabs upon 'Aly-ibn-Abu-Tâlib.

[20] The Lion of God. Surname given by the Prophet to his uncle Hámzah-ibn-'Abd-el-Múttalab, who was slain at the battle of Ohod A.H. 3.

[21] The Prince or first of the Martyrs. I have not been able to discover to whom this title was applied.

[22] Possessing two wings. At the battle of Muta (A.H. 8) the Muslim general, Zaïd, who bore the Prophet's standard, was killed. He was succeeded by Ja'afar-ibn-Abu-Tâlib. A sabre stroke deprived him of his right hand, with which he held the standard. He then took it in his left hand, which he also lost. He then held it between his mutilated arms until he fell mortally wounded. The Prophet was greatly moved on hearing of his death, and said, "Of a truth, in the stead of those two hands which he has lost, God has given him two wings, with which he now traverses Paradise amongst the Angels."

[23] The Sword of God. Surname given to the great commander Khâlid-ibn-el-Walîd.

HOW EL-ASMAÏY OVERCAME THE AVA-RICE OF THE KHALÎFAH EL-MANSÛR.*

IT is said that he could remember a poem having once heard it, and he had a Mamlûk† slave who

---

* Upon the death of 'Abd-Allâh-Abu' l-'Abbâs, es-Saffâh, his brother Abu-Ja'afar, el-Mansûr, was proclaimed Khalîfah, A.H. 136 (A.D. 754). He was inaugurated at el-Hâshimiyyah the following year with all possible demonstrations of joy on the part of his subjects. He died at el-Kûfah, A.H. 158 (A.D. 774), while on his way to perform the pilgrimage to Mekkah. His body was carried to the last-mentioned city, where, after a hundred graves had been dug in order that his sepulchre might be concealed, he was buried. He lived sixty-three, and reigned twenty-two, lunar years. He was a prince of great prudence, integrity, and discretion, and was also considered magnanimous and brave, and extremely well versed in the acts of government ; but these good qualities were sullied by his extraordinary covetousness, and occasional implacability and cruelty. He obtained the surname of Abu-Dauwânik on the occasion of his ordering a capitation tax of a dânik to be levied upon the people of el-Kûfah to defray the expense of digging a ditch or entrenchment round the town for the security of the place. In A.H. 145, el-Mansûr laid the foundations of the magnificent city of Baghdâd on the Tigris, which city, after its completion in A.H. 149, he constituted the capital of the Muslim empire. He is said to have left behind him in his treasury six hundred million of dirhems, and twenty-four million of dinârs.

† A Mamlûk was one who having been free-born, became afterwards a slave ; *e.g.*, captives taken in war.

could commit to memory anything that he had heard twice, and a slave-girl who could do the same with what she had heard three times. And el-Mansûr was so extremely miserly that he had gained the appellation of el-Dauwânik, because he reckoned even to Dauwânik.* And one day there came to him a poet bringing a congratulatory ode. And el-Mansûr said to him, "If it appears that anybody knows it by heart, or that any one composed it, that is to say that it was brought here by some other person before thee, we will give thee no recompense for it. But if no one knows it, we will give thee the weight in money of that upon which it is written."

So the poet repeated his poem, and the Khalîfah at once committed it to memory, although it contained a thousand lines. Then he said to the poet, "Listen to it from me;" and he recited it perfectly. Then he added, "And this Mamlûk too knows it by heart." And verily the Mamlûk had heard it twice,

---

* *Dauwânik;* Sing : *Dânik;* the sixth part of a dirhem. The title of Dauwânik applied to the Khalîfah would be as if an emperor of the present time should gain the sobriquet of *Farthings.* Even to this day, amongst the Arabs, a person of reputed means is looked on as miserly who reckons copper money with minuteness and care.

once from the poet, and once from the Khalîfah. So he repeated it. And then the Khalîfah said, "And this slave-girl who is concealed by the curtain, she also recollects it." And to be sure the slave-girl had heard it three times. So she repeated every letter of it, and the poet went away unrewarded.

The historian continues: Now el-Asmaïy * was among the intimate friends and table companions of the Khalîfah. And he composed some difficult verses, and scratched them upon a fragment of a marble pillar, which he wrapped in an Abâh,† and placed on the back of a camel. Then he disguised himself to the appearance of a foreign Arab, and fastened on a Lisâm‡ so that nothing was visible but his eyes, and came to the Khalîfah, and said, "Verily I have lauded the Commander of the Faithful in a *kasîdah.*"§

Then said el-Mansûr, "O brother of the Arabs! if it has been brought by any one beside thee, we will give

----

* See Note *, p. 116.

† Camel's wool cloak.

‡ A piece of cloth worn over the face by travellers as a protection against the scorching winds and dust of the desert.

§ A poem peculiar to the Arabs, which contains not less than sixteen distichs, and may contain a hundred.

thee no recompense for it.   Otherwise, we will bestow on thee the weight in money of that upon which it is written."

So el-Asmaïy recited this *kasîdah :* *

By the piping voice of the Bulbul, By water and by flowers,
By the glint of a twinkling eye, By thee, O my master,
My chieftain and my lord, The lover's heart is moved.
How often has enslaved me, The gazelle of Ukekeelee,†
From off whose cheek by a kiss, I have culled the blushing rose,
Saying, Kiss, O! kiss, O! kiss me.   But she sped not to embrace
    me,
And cried, No.   No.   No, no; Then rose and quickly fled me.
To the caresses of this man, The maiden yielded tremblingly,
And crying cried a cry, Woe! ah woe! ah woe is me!—
—Lament not thus, I said, Rather reveal thy pearls.‡

* I am sadly aware that the following translation of el-Asmaïy's *kasîdah* is utterly inadequate.   I can only plead that rich and beautiful though our English language is, it lacks the intricate alliterative turns peculiar to the Arabic.   Moreover, el-Asmaïy, who was the most celebrated philologer of his time, and was considered a complete master of the Arabic language, appears to have taken no little pains to render this poem (by means of those same alliterative turns) as difficult as possible.   Any one on reading the original must acknowledge that had the Khalîfah been able to seize the full sense of the words alone on hearing them for the first time, his mental power would have been extraordinary—to have committed the lines to memory it would have been marvellous.

† With Arab writers and poets the gazelle is a favourite simile for a pretty woman.   'Ukekeelee would be the name of the tribe or family.

‡ A poetical way of saying, Laugh instead of crying.

When saw she 'twas a grey-beard, Desiring yet a kiss,
Not satiate with caresses, She sought his fond embrace.
And at this moment cried she, Hasten and bring the sweets !
Whereat a youth refreshed me, With wine as honey soft,
More fragrant than carnations, Within a lovely bower,
Than roses or the cypress, In my nostrils was its odour.
And the lute thrummed and thrummed to me, And the drum
    rumbled low ;
The dancers swayed, swayed, swayingly ; The clappers clapped,
    clapped, clappingly ;
The mutton roasted frizzlingly, On leaves from quince-tree
    plucked ;
The turtle-dove cooed ceaselessly, Reiterating wearyingly.—
* Yet now upon a wretched ass, Thou mayst behold me borne.
Upon three legs it hobbleth, Hobbleth as do the lame.
And men throughout the market, With pebbles stoned my camel :
And coming round affrighting me, They followed and preceded
    me ;
But fleeing, on I passed, Though dreading the ass should fall,
To meet in face the king, The honoured, the revered.
So shall he order me a robe, Red as is my red blood ;
In walking I shall raise it, Glorying in my train.
I am 'Almaï the Polished, Whose tribe dwells in el-Máwsal ;
My education surpassing all, I have composed a beautiful ode :
In its opening words I say, By the piping voice of the Bulbul.

The historian continues : And it was so difficult
that the King could not remember it. And he looked
towards the Mamlûk and the slave-girl, but they had
neither of them learnt it. So he cried, " O brother of

* Though in times past all these delights were mine, poverty
has brought me to my present condition.

the Arabs! bring hither that whereon it is written, that we may give thee its weight."

Then said the Arab, "O my lord! of a truth I could find no paper to write it upon; but I had, amongst the things left me at my father's death, a piece of a marble column which had been thrown aside as being useless to me, so I scratched the *kasîdah* upon that."

Then the Khalífah had no help for it but to give him its weight in gold. And this exhausted all that there was in the treasury of his wealth. And the poet took it, and departed.

And when he had gone away, the Khalífah said, " It forces itself upon my mind that this is el-Asmaïy." So he commanded him to be brought back, and uncovered his face, and lo! it was el-Asmaïy. And the Khalífah marvelled at him and at his work, and treated him according to his wont.

Then said el-Asmaïy, "O Commander of the Faithful! verily the poets are poor and are fathers of families, and thou dost debar them from receiving anything, by the power of thy memory, and the memories of this Mamlûk and this slave-girl. But wert thou to bestow upon them what thou couldst easily spare, they might with it support their families, and it could not injure thee."

ALLÂH IS ALL-KNOWING!

WHAT HAPPENED TO EL-MANSÛR WHILE ON PILGRIMAGE TO MEKKAH.

EL-GHAZÂLY,* and ibn-Bilyân, and others besides them, relate that Abu-Ja'afar, el-Mansûr, being on pilgrimage at Mekkah, lodged at the Bait-en-Nádwah.† And he was accustomed to

---

* El-Ghazâly was the surname of two brothers natives of Tûs (a place in Khorassân composed of two towns, Taberân and Nawkân), both of whom were celebrated doctors of the sect of esh-Shâfaiy. I imagine that he upon whose authority the following tale is given was Abu-Hamid, el-Ghazâly, the more celebrated of the brothers, who was born A.H. 450 (A.D. 1058-9), and died A.H. 505 (A.D. 1111). For four years he held the professorship in the college, built at Baghdâd by Nizâm-el-Mulk, the Wâzir of Málik-Shah (the third sultân of the Seljûk dynasty), called the Nizamiyyah. His writings upon learned and scientific subjects are very numerous.

† *Bait-en-Nádwah.* In the time of the Prophet this was the building in which the infidel nobles were wont to assemble and hold discussions with the Prophet and his followers. After the banishment of infidels from Mekkah, the Bait-en-Nádwah became the lodging-house for nobles and great men when on pilgrimage.

circumambulate The House* before dawn. And he went out one night at that time, and whilst he was performing his Tawwâf, lo! he heard a voice which said, "O Allâh! I bewail to Thee the increase of corruption and depravity on the earth, and on his account who through covetousness comes between his people and their rights."

So el-Mansûr quickened his pace until he had filled his ears. Then he returned to the Bait-en-Nádwah, and said to the chief of his guard, "Verily a man is performing Tawwâf at The House. Bring him to me."

And the chief of the guard went out, and found a man at the el-Yémeny Corner,† and said to him, "The Commander of the Faithful wants thee." So the man went in to him, and el-Mansûr asked, "What

---

* One of the most important rites performed by pilgrims to Mekkah is the Tawwâf, or circumambulation of the Ka'abah (House of God). Seven circumambulations complete one Tawwâf, and this is incumbent upon every pilgrim. But the greater the number of times it is performed, the greater his holiness. The hour *Sahrí*, which I have translated "before dawn," is the time after the night, as reckoned by Muslims, has past, but before the morning star has risen. This is the hour generally chosen by persons of high rank for performing Tawwâf, as at that hour but few of the common pilgrims, who later in the day crowd to perform that rite, are present.

† The corner of the Ka'abah facing the south.

was that I heard thee lamenting to Allâh a while ago, concerning the increase of corruption and wickedness in the land, and who is the man who through avarice stands between his people and their rights? For, by Allâh! that wherewith thou hast filled my ears has sickened me."

The man answered, "Of a truth, O Commander of the Faithful! he who has united himself with greed until he stands between his people and their rights, in consequence whereof the cities of God are filled with oppression and violence,—he is, thyself."

"Woe be to thee!" cried el-Mansûr. "How is it possible that I should have joined myself to covetousness when the yellow and the white * lie at my door, and I hold the world in my grasp?"

"The Lord be praised, O Commander of the Faithful!" the man replied; "but has any one shown so much avarice as thou? Allâh constituted thee guardian of the affairs and possessions of the Faithful; but thou hast neglected their concerns, and hast devoted thyself to the accumulation of their wealth. And thou hast established between thyself and thy subjects a barrier of plaster and bricks and armed

* Gold and silver.

guards, and hast commanded that only Such-an-one or Such-an-one should enter thy presence. These men thou hast kept entirely to thyself, and hast laid thy commands upon thy subjects through them. And thou didst never ordain that the oppressed and the starving and the naked should come to thee, though there is not one amongst them but has a right to this very wealth. And these men whom thou chosest for thyself, and didst set over thy subjects, having observed that thou didst amass the money without distributing it, have said, ' This man betrays the trust of Allâh and His messenger, so why should not we betray his trust ?' And they have agreed together that they will only send thee so much as they choose of the people's money. And by this means they have become sharers with thee in the empire, and thou art careless regarding them. And if one who has been oppressed comes to thy door seeking thee, he finds a man appointed to look into the affairs of those who are injured. And if the tyrant be one of thy friends, this man excuses him to the sufferer, and puts him off from time to time. Then if he perseveres, and thou hast beheld him appealing in thy presence, thy satellites beat him with a terrible beating, that he may be

a warning to others. And thou, knowing of this, dost
not disapprove. But verily if a wrong were brought
before the Khalîfahs of the Benu-'Omeyyah who preceded thee, they remedied it immediately. And of a
truth, O Commander of the Faithful! I journeyed
once to China, and found upon my arrival that the
king of the country had lost his hearing. And he
wept. And his wazîrs said to him, 'What makes thee
weep, O King! Let not Allâh cause the eyes of the
King to overflow, except for fear of Himself!' The
King made answer, 'I weep not for the misfortune
which has befallen me. I weep because the victim of
tyranny may now cry at my door, and I cannot hear
him.' Then he went on, 'But if my hearing has gone,
verily my sight remains. Proclaim among the people
that no one shall clothe himself in red unless he be
oppressed.' And he would mount his elephant every
morning and evening, and ride through the city, lest
perchance he might meet with one clad in red garments, and knowing him to be wronged might succour
him.* This man, O Commander of the Faithful, was

---

* The habits of the King of the Celestial Empire must by this
account have changed more in the course of centuries than is
generally supposed !

an idolater, whose benevolence entirely overcame him
in his zeal for the good of idolaters ; whilst thou art
a true believer in God and His messenger, and art
cousin to the messenger of Allâh. O Commander of
the Faithful ! there can be but three reasons for which
thou dost accumulate money. If thou sayest, 'I
amass wealth solely for the good of the kingdom,'
verily Allâh will set before thee the example of
kings in ages preceding thee. All that they had
heaped up of wealth and men and provisions, availed
not what time Allâh willed upon them that He willed.
And if thou sayest, 'I only collect it for my son,'
verily Allâh will show thee an example amongst those
who have been before thee, that whoso accumulated
riches for his child, did not in any way increase his
wealth ; but, contrariwise, he sometimes died poor
and wretched and despised. And dost thou say, 'I
only gather treasure together to raise my position,'
that is the highest position in which thou art already,
and by Allâh ! there is but one station above thy
station, and to this thou canst attain solely through
practising holiness."

Then el-Mansûr wept bitterly, and cried, " But
what can I do, when of a truth the pious flee me,

and the virtuous draw not nigh me nor enter my presence ?"

The man replied, " O Commander of the Faithful ! open thy door, and cast down the barrier, and succour the oppressed, and exact only such money as is right and proper, and distribute it with justice and equity ; and I will be surety that he who has fled will return to thee."

Then said el-Mansûr, " We will do this if it please the Most High God."

And at this moment came the Muazh-zhin calling to prayers. So el-Mansûr rose and prayed ; and when his prayer was ended, he sought the man, but found him not. So he said to the chief of his guard, " Bring the man instantly to me."

And the chief of the guard went out seeking him, and found him at the el-Yémeny corner, and said to him, "The Commander of the Faithful requires thee."

" It is impossible for me to come," he replied.

" If thou dost not," said the other, " he will cut off my head."

But the man answered, " It is also impossible that he should cut off thy head."

Then he drew a piece of inscribed parchment out

of a traveller's provision-bag that he had with him, and said, "Take this. Verily it contains a prayer of deliverance. Whoso prays it in the morning and dies that day, dies a martyr; and whoso prays it in the evening, and dies that night, dies a martyr."* And he added further of its great excellence and rich reward.

So the chief of the guard took it and came with it to el-Mansûr. And when the latter saw him, he cried, "Woe upon thee! Dost thou understand magic?"†

He replied, "No, by Alláh! O Commander of the

---

* According to Muhammadan belief, there are two kinds of martyrs, viz., martyrs of this world, and martyrs of the world to come. The former are those who die in battle, or are slain for the truth's sake. Their souls depart at once to Paradise, where they inhabit the crops of green birds. The soul itself enjoys not, but as the bird eats, and drinks, and enjoys, the soul partakes of and feels enjoyment. The latter are saints and holy men who through purity of life are exempted from the terrors and torments of the tomb. Their souls also go direct to Paradise, where they exist in a state of calm though negative enjoyment; that is to say, they wander amongst the trees and shrubs of the beautiful gardens, but taste not of their fruits, and drink not of the limpid streams.

† It is to be understood (so my Sheikh informed me) that el-Mansûr had wished to kill him, but found himself unable to do so.

Faithful!" And then he told his tale, and el-Mansûr ordered a thousand dinârs to be given to him, and commanded that the prayer should be published; and this is it:

"O Allâh! like as Thou in Thy greatness hast shown mercy above all who are merciful, and hast raised Thy might above all who are mighty; and as Thy knowledge of what is beneath the earth is as Thy knowledge of what is above Thy throne; and as the unuttered words of the heart are unto Thee as those which are proclaimed, and spoken words as those which are secret; and as all things submit to Thy power, and all having dominion humble themselves under Thy dominion; and as the ordering of all things in this world and in the world to come is in Thy hands,—cause that I may be brought in gladness out of all the grief and misery which I have borne at morn and at eve. O Allâh! if Thou pardonest my sins, and overlookest my transgressions, and coverest my evil deeds, inspire me to ask of Thee what through my shortcomings I am not worthy to ask. I pray to Thee in confidence, and I ask of Thee without fear. For Thou art my Benefactor, and I am my own undoer in what is between me and Thee. Thou hast shown

Thy love to me by happiness when I should have made Thee hate me by disobedience. But my trust in Thee produced in me rashness toward Thee. Restore me therefore to Thy grace and Thy mercies, for Thou art the Compassionate, the Pitiful."

'ABD-ALLÂH-IBN-MARWÂN'S ADVENTURE WITH THE KING OF NUBIA.

EL-MANSÛR was talking one day in his Assembly of the decline of the empire of the Benu-'Omeyyah, and of what had befallen them, and of how they had lived in happiness, but died in misery. And Ismâîl-ibn-'Aly, el-Hâshimy, said to him, "Verily 'Abd-Allâh-ibn-Marwân-ibn-Muhammad,* is in thy

---

* See Translator's Note, p. 235. I find various accounts of the fate of 'Abd-Allâh-ibn-Muhammad. Abu-Ja'afar, et-Tábary, and el-Makín assert that Muhammad left behind him two sons, 'Abd-Allâh and 'Abd-el-'Azîz ; the former of whom was, after his father's death, taken and imprisoned, and so remained until the Khalîfate of Harûn, er-Rashîd, when he was released from his confinement, though he was still loaded with irons ; and that he died childless, and was buried at Baghdâd. D'Herbelot, on the other hand, states as follows : " Il (Marwân-ibn-Muhammad) regna cinq ans ou environ, et les Abbasides firent mourir aprés sa mort tous ceux de sa Maison qu'ils putent avoir entre les mains. Il y en eut un cependant, lequel s'étant sauvé en Egypte, de là en Afrique, et passant en Espagne, y fonda une seconde Dynastie des Ommiades, qui prirent aussi en ce pays-là le titre des Khalifes." D'Herbelot says elsewhere that this founder of the dynasty in Spain was 'Abd-Allâh. But in another place again throws doubt upon this statement by saying, " Il est vray cependant que Marvan le dernier de ces

prison, and knows a story concerning the King of Nubia. Send for him and ask him about it."

So they brought him, and he cried, "Peace be upon thee, O Commander of the Faithful! and the mercy of God and His blessing."

El-Mansûr replied, "To return a salutation implies security, and that is not my intention. Nevertheless, be seated."

So 'Abd-Allâh sat down, and el-Mansûr inquired, "What is thy story about the King of Nubia?"

"O Commander of the Faithful," he answered. "I was the heir-apparent to my father, and when thou didst pursue us I sent for ten of my slaves, and placed in the hands of each one of them a thousand dinârs, and equipped five mules, and fastened a jewel of great price within my girdle, and fled to the land of Nubia. And when we drew near, I sent one of my slaves, saying to him, 'Go to this King and salute him, and crave protection for us, and buy us

Khalifes laissa deux enfans nommez A'bdallah, et, Obeïdallah, (not 'Abd-el-Azîz) qui s'enfuirent en Ethiopie. Ben Schúhnah écrit qu' O'beïdallah fut tué sur le chemin, et qu' A'bdallah qui y arriva, vêquit jusqu'au temps du Khalife Mahadi l'Abbaside, et y mourut sans enfans."

Such conflicting statements as these are among the difficultie which beset the student of Arabian History.

some provisions.' So he went off, but was absent so long that I began to grow suspicious of him. Presently, however, he returned, and a man with him, who came in and saluted, and said, 'The King sends thee greeting, and asks, Who art thou, and what has brought thee to my kingdom? Art thou come to make war, or dost thou desire to join my religion, or suest thou for my protection?'—So I answered him, 'Return to thy King and say unto him, I am not come to make war, and I do not desire thy religion, for I am not of those who seek to change their religion,—but I come imploring protection.' So the messenger went away, and afterwards returned and said to me, 'The King says, I am coming to thee to-morrow; and let no new anxieties come into thy mind, nor any care about provisions.'

"Then said I to my companions, 'Spread out the carpets.' So they spread them out, and I prepared to receive him the next day. And behold! he drew near, and verily he wore two striped robes; one of which was wrapped around him like an Izâr,* and the

---

* The Izâr is a cotton cloth six feet long by three and a half broad. It is wrapped round the loins from waist to knee, and knotted or tucked in at the middle.

other hung about him like a mantle. His feet were bare; and with him were ten men with javelins, three of whom went before him and seven followed. So I despised his condition, and questioned within myself as to his murder. But whilst he approached, behold! there appeared a vast multitude, and I exclaimed, 'What means this?' They said, 'It is horsemen.' And therewithal came ten thousand bridles. And the horsemen arrived at the moment of the King's entrance, and ranged themselves round about us. And when the King had entered he sat down upon the ground; so I inquired of his interpreter, 'Why does he not sit upon the place which I have prepared for him?' And he asked the King, who replied, 'Tell him, verily I am a king; and he whom Allâh has raised to be king over his slaves should humble himself before Allâh and His might.'

"Then he scored the ground with his fingers for a while, but presently lifted up his head, and said, 'Ask him: How comes it that you have been deprived of this kingdom which has been snatched away from you, and you the men most nearly related to your Prophet?' I answered, 'He who is more nearly related to him than we, came and pillaged us, and overcame us and pursued us. And I fled to thee seeking protection, first from Allâh, then from thee.' He said, 'But why do you drink wine which is forbidden you?' I replied, 'That is the deed of slaves and foreigners who have entered our religion and our kingdom without our wish.' He continued, 'But why do you put saddles of gold and of silver upon your riding-steeds and war-horses when that is forbidden you?' 'That is the act,' I made answer, 'of slaves and foreigners who have come into our religion and our kingdom without our desire.' 'But why,' he went on, 'when you go out hunting and pass through villages, do you, with blows and ill-usage, impose upon their people tasks which are impossible to them; and as though this were not enough, you must needs also trample down their crops in the pursuit of one partridge of which the value is half a dirhem, when it is forbidden you to impose heavy burdens and to inflict chastisement?' I said again, 'That is the doing of slaves and attendants and their followers.' He answered, 'No; for you still wish to make lawful what God has declared to be unlawful, and you bring yourselves to do what God has forbidden you. And it is He who has wrested

u

from you your wealth, and clothed you in misery, and
has aided your enemies against you. And His vengeance has fallen upon you, and is not yet accomplished. And I fear lest punishment descend upon
thee if thou wert one of the oppressors, and that with
thee it also embrace me, for of a truth when vengeance comes it comprehends all. Depart therefore
after three days ; for of a truth if I find thee after
that time, I will seize what thou hast with thee, and
will slay thee and thine.' Then he rose and left me.
And I remained for three days, and then returned to
Egypt, where thy vicegerent laid hands on me and
sent me to thee. And here I am, and death were
dearer unto me than life."

Then el-Mansûr was softened towards him, and
thought to release him. But Ismâîl said to him,
" Upon my neck be the consequences of this."

" What dost thou advise ?" asked el-Mansûr.

He replied, " That he should be sent down to one
of our fortified houses, and that what is executed
upon those who resemble him, should be executed
upon him."

And this was done to him.

THE WITTY ARAB.

EL-MANSÛR was preaching one day at Damascus, and said, "O ye people! it is incumbent upon you to give praise to the Most High, that He has given me to reign over you. For verily since I began to reign over you He has taken away the plague which had come amongst you." But a certain Arab cried out to him, "Of a truth Allâh is too merciful to give us both thee and the plague at one time!"

HOW IBN-HARÎMAH WAS SAVED FROM PUNISHMENT.

IBN-HARÎMAH went into the presence of el-Mansûr, and offered him congratulations. And el-Mansûr said to him, "Ask of me thy desire." So he replied, "That thou shouldst write to thy vicegerent at el-Medînah, that should he find me drunk he is not to punish me."

"There is no means of escaping that," said el-Mansûr.

"I have no other wish," said Ibn-Harîmah.

So el-Mansûr commanded his scribe, "Write to my vicegerent at el-Medînah: If the son of Harîmah is brought to thee drunk, flog him with eighty strokes, but flog him by whom he is brought with a hundred strokes."

And the guard found him drunk; but they said, "Who would buy eighty with a hundred?" So they passed on and left him.

THE GENEROUS CREDITOR.

A HMED-IBN-MÛSA* is reported to have said,
"I never saw a man of more firmness of
character, or greater knowledge and clearness in argument, than one of whom word was brought to el-
Mansûr that he held possession of certain goods
belonging to the Benu-'Omeyyah. So el-Mansûr
commanded er-Rabîià, his chamberlain, to have him
summoned. And when he appeared before him, el-
Mansûr said, " It has been reported to us that thou
holdest a deposit of money and arms belonging to the
Benu-'Omeyyah. Produce it, therefore, that we may
place it in the Bait-el-Mâl."†

* Ahmed-ibn-Mûsa-ibn-Abi-Máryam, el-Luluy, a member of
the tribe of Khuzâàh, was a teacher of the Kurân readings and
the Traditions. The date of his death is not mentioned by Ibn-
Khalikân.

† See Note *, p. 22.

Then said the man, "O Commander of the Faithful !
art thou heir to the Benu-'Omeyyah ?"

"No," replied el-Mansûr.

"Then why," continued the man, "dost thou seek
for information concerning those possessions of the
Benu-'Omeyyah which are in my hands, if thou art
neither their heir nor their executor ?"

So el-Mansûr was silenced for a time, and then
remarked, "Verily the Benu-'Omeyyah oppressed the
people and forced money from the Muslims."

To this the man replied, "It is necessary, Commander of the Faithful, that eye-witnesses whom
the judge can (by reason of their respectability)
receive, should testify that the goods now in my
possession did belong to the Benu-'Omeyyah, and
that they are identical with what the Benu-
'Omeyyah forced from the people. For surely
the Commander of the Faithful is aware that the
Benu-'Omeyyah had wealth of their own besides
that which, according to the statement of the
Commander of the Faithful, they forced from the
Muslims."

So el-Mansûr reflected for a space, and presently
said, "O Rabîâ ! the man has spoken the truth. We

do not want anything from him." Then addressing the man, he added, "Hast thou a wish?"

"Yes," he replied.

"What is it?" asked el-Mansûr.

· "That thou," said he, "shouldst judge between me and him who denounced me to thee. For by Allâh! O Commander of the Faithful! I have neither money nor arms belonging to the Benu-'Omeyyah. But I was brought before thee, and I knew what thou art in justice and equity, and in following after right and forsaking oppression, and I was therefore confident that the speech of which I made use when thou didst ask me about the goods would be the surest and the safest."

Then cried el-Mansûr, "O Rabîiâ! let him be confronted with the man who denounced him."

So they were brought face to face. And the man who had been accused, said, "O Commander of the Faithful! this one took five hundred dinârs from me and ran away, and I have a legal document against him."

Then el-Mansûr questioned the other man, and he acknowledged the debt. So el-Mansûr asked, "What possessed thee to accuse him falsely?"

He replied, " I wished his death, in order that the money might be mine."

Then said the first man, " Verily, O Commander of the Faithful! I make a free gift to him thereof because that he has caused me to stand before thee, and has brought me into the presence of thy Council. And I give him another five hundred dinârs by reason of the words thou hast spoken to me."

So el-Mansûr praised his deed, and extolled him, and sent him back to his country highly honoured. And el-Mansûr always said, " I never in my life saw any one like this old man, nor one possessing greater firmness of mind, nor one who could overcome me in argument as did he ; nor have I ever seen clemency and generosity equal to his.

THE WAY IN WHICH EL-MÁHDY WAS ENTERTAINED BY THE ARAB.

TRANSLATOR'S PREFATORY NOTE.

El-Máhdy, the third Khalífah of the Abbasside dynasty, succeeded his father, Abu-Ja'afar, el-Mansûr, A.H. 158 (A.D. 774). He died A.H. 169 (A.D. 786), in the forty-second year of his age, having reigned ten years, one month, and fifteen days. Some writers affirm that his death was caused by an accident while hunting; but the more received opinion is that it was in consequence of eating a poisoned pear which was given to him by one of his favourite mistresses, for whom it had been prepared by a rival. He was a liberal and munificent, not to say prodigal, prince, as he dissipated in a short time the immense treasures left him by his father. He applied himself diligently to affairs of state; and was greatly beloved by his subjects on account of his impartial administration of justice and aversion to bloodshed.

IT is recorded that one day el-Máhdy went out hunting, and his horse ran away with him until he came to the hut of an Arab. And el-Máhdy cried, "O Arab! hast thou wherewith to feast a guest?"

The Arab replied, "Yes," and produced for him a barley loaf, which el-Máhdy ate. Then he brought out the remains of some milk, and gave him to drink ; after which he brought some wine in a bottle, and poured him out a glass. And when el-Máhdy had drank it, he said, "O brother of the Arabs ! dost thou know who I am ? "

" No, by Allâh ! " he replied.

" I am one of the personal attendants of the Commander of the Faithful," said el-Máhdy.

" May Allâh prosper thee in thy situation ! " returned the Arab. Then he poured out a second glass ; and when el-Máhdy had drank it, he cried, " O Arab ! dost thou know who I am ? "

He answered, " Thou hast stated that thou art one of the personal attendants of the Commander of the Faithful."

" No," said el-Máhdy ; " but I am one of the chief officers of the Commander of the Faithful."

" May thy country be enlarged, and thy wishes fulfilled ! " exclaimed the Arab. Then he poured out a third glass for him ; and when el-Máhdy had drained it, he said, "O Arab ! dost thou know who I am ? "

The man replied, " Thou hast made me believe thou art one of the chief officers of the Commander of the Faithful."

"Not so," said el-Máhdy ; "but I am the Commander of the Faithful himself."

Then the Arab took the bottle and put it away, and said, "By Allâh ! wert thou to drink the fourth, thou wouldst declare thyself to be the Messenger of Allâh ! "

Then el-Máhdy laughed until he lost his senses. And lo! the horsemen surrounded them, and the princes and nobles dismounted before him, and the heart of the Arab stood still. But el-Máhdy said to him, "Fear not : thou hast done no wrong." And he ordered a robe and a sum of money to be given to him.

"A WONDERFUL TALE."

EL-MUBÁRRAD * relates : As I was journey-ing from el-Básrah to Baghdâd, I passed by a lunatic asylum, and in it I beheld a madman than whom I never saw a more elegant or better dressed man. One of his hands was laid upon his breast; and as I drew near he recited, saying :

> Allâh knows that I am sad ;
> It is impossible to reveal my pain.
> Two souls are mine. One country
> Holds the one, another land the other.
> If I contemplate the Resurrection, even Patience' self
> Against its sternness nought avails.†
> And what my soul here present feels,
> That feels my soaring soul in upward flight.

* It is an anachronism to introduce the following tale in this place. El-Mubárrad was not born till more than forty years after the death of el-Máhdy.

Abu-'l-'Abbâs Muhammad, generally known by the name of el-Mubárrad, was a native of el-Básrah, but resided at Baghdâd. He was an eminent author, philologer, and grammarian. He was born A.H. 210 (A.D. 826); or, as some say, A.H. 207, and died at Baghdâd A.H. 285 or 286 (A.D. 900).

† Meaning that he was predestinated to his lot, and that nothing could change it.

So I said, "By Allâh! thou deservest praise. Allâh has richly endowed thee, O madman!"

Upon this, he seized hold of something to throw at me; so I placed myself at a distance from him. Then he exclaimed, "I recited to thee what thou dost like and approve, and thou sayest to me, 'O madman!' and dost league thyself with Fate against me!"

"I have done wrong," I said. To which he replied, "Thou art forgiven, having confessed thy fault;" and presently added, "Shall I recite to thee another poem?" I said, "Yes." So he began, saying:

> What slays more than separation from the beloved?
> And what more fills the lover's heart with woe?
> I myself brought to myself this pain,
> Which has surely o'ercome both heart and brain.*
> Alas! that I pass the night a captive
> Between two rivals—grief and wakefulness."

Then I said to him, "Thou hast done excellently, by Allâh! let us hear more."

So he continued:

> Did they search me, burnt would they find my heart;
> Or unclothe me, consumed would be seen my flesh.
> What is in me has weakened me and increased my grief,
> But to no one will I my misery unfold.

* Literally, *liver.* Arab poets suppose the liver to be the seat of love, and the heart to be that of reason. In European poetry, love resides in the heart, and reason in the head.

I said, "By Allâh! it is admirable. Let us hear more of it." To which he replied, "O young man! I perceive that each time I have recited verses, thou hast said, 'Let us hear more of it;' and this can only be because thou hast parted from a lover or a devoted friend." Then he added, "I believe in my heart that thou art Abu-'l-'Abbâs, el-Mubárrad. By Allâh! thou art he!"

I said, "I am he. But where hast thou known me?"

"Can the moon be hidden?" he asked; and then said, "O Abu-'l-'Abbâs! recite to me some of thy poetry, that my soul may be lifted out of its misery."

So I recited to him, saying:

I wept till the dew fell from Heaven for pity of me,
And my eyes wept for grief as the travellers departed.
O halting-place of the tribe! where has the tribe halted?
Whither the camels are driven, thither is driven my soul.
Rise, O Dawn! may Allâh water thee with dew,
And cause to descend upon thee heavy showers,
And for their sakes refresh thee! May the home be united!
May the re-union be complete and the cord rejoined!
Long lasted the pleasure, and her lover was near her
When times were propitious and busybodies asleep.
But times have changed from what I knew them,
For Time is a ruler, he has the power of change over men.

They departed, and with them departed my hope ;
Than distance no greater affliction can fall on one.
And the union is broken, and the heart is consumed,
And tears overflow, for the caravan has gone.
So was my heart when their camels departed,
As wasted by sickness or drunk with wine.
Though the camels had knelt, yet at dawn they arose,
And by hers my beloved one was borne away.
But her glance to a chink in her prison* she turned,
Looking toward me with tears from her eye streaming down.
O cameleer ! go slowly, that I may bid them farewell.
O cameleer ! in thy departure is my death.
By thy truth ! I shall never forget my intercourse with them,
Would I had known their long agreement to their deed !

Abu-'l-'Abbâs, el-Mubárrad, continues : "And when I had ended my poem, he asked me, ' What was their deed ?' I answered, 'Their death.'

"Then he cried with a loud cry, and fell down swooning. And I shook him, but found that he had really died. May God have mercy upon him !"

* The litter in which an Arabian woman of any rank is carried on camel-back when travelling.

Watson and Hazell, Printers, London and Aylesbury.

www.ingramcontent.com/pod-product-compliance
Lightning Source LLC
Chambersburg PA
CBHW031039120726
47905CB00007B/2243